Shafts of Light

ROB HICKS

Published in Australia by Sid Harta Publishers Pty Ltd,

ABN: 34 632 585 203

17 Coleman Parade, GLEN WAVERLEY VIC 3150 Australia

Telephone: +61 3 9560 9920, Facsimile: +61 3 9545 1742

E-mail: author@sidharta.com.au

First published in Australia 2020

This edition published 2020

Copyright © Rob Hicks 2020

Cover design, typesetting: WorkingType (www.workingtype.com.au)

Hicks, Rob

Shafts of Light

ISBN: 978-1-921206-51-1

pp318

A Note from the Author

At age twenty or so I decided I would write a book. Many years later after retiring from farm life I finally got around to it.

*My thanks to Kerry, Barbara and Luke and
all the team at Sid Harta for their expert help.
They have been a great help and inspiration.*

Chapter One

Jane and Alec

The sun elbowed its way through the clouds. Thin, bright shafts of light shone down, selecting, as if by some divine providence, various significant sites around the district. Today it shone on the little bridge just out of town.

'Today's the day Alec.'

'I'm scared.'

'We won't get another chance like this.'

'Are you sure Janey?'

'Too right. We'll wait for him at the bridge. The two of us at once, we'll fix him.'

'Are you sure he'll be on his own?'

'Yair, I heard him tell the other kids.'

Ever since Alec and Jane moved to the district they had been bullied by Jackson. He was only a little bit taller than Alec and only a year older but to a fourteen-year-old that one year was quite significant. Jackson always had his mates egging him on. Made him feel big and important. He would pull Jane's hair and take Alec's wrist in his two hands and twist one each way, and that hurt. Jane would try to intervene but he would just push her away. Once he even kicked her in the shins, much to the delight of his cronies. It usually ended with them riding home in tears.

Jane was two years younger than Alec, but she had a bit more fire, a bit more spirit.

They waited. Only on rare occasions did Jackson ride home by himself. Sure enough, here he came, alone, singing, with not a care in the world. As he crossed the bridge they sprang. They hadn't formed any sort of a plan, just acted on instinct. Jane grabbed the handlebars and Jackson skidded on the gravel. As he went down, they pounced on him like a pair of foxes on a rabbit. Jane tore his schoolbag from him and threw it in the drain. Before Jackson could get to his feet Jane jumped on his legs. She felt a rare thrill as he screamed with the pain. Her heart was racing now. The thought of all those weeks of being pushed around made her even angrier. Alec pushed his face in the dust. Jackson scrambled to his feet and started to run like the coward he was. Most bullies are cowards their mother had said, and at that moment Jane realised she was right. It gave her more incentive. He tried to get through the fence but Jane was too quick, he was half way through when she caught him. She was younger and smaller than Alec, but now, today, she was the stronger. She screamed at Alec, 'Come on Alec, get him.'

He grabbed a leg and together they dragged Jackson back. Jane pulled off one of his shoes and pelted it in the drain as well.

'Let me go, let me go.' Jackson's voice was full of panic now.

'You're not so good on your own, are you?' Jane's blood was fairly up now, she was really enjoying this. She kicked him in the shins,

'There, how does that feel?'

Jackson finally broke free, shirt torn from the fence, dust all over, blood on his pants from his skinned knees. He jumped on his bike and was away. Only then did they see Mrs. Taylor across the road in her garden, watching. She'd seen it all. As Jackson pedalled away, she laughed. She knew the story. Didn't like the Jacksons, especially that kid, although she knew it wasn't his fault, he was a pain, he was only doing as he had been taught, doing what his parents had let him get away with. Jane thought of another thing her mother had said about bullies. They only get away with it if by-standers do nothing. How true that was.

With only about a hundred children in the school the story soon went around. Two of Jackson's mates had seen him pedalling home with only one shoe, no schoolbag, bloodied knees and teary eyes, and a couple of minutes later along had come Alec and Jane, bloodied knees also and dusty, but laughing. The two boys had figured it out. The attitude towards Jackson changed quite quickly. Surprisingly quickly. There was quite a titter when Miss Hammond asked Jackson how his books had become wet. He had sneaked back later and retrieved his schoolbag and shoe. It soon became obvious that nobody liked Jackson, they just hadn't been prepared or had the courage to stand up to him. Different story now. His mates gravitated towards Alec, and Jane found she had some new friends amongst the girls.

Alec and Jane started to like their new home.

Miss Hammond was organising the end of year break up concert. She wanted as many of the children as possible to take part. Some would play instruments, some would recite poetry or read stories they had written. Some would sing. She formed a group into some sort of choir, comprised mainly of those who weren't involved in other acts. The first practice session was a bit of a shambles until she tried some Christmas carols. They knew the words and tunes of those and she was quite excited as she played, to hear their little voices come together in reasonable order, pretty much in tune echoing in the empty hall. Alec and Jane hadn't been selected for any items on their own so inevitably they found themselves included in this choir. Not really a choir, more a group of mixed voices.

Miss Hammond hadn't expected much but after a couple of verses of Silent Night she became aware of a couple of voices which came through above the rest. With her keen ear for music she could hear them quite clearly. She recognised some real talent there somewhere. It didn't take long for her practiced ear to realise it was, indeed, Jane and Alec. She asked them to sing a couple of verses as a duet, unaccompanied.

Their pitch was perfect. They hadn't sung much at home, just occasionally they would sing with their mother as she went about her daily chores. Miss Hammond decided they should sing at the concert. Jane and Alec liked the idea. Singing was fun. Much better than all those books and writing and stuff.

Concert night came. First a poetry recitation, then a piano solo followed by some tap dancing by four of the girls, leading up to a couple of Christmas carols by the group after which Miss Hammond announced simply that Alec and Jane would now sing. She knew they would be the star act. They had been great at practice but she'd been a bit worried about their reaction to a hall full of people. She needn't have worried.

They stepped forward to the microphone and as they had practiced, Miss Hammond played just one chord. There was still a little shuffling and murmuring in the hall as Jane started to sing. Her voice was strong, powerful for one so young. It carried to the back corners of the hall with ease, perfectly on pitch as she had always been at practice. After just one line of 'Once in Royal David's City' there was complete silence, not a whisper, not a murmur, not even a shuffle in the audience. Every eye was on her. She sang the first verse alone, Alec sang the second, then they sang the third verse as a duet. They sang as one, absolutely perfect in tune and timing, every word clear and precise. The applause was spontaneous, loud and prolonged. Miss Hammond congratulated herself on her choice of song. It was exactly right.

She looked across the audience, saw old Granny Hislop

leaning forward and was completely staggered to see her wipe a tear from her eye.

'Imagine that,' she thought, 'maybe that tough old girl has some sensitivity after all.'

At intermission all were full of praise for the two young singers and many asked Miss Hammond if there was to be another number from them. After some discussion with Alec and Jane they decided to sing Silent Night and even without rehearsal they were still perfect in timing and pitch, and equally well received by a very enthusiastic audience.

Chapter Two

Jane at 15

Jane didn't much like Ferret and Fox, two boys Alec had begun to knock about with. Unlikely mates for Alec, they were a rough pair in lots of ways. Jane had spoken to Alec about them once or twice, but he wasn't ready to listen. He thought they were all right, sure they were a bit unruly at times but Alec couldn't see any harm in that. Jane saw things quite differently. She couldn't understand how Alec had come to be mates with them. She felt Ferret had earned his nickname. He was the sort of bloke who would, like a mongrel dog, sneak up behind you and bite you on the ankle. And Fox had a surname which suited him perfectly. Strange how that happened sometimes. She thought he was a creepy, shifty type of individual. One who couldn't be trusted, one who would be your mate till things started to go a bit wrong, then, suddenly he wouldn't want to know you.

Jane and Alec were often left to their own devices at weekends. Usually on Saturdays their parents would go to the races somewhere and leave them to do whatever they liked. It was one such Saturday that things came to a head. Jane and Alec were home alone when Ferret and Fox drove up to the house. That alone spelled trouble as neither of them owned a car and not only that, neither had a driving licence. They came to the door. Ferret was the first to speak,

'Want to come for a spin Alec?'

'I dunno, where're you going?'

'Oh, just anywhere.'

'Whose car is that?'

'It's my mothers.'

'She knows you've got it?'

'Nah, she's away, but she wouldn't mind.'

'You sure about that?'

Fox chimed in, 'Yeah, it'll be right. What she doesn't know won't hurt. Anyway, we'll be back in an hour or so. She won't even know we've taken it.'

Jane stood silently listening to all this. Watching Alec all the while.

'But no-ones got a licence.'

'So, what,' said Ferret. 'We'll go on all the back roads. Come on, it'll be a buzz.'

'Yeah, O.K. Wait till I get my wallet.' He went to his room and came back all ready to go, only to find Jane standing in the doorway. He started to brush past her but she didn't budge.

'You're not going Alec. That'd be a stupid thing to do.'

'Aw, come on Jane. It's just a bit of fun.'

'No Alec, you're not to go.'

He stepped back a little. Jane was standing with her

hands on her hips. Defiant. The other two were waiting on the veranda, listening. Ferret was impatient.

'Come on Alec. Let's go.' Jane stood, watching Alec and at the same time she spoke to Fox and Ferret over her shoulder.

'You two piss off. You're not taking Alec anywhere, and if you've got any sense at all you'll take that car back and forget about joyriding. You're heading for trouble.' She turned then as she spoke and stood, with her hands still on her hips as she continued her verbal barrage. 'Stand back and have a good look at yourselves before you do someone some damage.' Her voice was sharp. One of those no-nonsense sorts of tones, the sort of voice which said — you'd better listen, you'd best not reply, anything you say will only make things worse. Jane was quite a bit smaller than any of the boys but the two on the veranda had taken a pace or two back when she turned.

There is something quite scary about a female in full voice. Standing there she seemed to grow about a foot taller. It seemed as though her voice would blister the paint off the walls. She presented an imposing, even frightening presence. The two boys retreated to the safety of the car. It seemed to be the best plan. Jane saw them well out of the way, then turned back to Alec. He went to push past a second time. She didn't move. Sure, they'd had their differences every so often and were quite firm with each other but this was very, very different. She stood her ground in the middle of the doorway, still with hands on hips. She wasn't nearly as big as Alec but it was plain to him that she wasn't going to move. By now there were tears streaming down her face. She spoke through her tears, her voice strong and forceful despite the tears.

'You're not to go Alec. I won't let you.' Alec was transfixed. He had never seen her like this. Standing there, unmoving, she presented a formidable figure. After a few seconds he realised she was right and he also realised how much she thought of him, how much she cared. He stepped forward, took her in his arms, gave her a hug and said, 'You know sis, I think you're right.' He stepped out to the veranda and called out to the boys,

'I think Jane's right. I'm not coming.' He was still standing there as they drove off.

'I'm glad you did that Alec. Nothing good could've come of going with them. And I don't believe anything good can come of you mixing with them. They're bad news. I think you're going the wrong way getting tangled up with them.'

Alec thought about this a while and decided Jane was right. Even though she was younger than him he respected her common sense. She was in fact very mature for her age. He started to appreciate how mature she was. He was glad he'd listened to her, especially later when he heard Ferret's mother had found that they had taken her car and she did mind. She was in fact furious. They had put a small scratch in the front mudguard. Not much of a scratch but Ferret's mother had seen it and questioned Ferret.

Two days later Alec talked to Ferret and Fox at school,
'What'd you do last Sat'd'y?'

'Well we didn't go far. Just sat and talked for a while. Then took the car back.'

Neither would admit it but they decided Jane was right.

Alec saw less of them from then on.

Jane and Alec became regular entertainers as their reputation as singers spread and they were often asked to sing at the local dances or with the band at the pub at weekends. Their appearances became sporadic as they grew older and left town to further their education, Alec to university and Jane chose to attend a dance academy.

When their elderly aunt died there was some doubt as to whether they would get home for the funeral. As the family and other relatives of the deceased gathered in front of the church there was some discussion on the possibility of Jane and Alec getting there.

'I do hope they make it' was the comment of the other Aunt.

The other aunt had her family nearby, including a very precocious five-year-old, little Norman, a little boy who seemed to be always on the move as little boys of that age are wont to be. Later during the service,

'Sit still Norman,' his mother pleaded.

The minister was in full voice, praying with some divine enthusiasm. 'Dear Lord, forgive us ....'

'Who's he talking to Mummy?' was little Norman's question, in a stage whisper which could be heard quite well through half the church.

'Quiet dear, he's talking to God.' A few seconds later as

his mother sat with her head bowed and eyes closed, little Norman was crawling around beneath the pews calling,

'Where are you God?'

'Sit still Norman,' his mother pleaded again. But Norman wasn't to be deterred.

'Without Thee,' the minister intoned, 'we are but dust....'

'What's butt-dust Mummy?' was the next question to carry around the church.

'Sit still Norman,' his mother pleaded, and she produced a book and some coloured pencils she kept for just this sort of occasion. This kept little Norman quiet for a while and when, during a short break after the praying had stopped his mother asked,

'What are you drawing Norman?'

'I'm drawing God.'

'But nobody knows what God looks like.'

Norman kept drawing with his usual intensity and said, 'They will when I finish this.'

The minister paused. He had to grin at that.

The church was three quarters full and after the praying and the eulogy the minister had seen what the congregation hadn't. He'd seen Jane and Alec arrive late and slip quietly into the back row. The minister announced that they would all sing Amazing Grace and it only took about three bars for Jane and Alec's voices to rise above the rest and produce looks of relief among those in the family. The minister was quite a 'with-it' sort of bloke. He'd heard Jane and Alec sing on quite a few occasions and after the first verse he signalled the congregation to stop singing and Jane and Alec sang the rest of the anthem, still perfect in pitch and timing as they had always been.

Jane didn't much like the clergy, didn't much like men in dresses as this minister chose to dress, felt that if men wanted to wear dresses they would do well to save it for the Mardi Gras or some similar occasion, but she was quite pleased that this minister had had the presence of mind to signal the assembled people to let her and Alec sing.

After the service the deceased's sister came and spoke to Jane and Alec,

'I'm so pleased you two made it, my darling sister would have been so thrilled to hear you sing.' She stood for a second, wiped a tear, then moved on.

Chapter Three

Jane and Alec

They had been pretty close as children and had kept regular contact when Alec had gone to university and Jane to a Dance Academy. Alec had become a minister and married Evelyn. Jane became a member of a chorus, dance troupe travelling from town to town, putting on shows for one or two nights at a venue then moving on, or travelling to all the local shows. Each town had an annual show and they would set up their tent and perform. Jane preferred these days as compared to the times when they would do just one performance in the town hall or theatre because, at the shows, they performed several times, afternoon and evening.

Thomas Jamieson was a member of the cast who also sang and danced. It wasn't long before they fell in love and were married and had a son.

Alec didn't approve of Thomas and didn't approve of the life style his sister was leading. He'd said on many occasions he felt they were going nowhere. 'There's no future in what you're doing sis' he'd said. But, of course, she had taken no notice. She was a free spirit and life was a breeze. Travelling, dancing, drinking, though not enough to be a problem until the night of her twenty-seventh birthday. She'd had a few more drinks than usual but still elected to drive, crashed the car and killed both Thomas and their son. She had very little injury, just a few minor cuts and bruises but the Ambulance men could not do anything to save Thomas and their son. Thomas was killed outright and their little four-year-old boy died in her arms.

It was soon after that she started drinking heavily. They were living in the country then. She had given up the dancing and come to live in a town near where Alec was the local parson. Sometimes Alec would go to her place and find her collapsed on the floor or sprawled on the bed. He would get calls from a pub or club or even the police asking him to come and take her home. Then one day she disappeared. Just packed up and left. She left him a note saying she needed a change and went off without a word to anyone.

He'd tried everything he knew to find her. The travelling troupe, her old school friends, anyone he could think of whom she might contact, notices in the papers. He tried for months but had to concede in the finish he wasn't going to find her till she wanted to be found. The police said since she had left a note and no foul play was suspected, they could only list her as a missing person. That was it, nothing else.

Chapter Four

Scott

Scott's shyness stemmed from his childhood. Being an only child, he'd had a smorgasbord of an upbringing — a bit from here and a bit from there and yet a bit more from somewhere else.

His mother had left when he was about ten years old. He never understood why. He always remembered her as a pleasant, happy soul, always busy about the house, or outside in the garden, or out driving a tractor or fixing a fence as nearly all farm women did. Then, one day, she left. She hadn't given even a hint that she was going to leave. She just sat down with him one morning and said she had to go away. She had tried to explain that she had to do other things. He sort of understood that and he took that O.K. but when he asked her how long she would be gone and she replied she didn't know he became very scared. He remembered the day. Remembered sitting on the veranda of the house bawling his eyes out as she drove off.

He was always looking for her to come down the road or when he came home from school sometimes, he would rush into the house feeling quite sure she would be there. He would ask his father or the lady next door when she might be back and usually would get a very vague, non-specific answer. He became accustomed to coming home to an empty house. It was worst in the cold weather. He remembered when his mother was there, he would come home from school cold and hungry and there she would be, waiting for him. The house would be warm and she would have some biscuits or a sandwich for him to eat, and she would ask about school or she would chatter on about whatever came into her head. She was a bit of a chatterbox his father often said. Now all that was gone. In the space of a day, without warning, all those nice things disappeared and he was left with an empty house and a broken heart.

He spent a lot of time alone. The school bus let him off about two kilometres from home and he would ride his bike from there. Sometimes, on his own, he would ride very slowly, stopping a few times because he knew he would be going home to an empty house. His father would usually be out in the paddocks somewhere, working and would not get in till nearly dark, so he would have to find something to do, often for a couple of hours.

Whenever he could he would ride home with the two boys from next door. Go to their place and play. Their mother was always kind to him. He loved those times. Their mother would have scones and cakes or biscuits or some other goodies which he never had at home and she always made him feel welcome, made him feel he was a bit important as she was always treated him the same as her own boys. She understood the trauma this young boy was going through. She was angry at his mother for leaving the lad just when he really needed her.

He would stay as long as he could until she sent him home, usually just before dark. He'd ride home with tears in his eyes but always composing himself before he got home. He didn't want his father to see him like that.

His father rarely mentioned her but Scott knew he was suffering too in his own way. Sometimes Scott would find him just sitting on a box in the shed, staring into space. Sometimes he would hardly speak for hours. At some point Scott came to realise his mother was not coming back. He gradually absorbed that fact into his daily life and eventually he stopped asking after her. With that sort of childhood, it was not surprising Scott had difficulty relating with girls, since he was an only child and with the next-door neighbours being boys. He did however communicate quite well with older women even though his mother had left when he was young. No doubt the mother of the boys next door had a big influence on his growing up. She had always been there for him.

There rarely seemed to be any girls in his life so Scott felt uncomfortable treating them as friends. For nearly all his school life Scott had the impression that if he spoke to a girl for more than a minute or so it meant she was your girlfriend, more than just a mate or friend. Somehow the communication was different. Different to talking to another boy. He somehow couldn't get it into his head that a girl could be just a friend or a mate. He noticed how different it was with boys who had sisters. They could easily relate to girls, just simply talk to them.

It needn't have been that way for him of course, and it shouldn't have been, but for Scott that was how it was. Girls seemed to be a separate species, totally alien in his world. He was particularly unsure of himself in the presence of strong, confident girls. Girls like that made him want to duck away at the first opportunity. He gave the girls the impression that he didn't like them which was far removed from the truth.

Two of the girls in his class had even confronted him one day saying they both wanted to be his girlfriend and he should pick which one he wanted. The fact was he was very keen on one of them, but she was one of those strong, confident girls, one who made him feel very insecure, and being unable to let her know, he picked the other one.

Chapter Five

The Pram Lady

And so, it was. Scott at age eighteen had decided he didn't want to stay on the farm and had made a move to Archerville, a small town about a two-hour drive from the home farm. Archerville was a typical small town, if such a place exists. A town with a population of about three thousand, one pub, a supermarket, the usual shops and small businesses. The railway was a big factor in keeping the town connected to neighbouring towns and employing several people.

Scott had found a job as a labourer with Harry Fielding, a local concrete contractor. He left home on the Saturday to start his new life. Sunday morning found him in a small shop buying milk. Scott was never at his best on Sunday mornings. Today he was a little worse than usual. He'd spent Saturday packing, driving to Archerville and then moving his gear into his rented flat, and finally tumbling in to bed quite late, two o'clock in fact, and even then, tired as he was, he was unable to sleep.

He'd lain awake for some time listening to the sounds of the town. New sounds, unfamiliar sounds — a train whistle, the bells of the wig-wag signals as the train crossed the main road, voices of people walking past, a car with motor revving and music thumping its way down the street, the banging of car doors as the people next door came home after a night out and then their 'goodnights' carrying clearly in the night air. There was nothing like that to keep one awake back home. Only occasionally, a dog barking.

It was just the usual Sunday morning one might expect in any small Australian town. People strolling to the shops, or just talking, passing the time of day, always taking time to stop and chat. Even though they saw each other most days, there always seemed to be something to chat about. And kids playing in the park, on skateboards or throwing sticks for some useless dog to fetch. Maybe not really a useless dog, for it kept the young ones amused with its antics.

People were occupied doing things, important or otherwise. Digging in gardens, mowing lawns, lawns which seemed to suddenly require attention of a Sunday morning, or sweeping. Doing the things which keep a town thriving. And thriving Archerville certainly was in its' own quiet way.

It was a typical Sunday morning. The sun elbowed its way through the clouds. Thin, bright shafts of light shone down on Archerville, selecting, as if by some divine providence, various significant spots

It was not surprising that Scott had taken a few seconds in
the little shop that morning to realise he was witnessing a
hold up. A long-haired youth was threatening the lady atten-
dant with a knife. Scott had become aware of the young man's
agitated voice at the counter near the door. Presumably he
hadn't seen Scott rummaging through the magazines at the
back of the shop. Scott was normally a placid sort of young
man but this caused a prickling sensation of anger to spread
through him. Something inside him snapped. His reaction
was impulsive. He let out a wild yell, somewhat like an angry
drover yelling at an errant cattle dog, and charged down the
shop. The felon swung around; his mouth dropped open as he
saw Scott thundering towards him. In an instant his position
had changed from aggressor to potential victim, his expression from nervousness to amazement, then to absolute terror.
He dropped the knife and raced out the door. Scott reached
the street only a few paces behind.

'Bloody coward,' he yelled.

The young man ran, partly for fear of being apprehended
and charged, but probably more for fear for his ultimate
physical safety. Given Scott's attitude, that fear was probably
justified. Brought up in the bush, where honesty is normal
and expected, the act he had just witnessed was abhorrent
to Scott. He was desperately keen to catch this would be thief
although he hadn't any real thought as to what he might do
when he did catch him.

It may have been a fairly even contest, the one running in fear, the other in anger, but the chase only lasted a few seconds. They reached the corner at just the same time as a lady pushing a pram. The long-haired youth side stepped, but Scott, fit and nimble though he was, could not avoid a collision. He knocked the woman down. His brain had been racing fast, but now it raced even faster. Stop or go on?

He dashed on, thinking, 'Someone will see to her, I'll catch this mongrel then come back.' However, a few strides later a quick look back changed all that. The lady was lying quite still on the footpath and the pram was rolling towards the road. No hesitation now.

Scott caught the pram easily enough, and by the time he wheeled it back, half a dozen people had gathered around the lady. She was still down and someone was kneeling beside her. Clearly, she was injured in some way. Nobody in the group was interested in Scott. Probably, nobody had seen Scott knock her down.

Scott sat on a low fence to catch his breath and contemplate the events of the last few minutes. So much had happened in such a short time. The whole episode had probably only taken two or three minutes, but those two or three minutes and the consequences were to have a lasting effect. The ambulance came and he realised as they were loading the woman into it that he hadn't really seen her, he hadn't seen what she looked like. All he had seen in his rush was a vague blur of a thin woman in a long dark overcoat and some sort of a beret, pulled down, covering half her face.

The ambulance prepared to leave when Scott, quite recovered now, called,

'Hey, what about the baby?'

A man who had been helping the ambulance men looked at Scott for a second, then spoke to the driver. The ambulance drove off and the man approached Scott. He was a middle-aged man with thinning wispy hair, wearing an old suit with holes in the elbows and patches on the knees, a shirt with a frayed collar and a tie, of all things, a tie. On his feet, a pair of worn out sand-shoes. Scott was mystified. Why wasn't anyone interested in the pram?

'I'll take that, I know where she lives,' was all the man said as he took charge of the pram. Only then did Scott look into the pram. The surprises of the last half hour or so were compounded when he did so. Inside was a large rag doll surrounded by some parcels wrapped in newspaper, two or three wine casks and several bottles of cheap spirits. The man started shuffling off with the pram but Scott somehow couldn't leave it at that. He felt a responsibility to the lady he had knocked down, an obligation to do something for her even though he felt it was quite reasonable for him to have chased the thief. Wouldn't any decent person do the same given similar circumstances? Maybe not. Maybe some would have found a reason not to give chase. Be that as it may Scott still felt a 'duty of care', a phrase he remembered from somewhere.

He walked with the man up a slight incline. The man had a slight limp, and it wasn't long before the slope of the road had an impact and he began to struggle a little. Scott took over and soon found it difficult enough too. The pram was heavy to push, the wheels stiff from a lack of oil and a certain amount of distortion. Scott wondered how that thin wisp of a woman had managed. The man was unresponsive to Scott's questions. Where did the lady live? Did she live alone? Should we notify someone? These inquiries were answered with not much more than grunts. The man pointed — left at the corner. Three houses down he pointed to a gate, a very tired looking gate in a very tired looking fence, held up in places by a tangle of uncontrolled rose bushes with tentacles reaching out to catch the unwary. A cracked cement path led to a dilapidated weather-board house. They went down the side and round the back. The front had been bad enough but the back was a complete shamble. Overgrown with rank grass, a scraggy lemon tree, a leaning shed, a leaning verandah with rotting floorboards. Once again, the man pointed and Scott realised, he was to push the pram into the corner where the floorboards had long before disappeared. The man muttered, 'That'll be right there,' and then 'Thank you' as he headed for the gate and shuffled off up the street. Further conversation was obviously not going to be encouraged. Scott just stood and stared. Was this real? He felt he must at least tell someone, someone must care.

He became aware of an elderly lady in the front garden of the house opposite. She was simply standing, looking, motionless, as though she didn't want to be noticed. He wandered over slowly. She looked as though she was ready to duck out of sight so Scott started to speak from the middle of the street.

'Do you know the lady who lives there?'

'Yes. Has something happened to her?'

Scott related the story of the morning and the woman simply said 'Oh' and made to go inside.

Scott asked quickly, 'Is there someone I should notify?'

'I think she has a brother in the city somewhere, I don't really know.' After this quiet reply the lady was gone.

Scott returned to the accident scene. He recalled a young man coming out of a house across the street when the ambulance had arrived. He found the young man still at the front fence and at last found someone who would communicate in sentences of more than two or three words. Yes, he did know a little bit about the lady with the pram. She was Mrs. Jamieson and she wasn't as old as most people believed.

'It's the booze you know.' This comment came from a female voice behind the screen door. As Scott turned a middle-aged lady pushed the screen door open and carried on the conversation from a range of about fifteen paces. Yes, there was a brother but she wasn't sure where he was. No, he'd never been around here in all the time she'd known Mrs. Jamieson, and yes, they would probably have taken her to the hospital.

Chapter Six

Mrs Jamieson

The lady at the hospital reception was middle aged with small round glasses and her hair tied back in a bun. She was rather pleased to see Scott. Perhaps he could help with the paper work. They had admitted her but hadn't any details.

'You see dear, the ambulance was in the area, coming back from a false alarm when they got the call. That's why they were there so quick. Beat the police and all.'

'Police. Bloody hell, I didn't think of them. I suppose someone called them.' In all the confusion he'd forgotten that the police would need to talk to him about the hold up. He gave the lady as much information as he could then found a phone-box in the foyer, rang the police and arranged to make a statement. The ward sister wouldn't let Scott see the old lady but she did assure Scott that she was reasonably O.K. and was resting comfortably. She was very pleased that Scott could at least put a name to her patient.

By the time Scott left the hospital, and finished making his statement to the police he was surprised to find it was one o'clock, three hours since he'd left his flat. Perhaps I'll just start Sunday over again. He went back to the shop.

'Do you still want the milk?' the lady behind the counter said with a silly grin. She was a very attractive lady with a beautiful, confident smile, a twinkle in her eye and a little bit of cheek in her voice. Scott had forgotten he'd put a carton of milk on the counter before he'd gone to the magazine section of the shop.

A small, slightly stooped man wearing horn rimmed glasses with very thick lenses appeared and began to thank Scott profusely. The lady's attitude intrigued Scott. Here was the woman who had been threatened with a knife, not just a pocket knife either, it had been a long-bladed dagger looking thing, treating it as a regular occurrence and seemingly quite unconcerned, while the man who wasn't even there when it happened, was showing all the emotion.

After introductions, I'm Scott, I'm Eldred, and this is Laura and handshakes all round, Scott found himself telling the story of the pram lady yet again. The man was more interested in thanking Scott. He thanked him again and again, saying a lot of people would have just let it happen and he was so pleased that Scott had been in the shop, and generally rambling on to the point where Scott was becoming embarrassed. The lady, Laura, was quite unperturbed.

'You'll have to stop chasing people out of our shop like that you know, it's not really good for business,' she said with a grin and a wink. She was incredible. Scott looked at her more closely. She was probably about fortyish. Her sparkling eyes showed a carefree confidence and she looked as if she would laugh her way through any situation. What an odd couple they made. He looked to be quite a bit older than her. Maybe they weren't a couple, perhaps she just worked there. But, no, she'd said 'our' shop.

Then he saw her look at Eldred and in an instant Scott knew they were a couple. Her eyes showed her feelings. The look only lasted a few seconds but in those few seconds she showed all the love any woman could have for any man. Scott could easily have missed that look and been left wondering.

It was Monday night before Scott rang the hospital, only to be told Mrs. Jamieson wasn't having any visitors. The same response on Tuesday prompted Scott to go to the hospital. He asked the matron to tell Mrs. Jamieson he was here and ask her would she see him for a minute. Twice the answer came back, 'No.'

'Please tell her I'll wait.'

That did it. Matron said she had relented and would see him.

All Scott could see was a wizened little face with very sad eyes peeking out of the bed clothes. She'd probably been pretty once, but her face showed the signs of a pretty rugged life. Scott tried to estimate her age but, not being very good at that sort of thing at any time, found himself without any real idea.

'Thank you for seeing me. I just wanted to say sorry for the trouble I caused you.' All he heard was a barely audible, 'It's O.K.'

'Is there anything I can do? Anything I can get for you?'

'No thanks. It's all right. I'm O.K.'

This reply was just above a whisper. Her small thin body hardly seemed to make a bump in the bed. A memory of visiting an aunt in hospital came back to Scott. She had been small and frail too. Scott moved closer to the bed, close enough so as not to miss anything she might say.

'Can I come and see you again?'

At that moment the Matron came and said, almost as an order, 'You'd best leave now, she needs her rest.' There was a quiet 'It's O.K.' from Mrs. Jamieson. The matron left. Scott experienced a feeling of closeness to this lady. Her thin sinewy hand lay on top of the bedclothes and on an impulse Scott reached out and took it in his. She looked surprised but didn't withdraw it, instead murmured, 'Stay a while.'

He pulled up a chair, took her hand again and told her the story of the would-be hold-up, the chase, the crash, then helping the man with the limp take her pram home.

'So, you've seen where I live then. I'm surprised you would want to come and see me after seeing that.'

'After all the bother I caused I just wanted to see that you were all right, it doesn't matter to me where you live.' Her eyes brightened a little.

'Thank you.'

He didn't stay long. Now that he had broken the ice, he thought it best to keep it short, there would be time later for a longer visit.

He visited her regularly always wondering why they were keeping her in hospital. He had become friendly with the matron and found the gruff exterior was only a surface thing and beneath it was a genuine caring lady, but even then, any questions about Mrs. Jamieson's condition were met with a very non-committal, 'She needs rest.'

Scott accepted that he was not going to be told anything by the staff. Indeed, he knew enough about hospital rules to know this would be the case, but he did think he may have been able to somehow elicit some sort of information. But it was not going to be. He wasn't going to get even a little hint so he had to leave it at that.

Chapter Seven

Jock

Scott's job with Harry Fielding entailed early starts and fairly hard work with the concreting, but it suited him for the time, although he realised there were no real long-term prospects, unless one day he became his own boss and took on jobs by himself, but he wasn't thinking that far ahead. At the moment he was quite happy to have a job which paid him enough for the rent and his food and a bit of booze and to have something left to put away at the end of the week.

He'd found a place in the local cricket team. He'd been in the pub one night after work — he'd very quickly discovered that that's where one finds out anything that's going on in a small town — and had inquired about the local cricket team and was assured by Jock the barman that he would be very welcome to come down and meet the boys.

'In fact, I can guarantee you of a game on Sat'd'y if you're free. You can have my place, I'm no good at it, I just play to make up the numbers.'

So it was that unexpectedly he'd become a regular in the team and Jock was still making up the numbers, despite his inability with either bat or ball or his lack of judgment in the field. They were always short of players. Scott saw Jock in action in the first match he played. Jock was fielding at fine leg, the spot where the worst fielders were usually stationed and the ball had been hit wide of Jock who took off after it. Jock lumbered rather than ran. It took him about twenty or so paces to get up a head of steam as he threw one foot after the other like a square gaiting track horse. Jock wore a big floppy hat and as he ran it would sometimes flop down in front of his eyes, as it did on this occasion, causing Jock to run right on past the ball and then stop and look back in time to see it trickle into the fence five yards behind him. Scott had seen a lot of people playing a lot of different sports, but he'd never seen anyone as uncoordinated as Jock. The team didn't expect much of him, and of course they didn't get much either.

Scott had become quite popular, not only because of his prowess with both bat and ball, but also because he had a car big enough to take half the team when they travelled to away games. A bit squashed but he usually somehow managed to get five or six in the car. They were a mixed bunch, some farmers who travelled in farm utes, usually two or three young kids and the inevitable old brigade, one or two blokes who were just 'making up the numbers.' There was one snooty, stand-offish joker who always seemed to find some way of taking his own car when they played away and not take any of the other players. He would always be going to be 'late on Saturday, so you blokes better go on, and I'll see you there' but somehow, he seemed to manage to be there on time. Funny thing that. Scott wondered why the prick didn't come right out and say it. He just preferred to be on his own. The rest of the team had learnt to accept it. It had been going on for a lot of years, so now they didn't even bother to ask him. Everyone was eagerly waiting for the day when he couldn't take his own car and had to condescend to travel with them. That was going to be a very interesting day.

Chapter Eight

Ned

After cricket one day, Scott met Bob Creewell. In the pub after the game. On this occasion Bob was having one of his sessions at the bar. It didn't happen very often, but occasionally he would break out, usually he'd be on his own, away from the influence of his wife, Jocelyn. Not that there was any problem between them, it was simply a fact that when they were together, Jocelyn did most of the talking, and she was very good at it. Nothing objectionable but she just chatted on. There was rarely a silence when she was about. This afternoon was one of those occasions when he was at the pub without her and was thoroughly enjoying himself.

He was drinking with Terry, a local farmer, a big man with a wide brimmed hat pulled down flat above a pair of thin rimmed glasses which seemed to be surrounded by an enormous, unkempt beard, so that all that was visible of his face was a pair of bright blue eyes and a set of molars which would be any dentists delight. Scott had met him before.

Terry introduced Scott to Bob and they had had a couple of drinks when Ned Brannigan walked past. Scott had seen Ned a couple of times about the town and was interested to know who he was.

'Who is that bloke?' he asked as Ned walked past.

Bob turned but Ned had gone.

'What'd he look like?'

'Fairly solid sort of joker. Wearing an old coat and battered hat.'

'Sounds like Ned Brannigan.'

'Yair, it was Ned,' said Terry. 'He's a bit of a clown. One of those sort the town could do without.'

'Actually, you're quite wrong. I have to defend him. I think he's a very clever man. I reckon people would do well to listen to him a bit.'

'But some of the things he comes out with are way off beat.'

'Yair, that may well seem to be the case, but sometimes those way off beat ideas can be very pertinent. People tend to dismiss his ideas without giving them a second thought. Probably because he's often so blunt and tactless they've made up their minds before he speaks. They're not prepared to say — hang on, he could be right, and, well, he just might be right.'

'Like when?'

Bob Creewell was warming to his subject. He'd had just enough booze to be in a talkative frame of mind. When he got started, he was pretty hard to stop. Two or three others had come closer to listen and Terry was egging him on a bit. He didn't need much encouragement.

'Well, what about the time that damn fool politician came here and tried to convince everybody it would be a good plan to close the Ag. Department office and depot and have a bigger one way to buggery somewhere. He had a lot of people agreeing. Even that dill who was Shire president at the time seemed to be in favour of it. What was his name?'

'Coxon.'

'Yair, that's the bloke. Gawd he was a disaster. Just as well he was only there for one year.'

'What about the politician?' Scott asked,

'Yair, what about the politician?' someone echoed.

Bob knew they were having a bit of fun with him, but he didn't mind. It was all in good spirit. He just kept right on, knowing they really didn't care much what he said, that they just wanted to keep him going.

'Yair, that bloody useless politician. He had most of them convinced 'til Ned got to his feet. Remember, there was a bit of shuffling when he started but he soon pointed out that it would mean loss of jobs and the locals would always have to travel to get answers to their problems. Remember he said how it was hard enough to get answers as it was without having to travel miles. By the time he'd finished there was dead silence. Then they clapped, and I clapped with 'em. He won 'em that night 'cos he was absolutely right. He could see it would be bad for the town. You know, lost jobs and loss of a valuable service.'

One of the men listening spoke up.

'You're right about that. I remember it well. I reckon some parasite had got in that politician's ear. Someone was going to make a quid out of that little exercise.'

Bob went on, there was no stopping him now.

'Remember Ned said — and you Mr. Coxon seem to be in favour of this, and remember Coxon stammering and spluttering — Well.... I er.... I only want what's best for the town. And that was Ned's big chance and remember he said — The best thing you could do for the town would be to resign and let someone else do the job. He was right that time and I tell you what he was the only one with guts enough to say it. That Coxon was useless. I don't know how we got saddled with him in the first place.' Terry spoke up,

'That's right. And nobody got up to disagree. And Coxon did resign at the next election. He must've got the message.'

Scott didn't find out the outcome of the Ag. Department story. A commotion had started in front of the pub. For a start nobody took much notice, but the voices became louder and more agitated. Bob and the others at the bar ventured out to the footpath. The main agitator was a big man. A very big man brandishing a cricket bat and advancing towards a couple, standing, cowering with their backs to the pub wall. The man of the couple was shorter and obviously quite a bit older than the man with the cricket bat. The woman younger, probably the older man's daughter. He was standing in front of her trying to shield her as best he could. The big man who was letting forth a stream of abuse, directed at the woman,

'You little bitch. I should never have trusted you. You've let me down for the last time.'

He advanced another couple of steps. At that moment Ned re-appeared. He'd heard the ruckus and had come back. He pushed through the onlookers who had gathered and without breaking his stride walked straight towards the big man. Ned didn't say a word, didn't even raise a hand, just headed straight for the big man who turned as he saw Ned approaching. He faced Ned with a questioning look. A wondering look. Ned's advance took the big man completely by surprise. He didn't try to defend himself, in fact he didn't really think he needed to.

Ned was a few inches shorter than him and was walking as though he would walk on past. The man stood with the cricket bat in one hand, the other held casually in front of him. Without breaking stride, Ned drove his fist into the man's stomach and as he went down smashed a fist to the side of his head. Ned's method of dealing with the situation was perfect. Big and all as he was, the man finished in a crumpled heap.

Ned stood over him and when he thought the man was ready to listen, he spoke in a strong, steady tone,

'Right. I don't know who you are but I think you might appreciate that in this town we look after each other. There's no place for the sort of stuff you just tried on. Why don't you just piss off out of here and don't bother coming back.'

The man finally got to his feet, picked up the cricket bat and made towards Ned. Quite suddenly there were three other men beside Ned, all standing in front of the girl and her father.

Ned said, 'You can have one hit if you like, but you'd better make the most of it 'cos you'll only get one.' The man looked about him then back at the men. Bob was one of the three and he said quietly,

'Might be best if you do what Ned said. Just leave now and there'll be no more problem. And, er, don't even think about coming back. Get out of town and stay out. You're not welcome here.'

Big and all though he was he headed for his car, rather like a dog that's just had a boot from an angry owner. He was visibly cowering, like most bullies tend to be when confronted. Two of the men walked with him to his car.

Ned turned his attention to the young woman.

'You O.K?'

Still shaking she nodded.

Her father was first to speak,

'I can't thank you enough for that. We'll be thankful to you forever. I'm not sure how we would have coped without you. I've seen him angry before but never like that. Thank you, thank you, thank you.'

Ned brushed off the thanks. That wasn't important to him.

'You're new here, you staying in town?'

'Yes, only been here a week. Thought we'd get away from him, but it didn't take him long to find us.'

'Well, you see how things work in this town, any more strife from him and you let someone know. We're here to help.'

The girl finally spoke,

'I can't thank you enough.' Then after a pause, 'I think we might have just found a good place to be.'

Chapter Nine

Alec and Evelyn

Scott continued to visit Mrs. Jamieson regularly. Each visit they chatted more freely. She was becoming a significant part of Scott's life as indeed he was of hers. Conversation came easily between them. Conversation about life in general, about Scott's life, Scott's family, hospital life, life around the town, but his questions about her own life were met with only vague answers, usually followed by a silence or a shift in the direction of the conversation. Although only nineteen, Scott was a rather mature young man and so after this had happened a couple of times, he decided this was a subject best not pursued and probably best not even raised.

Each day she seemed a little brighter but always her face showed suffering, as though she had some sort of pain deep inside. He kept wondering how long she might be kept in hospital and above all, why she was being kept there. Obviously, there was more to it than the accident. He got a little clue one day when two nurses came in and said they needed him to leave now because they had to 'do her legs'. Matron was still not forthcoming with any information.

'I'm glad you come to visit; she needs a friend. She doesn't have other visitors,' she'd said.

All that changed, however, a couple of days later. When Scott called there were a couple of people seated by Mrs. Jamieson's bed. Scott held back when he saw them and was about to leave when Mrs. Jamieson saw him and beckoned to him. Without anything being said, Scott detected something uncomfortable between them, a distinct tension in the room. The man rose and extended his hand saying, 'Hello, I'm Alec and this is Evelyn.' Scott introduced himself and noting the small silver cross in the man's lapel thought — Hell, a bloody parson. He didn't much like the clergy or church people in general for that matter, having been compelled as a child to sit in a tiny church at three o'clock each Sunday, summer or winter, sweltering or freezing, he hardly remembered there ever being anything in between the extremes, listening to various parsons or local preachers droning on and on and on with sleep inducing sermons.

Then he had a sudden thought. Had she called for a priest? Had she taken a turn for the worse? She looked just the same. Why was this joker here? 'Are you O.K.?' How often had he asked that?

'Yes thanks,' came the quiet reply.

Silence followed. One of those silences which lasted

a few awkward seconds yet seemed like hours, till Mrs. Jamieson said,

'Alec is my brother.' He remembered then the neighbour saying something about a brother somewhere in the city. Scott wondered why it had taken her brother so long to call. He could feel the tension, it seemed to get stronger, the air thicker, the atmosphere heavier. Scott decided he would rather be elsewhere, anywhere else really. He left quickly. Outside he took a couple of deep breaths, feeling very relieved to be out of there.

The next day he met Alec and Evelyn coming out the main door. Alec nodded and paused as if to talk but Scott just acknowledged them and walked on. Even though he had only spent a few minutes with them the day before, he felt oddly uncomfortable in their presence. It was more so him than her. He seemed to be a little aloof with a kind of forced smile and she, a shy withdrawn lady, who, although reasonably tall, seemed insignificant. It was as if she wanted to stay in the background, un-noticed, eyes averted, just content to follow her husband like a well-trained sheep dog follows its master. First impressions are usually lasting impressions and often quite accurate assessments but Scott was later to find how wrong he was.

Next day Scott went to visit Mrs. Jamieson. He went to her bedside as he usually did and tried to keep things as they normally were. He didn't mention Alec and Evelyn. Given the previous uncomfortable scene, and her previous reluctance to speak of her past, he felt it may be unwise.

No doubt she would talk about them when she was ready. There followed a few more days of wondering for Scott, about the brother and about what was keeping her in hospital. He'd become quite fond of her, thought of her as a sort of 'aunty', like he'd thought of the mother of the two boys who lived up the road out at the farm when he was growing up. She seemed to fit in to that same category, so it was natural that he felt concern for her. What was her real problem? Why the tension between her and her brother? These questions were getting very difficult to hold back.

She was brighter at the next visit, had a bit more colour in her cheeks. To hell with it he thought, today was the day to ask.

'Mrs. Jamieson, please tell me what is happening, why are they keeping you here?' There was a long pause as she considered the question, then she said simply,

'They found something wrong with my legs.'

'What sort of something?'

'Ulcers.'

'Anything to do with my knocking you down?'

'Oh heavens no. Have you been thinking that?'

'Yes.'

'I'm sorry, I should have explained to you sooner. This is separate altogether. I suppose I haven't been looking after myself very well.'

'How long will you be here?'

'Not much longer.' She fell silent after this last comment and Scott realised, he wouldn't get much more information, more questions would be out of order at that moment so he changed the subject.

'It's good your brother is about. I hope he'll be able to help a bit when you go home.'

She looked away, buried her head in the pillow and started to cry, quietly at first, but gradually the sobs got louder and longer and deeper. Heart breaking sobs. Her whole body seemed to be crying. She shuddered and shook as the sobs seemed to come from deep inside that tormented little body. He'd hit a raw nerve, a very raw nerve. He cursed himself. Why couldn't he have left it alone? What sort of a bloody idiot would keep on like he had? He sat still for a moment, not knowing what to do, then, on an impulse, he knelt beside the bed, took her hand and then rested his head on the pillow beside hers and gently stroked her cheek. She cried and cried and cried. Unshed tears, held back for a very long time now finally released. They had started as a trickle, then a few sobs, then built to an uncontrollable torrent.

Matron came in. She stood and looked for a few seconds, very sensitive to the situation. She'd seen all this sort of thing before and she knew it was best to leave them be. It was quite a few minutes before Mrs. Jamieson could speak.

'He mustn't see my place,' she blurted. Scott thought he had better keep going now, get it all out in the open.

'Hasn't he been to your place?' Then he thought — What a stupid question, but he had asked it more out of surprise than anything else.

'Last week was the first time I've seen him for about seventeen years.'

'That's a bit sad. How come that?'

'I left where I was living. Just wanted to get away for a while.'

'Oh.'

Scott left it at that for then. He knew by now not to rush things with her. Eventually he would be told the story, probably. If not, then, so be it. Probably best he didn't know, even tho' he was very interested, because he'd become quite fond of her and wanted to help her. It was part of his country upbringing even though one part of him said stay out of it, another, stronger part saw her as a friend and also as a parental figure, a sort of replacement for his own mother who had deserted him. His main concern was the care she would need when she came home. Who was going to be there to look after her then? Next time he ran into Alec and Evelyn he decided to ask them. They sat in the coffee shop and talked. He hadn't asked for, nor expected to hear Alec tell his sister's life story.

Scott felt he was intruding on Mrs. Jamieson's private life but Alec insisted on telling the story because he had seen how fond Scott had become of her and he thought it may help Scott to understand his new friend.

'She had a traumatic experience then she started drinking heavily.' Scott didn't ask what had happened, what the traumatic experience was. His innate shyness was still a big part of his makeup which made it difficult for him to ask, but he also felt it better not to ask, felt maybe it would be better if he didn't know, might be better if he waited, as he'd often done. Maybe one day it would come up and Mrs. Jamieson would feel she could tell him.

Alec got to the time when she disappeared and his search for her.

'How did you eventually find her ... here?' asked Scott.

'I guess we got lucky. She had a regular visitor at the hospital. He is the local parson. Besides you he was really the only person who called on her. She hadn't asked him to. He used to just stop as he was doing his rounds. One day she let it slip that she had a brother who was a minister and that was all it took. He asked her which Church and her brother's name. Both questions she eventually, reluctantly answered.'

Scott remarked,

'I can well understand you saying reluctantly. Sometimes I have great difficulty communicating with her, but I'm learning when to speak and when to shut up and wait.'

Alec continued, 'This minister chap asked would she like him to find me and she simply said to wait 'til she was a bit better but he took it on himself to look for me. Thought I would like to know. He told her he was looking for me and eventually she relented and told him to go ahead. He said it took him about ten phone calls over a few days to find me.'

They talked for a long time, Alec mostly, but Evelyn would sometimes interrupt either to correct him or maybe elaborate a bit. She did this with a strength which surprised Scott. She was direct and forthright and each time Alec would immediately stop and allow her the floor, usually only for a few seconds, with her choice of words and perception of things, that was all the time she needed to make a point or explain something. 'That's not right Alec' she would say and then correct him. He never questioned her. She would say things like tell him about the cats, or the holiday at the beach or some other thing and Alec would immediately tell that story. Scott realised Evelyn was a very strong lady. He had got her all wrong. By the end of the conversation Scott had quite a different appreciation of both of them, a feeling of warmth towards them.

As they left the coffee shop Evelyn said,

'Thank you so much for being here for our Jane. Alec and I are so pleased you are about. She has grown very fond of you.'

So, her name was Jane. That was the first time he'd heard anyone call her anything other than Mrs. Jamieson.

Chapter Ten

Marion Creewell

Between work and cricket and one or two evening sessions at the pub and visiting Mrs. Jamieson at the hospital, Scott managed to fill in his time quite easily, at the same time getting to know a few of the locals. Some of the cricketers talked about the monthly dance, held in the woolshed on one of the farms close to the town. First Saturday of the month. Scott went along with some of his cricketing mates. Although he could dance reasonably well, he was still quite shy with girls. He had some reservation about walking up to a group of people and asking a girl to dance in front of everyone. Because of all his reservation Scott would spend most of the evening sitting at the back while all his mates were dancing and clowning around.

'You're not much of one for the dancing,' one of his mates had said.

'Nah, I'm not much of a twinkle toes.'

It all came to a head one night when, between dances,

Scott suddenly found himself sitting with two of the girls. The music started and all the others in the group headed for the dance floor. The only ones left were Scott and the two girls. He really liked one of them. He knew her name was Marion Creewell. He realised she was the daughter of Bob Creewell whom he'd met at the pub. Everyone called her Cree and he knew her friend was Sheena something. He'd met Cree a couple of times and would have loved to dance with her but because of his shyness was unable to ask her in front of the other girl. Cree had figured that might be how it was and nudged her friend who got the message and took off. Scott asked her then. She was quite surprised at how well Scott danced. She wasn't backward in saying so.

'You can dance. I didn't think you could. How come you don't dance much?'

'Oh, I don't know. I s'pose it's because I'm not a very good dancer. You know, always treading on a girl's toes or something.'

'Well, we've done two rounds and you haven't kicked me yet, so I reckon you've not got anything to worry about.'

'Yair, well, sometimes I go O.K.'

'Sheena would love to dance with you.'

'Would she? Well how come she took off a minute ago?'

'She went 'cos I told her to.'

'How come that?'

'Cos, I wanted to dance with you and I figured with just the two of us there you'd nearly have to ask me. And you did and I'm glad you did.'

They danced in silence for a while. Then she said,

'Sheena would love to dance with you. So would Bess.'

Cree encouraged him to dance with the other girls. He gradually became more confident and joined in, all the time feeling thankful to Cree.

The two of them formed a friendship from that time. Scott was amazed how easily he was able to relate to Cree. He gradually came to realise that girls could be his friends. Just friends with nothing serious attached to the friendship. Just mates.

Scott was getting to know some of the locals but the one he really liked and wanted to spend time with was, of course, Cree. They were often together although not as a boyfriend, girlfriend combination. Just mates.

Chapter Eleven

Woodley

On one occasion Scott and Cree met in the street and decided to get hamburgers. They had driven into the supermarket car-park which was handy to the takeaway. Scott was about to park when Cree said,

'Don't park there.'

'Why not?'

'That's Woodley's car.'

'Er, yair, okay, so what?'

'Well, look at the bloody thing.' Scott looked. The car in question was a battered old Holden. There wasn't one panel intact. Each one had a dint or a scratch.

'And? So?'

'My father says never to park near a car like that. The people who drive heaps like that don't have any insurance, don't care who they hit and never pay for any damage they do. He says give them a wide berth, 'specially Woodley's crap heap.'

'Oh, ...okay, ...yair, I see what you mean.' They parked

further along. As they sat in the car talking and eating their hamburgers, Cree pointed to a man coming out of the supermarket.

'That's him.'

'Who?'

'Woodley.'

Scott saw who she meant, an untidy looking man wearing a grease stained boiler suit and a battered hat.

'What's he do?'

'Who?'

'Woodley.'

'What'd ya mean?'

'Woodley. What's he do for a job?'

'Oh, yair. He's got the garage. You know, fixes cars and that. Other people's that is. Not his own.'

'Oh.'

Woodley threw some shopping bags in the car and sure enough a few seconds later they heard the crunch of metal against metal. Woodley was about to drive away when a smartly dressed lady approached. Woodley looked at her and you could almost see the expression on his face saying — ah this one will be easy enough to convince there's no point in looking for repair costs. He got out of the car and greeted her,

'Sorry about that. I just misjudged it a bit.'

She confronted him from about arm's length, hands on hips. Scott was about to say something but Cree held up her hand. 'Shush a minute, this could be quite interesting.' The lady started, 'You were going to drive off, weren't you?'

'No, I was going to leave a note.'

'Like buggery you were. I was watching you. You had no intention of stopping.'

'Aw, come on, it's only a little scratch, it's not much.'

'It mightn't be much to you in that battered old shit heap of yours, but it's more than just a scratch to me. That'll cost at least two hundred dollars to get fixed.'

She was getting into her stride now. Getting really fired up. Woodley was on the back foot. He knew it wasn't going to be easy to get rid of this one. Usually a bit of a chat and a bit of a sob story and people understood he had no money and he couldn't afford a better vehicle and he couldn't pay much towards the repair.

Cree said,

'Looks like he might have met his match this time.'

'Aw, come on lady it's only a small mark.'

'...and you'll pay. I'm sick of useless bastards like you.'

He stood and said nothing. He was done and he knew it. By this time a few people were standing about, listening but pretending not to listen. All curious to see Woodley's reaction. Some of them had been his victims.

'Come on, what's it to be? Either you pay or do I call the police? I've got plenty of witnesses. You'll be in deep shit if I call the boys in blue. I bet that bloody thing isn't registered or insured or anything. They'd have you off the road in a flash.'

'All right I can see I'm not going to bluff you. What do you want?'

'Two hundred bucks should cover it.'

'Aw, fair go lady you know I can't pay that.'

'You piss about much longer and it'll be three hundred and I'll call the cops as well.'

'Okay, okay, you win, you win. Wait till I get my cheque book.'

'You never give up do you? You think I'm crazy? Cash, you old bastard. Cash.'

Scott and Cree sat staring at this scene, both quite surprised by the language this lady was using. She looked so prim, hardly the sort of lady to be so assertive. Cree began to giggle. Woodley opened the car boot and spent a few minutes rummaging around, finally coming up with some notes and some coin and slowly counted it into her hand.

'There y'are. That should cover it.'

'That's only a hundred and seventy. You've got more there. Give me the rest of it.'

'Ah, give me a break. That should be enough.'

She just stood still, with her hand still extended, waiting.

'Oh well. Okay.' He scratched in the boot again, finally coming out with just the right amount, and counted it into her hand.

'Right, that's it. Now piss off.' And he did. She watched him go and a funny thing happened. The few people gathered around clapped, and a few 'well dones' could be heard. She ran her hand over the scratch -

'My brother'll soon fix that. He's a panel beater.' The crowd dispersed, laughing.

Cree said,

'My Dad says Woodley is the perfect advertisement for contraception.'

Chapter Twelve

Jane

'I'll be going home at the week-end.' Jane said it with a little apprehension, a little doubt in her voice. Scott had looked forward to the day she was well enough to leave, but now it was at hand he too had some doubts. Would she be able to care for herself, in fact would she look after herself? Would she start drinking again? They had never talked about the booze. Another thing bothered him. He had never forgotten her words when talking about Alec, 'He mustn't see my place!' Those words had been said when she was in a very emotional state, the sort of time when true feelings and thoughts are apt to just spill out, unchecked, thoughts which at other times would most likely be kept in check, hidden away with the excuse — it's not that important or it'll keep, or I'll bring that up another time.

Scott was faced with a dilemma; would he tell Alec and Evelyn about Mrs. Jamieson's house? What to do? Tell or not tell? He made a decision, made it with the impulse of youth, he would tell.

Then he changed his mind. He would stay right out of it. Later, when he remembered Evelyn saying, 'Jane has become quite fond of you, he thought maybe there's another way, half tell, or tell with a proviso. Somewhere he had read a statement something like — a little less tact now can save a lot of headache later, or was its heartache, didn't matter which really — the idea was still the same. He wondered if that applied to him now. After some deliberation he realised there could be another way. He would go to her place and do a bit of a tidy up so that if Alec and Evelyn went there it wouldn't look so bad, outside at least. He'd intended to do that for her anyway. Harry Fielding liked early starts, so he was usually finished for the day by two o'clock. This is a regular feature of the concreting work. He headed around to her place immediately after work the next day. He hadn't been back since that day they had delivered the pram and he wasn't sure what he was going to do. He found the place easily enough but was in for a surprise when he got there.

In the driveway was a utility and trailer with rakes and shovels all neatly arranged in a rack and mowers and ladders and all the gear of a professional gardener or handy man. The grass had been cut, the gravel path weeded and raked, the roses pruned and all the prunings stashed in the trailer ready to be taken away. He wandered round the back. The pram was still where he and the old man had left it. Two men were working at the back of the house, one, a young chap about Scott's age, chipping some unruly grass, the other, an older man, doing some repairs to the guttering. By the amount of cleaning up they had done it was obvious they must have been there for a day or two before. The men told Scott a minister chap had hired them. They had met him on site and he was quite specific when he told them what he wanted.

So, Alec had been there. Scott felt a great relief. All that worry about telling or not telling had been for nothing. He also felt relief that the clean-up was being done properly. These men were professionals and were doing more and a far better job than he could have ever hoped to do.

Scott still felt he would like to do something and the thought of concreting the path crossed his mind. The more he thought about it the more logical it became. He could do the digging and boxing after work and get the boss to do the actual concreting. He discussed it with the handyman chap and he agreed to leave that part till Scott worked the idea out. As Scott was leaving, he caught a glimpse of the lady across the street peeking through the curtains. He hadn't given her a thought and then realised she would be wondering what was going on. He marched straight over. She didn't answer his knock. He knocked again and then finally he heard her shuffling up the passage. She half opened the door. He spoke into the dimly lit passage. All he could see was her outline, silhouetted in the light from a distant window.

'Just wanted to tell you Mrs. Jamieson is coming home at the week-end. We're just tidying up a bit. You know, make it a bit nicer for her.'

'Oh, that's good. She'll like that.' Scott knew from his

previous encounter that that would be about all the communication there would be, so he headed off, calling, 'See you' as he went.

It didn't take Scott long to prepare the path. He dug it out and borrowed some timber for the boxing from Harry. Harry was very good about the job. Scott had told his boss the pram lady story and Harry had been very helpful. Even insisted on coming around and helping Scott with the boxing, making sure the levels were right and the lines were straight.

'You'd better give me some idea of the price for this,' Scott had said. 'I don't think she's got much money, but anyway, I want to do it for her. I'll probably have to get you to take it out of my wages, if that's O.K. by you.'

'You don't have to pay me anything, that part is from me, but you will have to pay for the concrete. Those fellers seem to want money for their stuff. Strange thing that. Probably be about a hundred and fifty.'

'I haven't got that at the moment. Can you take it out of my pay?'

'Well, if it helps, I'll take it over three or four weeks. You know, sort of spread it out. That'll make it easier for you.'

'Will you do that? Crikey, thanks Harry, that'll be great, gee, thanks a lot.'

So, it was arranged, the boxing done, then the concrete poured all in a couple of days. All finished in time for Mrs. Jamieson's return.

Scott had arranged to drive Mrs. Jamieson home from hospital. Now he was faced with another dilemma, how to tell her about the repairs and tidying up Alec had organised.

He waited until the day before she was to go home, then just simply blurted it out.

'There's a surprise waiting for you when you get home.'

'Oh, is there. What sort of surprise?'

'Alec has organised some tidying up.'

'What sort of tidying up?'

'He's had the grass mowed and the roses pruned, that sort of thing.'

'Oh. So, he's been there then.'

'I don't know that; some men did the work. Actually, yes, he must've been there 'cos the men said he'd shown them what he wanted them to do. Yes, I guess he must have been there.'

'How did he find out where I live?'

'I don't know. I haven't seen him since that last time at the hospital. I guess in a small town it wouldn't be that hard to find out.'

'What?'

'To find out where someone lives.'

'Oh, yes, I suppose so.' There was a silence between them for a minute or two while Mrs. Jamieson thought of the shock her brother would have had when he first saw her hovel. She stared at the wall, her thoughts obviously far away, then like someone waking from a dream, coming back to the present she spoke in a resigned voice.'

'Ah, so you've been back there too.'

'Yes. I wanted to mow the grass or something but it'd all been done.'

'Oh.'

'Oh, and we organised a concrete path. Down the side and round the back.'

Silence again, and again her face took on that faraway look. The look he had come to know. When that happened, it was useless to try any further conversation, usually she became distant and the talk ceased, dried up, dried up to non-committal mumbling and prolonged, uncomfortable silences. This time however, Scott thought, to hell with that, I'll get her back to the present, the here and now, instead of letting her go away to some other place, some other life somewhere, shutting him out. Suddenly Scott had some doubts. Maybe I shouldn't have done the path. Maybe she's cranky about it. Bloody hell, if she didn't want that I'll be in the shit good and proper. He waited a while,

'I hope that was O.K.' He didn't think she was the sort that would get her knickers in a knot but you never could tell. Really, when he came to think about, he began to have some real doubts. Thoughts occurred to him that they may have invaded her space. Moved into her private world. A world which he supposed she'd kept to herself for years. He thought he'd better make light of it.

'Course, if it's not right we can come and take it away.' She still didn't speak. He took her hand. He'd often done that. It was a gesture she'd come to expect occasionally, and something she quite liked but this time she made to withdraw. He held on firmly,

'Don't shut me out please. I hate it when you do that.'

She looked at him, surprised.

'Do what?'

'Go away like that.'

It had become a part of her makeup over the years. Part of her defence when things became a little too difficult. She would just simply shut herself off, go away to a place of her own, not physically, but off to a silent place. Just go away. Thinking. It was probably at about this time that she realised she was important to him. In the short time she had known him she hadn't thought of that. She started to think back — what had he said about his mother? She had left when he was quite young. He hadn't talked about it much. She began to realise that maybe she was becoming a substitute mother. Hell, that's the last thing she wanted, having someone depending on her for something. She couldn't imagine having someone relying on her for anything.

Then another thought. My son would have been about his age. The thought of her son brought the tears on again. Once they started there was no holding them back. She hadn't told Scott about her son. The memory of the night she'd crashed the car always brought tears — feelings of guilt, of uselessness, thoughts of what might have been. Her husband had died immediately, but her son died in her arms, crying 'Mummy it hurts' gradually getting weaker and she, then the ambulance men unable to save him, unable to do anything for him. He was just two and a half years old. The tears slowly stopped, gradually dried up. She came back to normal after a few minutes.

'No, it's all right about what you've done. I'm sure I'll like it.'

He really did heave a huge sigh of relief, a very audible sigh. She just grinned at him,

'There's nothing to worry about.'

Scott wondered if they would ever be able to talk about those times when she withdrew. Wondered if she would ever tell him what had happened that caused her so much grief. Alec had given him a bit of a clue when he said something about a traumatic experience. He hated seeing her suffer the way she did. Maybe one day she would tell him.

They made arrangements for the next day. Scott had bought a dressing gown for her at a charity shop. He had taken quite a bit of time selecting it and even though it had only cost three dollars he was rather pleased she had it on when he called to pick her up. He wasn't sure what she had on underneath but her hair was nicely combed and she even had on a little lipstick. The nurses had made sure of that. They had become quite fond of her.

It was only a few minutes in the car. The 'goodbyes' and 'look after yourself' from the staff had taken longer than the trip home. Scott had made her promise, 'No more tears now,' he said, but it didn't quite work. When she saw the transformation to her place that Alec had arranged, she had had a little cry, but this time they were tears of joy, of pleasure and thankfulness. Scott had bought a few groceries for her. Just the usual basic things, bread, butter, milk, tea and some cold meat so she could make herself a sandwich or something. She had a little bag which he had also picked up from the charity shop. There wasn't much in the bag, just a few toiletries the nurses had organised. Scott carried these few things to the back door. He didn't want to go inside and also didn't want her to be in a position where she would feel obliged to ask him in, he felt sure she wouldn't want to, he imagined it would be pretty terrible, so he said, 'Will you be alright now? I'll call tomorrow if you like to see if you need anything.'

She took his hands then. It was the first time she had initiated any contact between them.

'Thank you for being so kind,' was all she said.

He felt the bond between them was suddenly strengthened. He could feel an uncomfortable moment coming and he didn't want that. Didn't want to break a very special time between them. He left quickly.

He called each afternoon on his way home from work. Each day bringing a few things she needed, going to the back door where he would sit on a log someone had long ago placed there, no doubt an intended part of a long-forgotten garden feature of some sort. She would sit on an old canvas chair which looked in imminent danger of collapse, and they would chat, sometimes only a few minutes, sometimes quite a long time. There was a mutual unspoken agreement. He didn't seek to go inside; she didn't invite him in. The pram was still there, untouched. Still the booze was not mentioned.

Gradually her health picked up, she put on a little weight, her cheeks coloured and her eyes had a bit of a sparkle. He discovered she had quite a sense of humour and they would often giggle together at some of her jokes. She was well enough to walk to the shops by now — it wasn't far.

One day Alec and Evelyn were there. They talked for a while and Scott left before them.

The next day the Pram was gone. Scott missed a day then sometimes two. She seemed to be getting on very well.

Chapter Thirteen

Jane

Then it happened. One afternoon he knocked on the door as usual. No answer. Probably at the shops, he thought, but then, no, she usually went to the shops in the mornings. He would have left then but it didn't seem right. Back door open, screen door unlocked. Then he heard movement, a noise of someone shuffling and a bit of a bump. Maybe she had visitors, but that would be unusual. Other than Alec and Evelyn that day he hadn't struck anyone else there any time he called and had not heard her mention anyone else. Although the house was dark inside, he could see part way up a passage which led from the back door. Then he saw movement. Saw her drift across the hallway from one room to the other, a ghostly apparition in the dimly lit hallway. There seemed to be only one person there. Then a crash and a curse. Another crash and then silence. He called out. Still silence. An ominous silence. A silence which made him shiver a little. He had to decide, leave or go in? He thought, I can't leave now, can't leave it like that, I'll have to go in. In the bedroom he found her sprawled on the floor, one shoe off, arms at odd angles where she had fallen. Around the room he saw a chair upturned, bedclothes pulled off the bed in a tangled heap, a half empty bottle of some sort of spirits, spilling on to the grotty carpet.

She lay there, eyes half closed, groaning, completely out of it, oblivious, unfeeling, unseeing, unhearing, sozzled, paralytic, blind rotten drunk.

What to do? He'd never seen anything like this.

Had no experience of it. At that moment she was a complete stranger to him. He didn't know her. She certainly didn't know him. Didn't know anything. The room was dark, only had one small window which was covered with an old faded curtain. He switched on the light. A dust covered shade hung around a weak globe. She hadn't moved. He straightened the bed clothes and with some difficulty, picked her up and laid her on the bed. On her back at first but then he remembered from somewhere that people can choke if they vomit when unconscious. He thought there would be a high likelihood of that happening, so he rolled her on her side with her head near the edge of the bed and her body across the bed so she wouldn't roll off, turned the light off and left.

He supposed this had often happened, wondered how long it took to wear off. He called back that evening. No lights on. Sneaked in. Peeked in to the bedroom. Flicked the light on. She hadn't moved but her breathing seemed O.K., deep and regular. He switched the light off and left. He was still awake at mid-night. Unable to sleep, and not likely to sleep, he got up and went round to her place again. This time the lights were on and he could see movement behind the curtains. A shadowy figure, she seemed to be moving quite normally. Relieved he went home to bed.

After a restless day at work, he called at her place on the way home. She answered his knock. Came out and started to chat as she usually did as though nothing was out of the ordinary. He was surprised to see how fresh she looked, not a trace of a hangover. He knew if he had had a night like that, he would have been still struggling in recovery mode, even well into the afternoon. Unsure how to proceed he let the conversation run along for a while then decided to face the situation head on. To abandon all pretence.

'I called yesterday. I heard you fall. I went in and put you on the bed.' He said it quietly, without any hint of drama or accusation, without any emotion at all, just a quiet statement similar to a comment anyone might make about the weather.

Her face fell. She just said,

'Oh.' Then after a pause of quite a few seconds, added,

'So, you know then.' Another pause, then,

'I'm surprised you came back today after seeing me like that.'

'I came back last night, twice.'

'Oh.' Another pause.

'The second time I could see you moving about. I knew you were O.K. so I didn't come in.'

Seeing her discomfort and feeling a bit uneasy himself he made a real effort to keep the tone light. He said with a half-smile,

'It wasn't easy either.'

'What?'

'Getting you on to the bed. You weren't helping me much.'

'Oh.' Then after yet another pause, 'I don't suppose you'll call much now that you know what I'm really like. I won't blame you if you don't.'

'I'm here, now aren't I? It didn't stop me today, and I can't see it stopping me tomorrow either. Did you think I would like you any less?'

She looked at him, thinking, I'd love a son like this guy. Then she thought — I wonder if my son would've been like him. She realised then; in the space of a few minutes she'd gotten over her grief for her little boy. All the tears she'd shed over that little feller suddenly became easier to handle. She felt then that maybe she'd finished her grieving.

She said in her quiet voice,

'Thank you,' then after a short silence, 'You don't seem to be all that surprised. How'd you find out?'

'The fact that they kept you in hospital so long made me wonder if there was something else, then I remembered the mother of a mate of mine had a similar thing. And then I remembered the stuff in the pram. Some bloke and I had brought it home. That's when the penny dropped.'

A silence followed between them. Scott felt comfortable with that silence. Mrs. Jamieson just sitting quietly and him wondering how to break it and yet not in any hurry to do so. He waited quite a while then asked quietly,

'How often does it happen?'

'That's the first time since I came home from hospital. I

thought I may have beaten it but it just crept up on me, and once you start you can't stop.'

'I'm here to help you know, if I can and if you'll let me.'

'Thank you.'

'Only, you'll have to tell me how. Just don't shut me out.' He felt as though he was taking a responsibility. Maybe that's what she needs, he thought, someone to take charge of her life for a while, someone to wield a big stick. It would have to be someone who really cared about her. Someone who could look after her a bit and show her she is important. Maybe I can do some of that. But, no, she really needs someone more her own age.

Chapter Fourteen

Chapman

They met at the dance one Saturday night, Chapman and Cree.

Chapman had found her name was Marion Creewell but he called her Cree like everyone did, and she called him Chapman like everyone did. He'd only come to Archerville a couple of months before. Quite quickly he'd found the Saturday night dance was a good place to meet the locals. That's where he'd first met Cree. Took a fancy to her straight off. She found him amusing, always good for a bit of a laugh. A couple of times they had met in the street, both times outside the milk bar. Each time they had talked for quite a long time. Each time Cree had hoped he would suggest they go for a drive somewhere, but somehow; he didn't seem to take any little hint she dropped.

She loved to hear him talk, took great delight in encouraging him. All sorts of funny things came out. Sometimes it was like turning the radio on to one of those interview programs when the interviewer didn't say much, just the odd question to keep the guest talking. Like the time they sat in his car and talked about disagreeing.

'Well, you know how it is,' Chapman had said, 'If you express an opinion there'll always be someone who'll disagree.'

'That's not always the case. It may happen sometimes but not all the time.' As soon as Cree said it, she realised she'd done exactly what he'd just said. She thought he may not notice, but no, 'There y'are, just like I said.'

'Just testing, I didn't think you'd notice.'

'My father said that.'

'What?'

'About disagreeing.'

'Oh, did he? I reckon your father must be pretty smart.'

'Oh, I don't know, actually he thinks I'm pretty clever. He said once he's got great admiration of my far-reaching knowledge on a wide variety of subjects.'

'He said that?'

'Well not exactly that, but that's what he meant.'

'What were his exact words?'

'He said I'm a bloody smart arsed little know-all.' Cree laughed at that.

Coming as he did from a farming background, he'd found a part time job on a local farm and was fitting in well there, and at other times he went fruit-picking, so he was always working at something. He told Cree he didn't want to be like some of the lazy bastards he'd seen who found it easy to just bludge on the unemployment money.

She was very popular with everyone so he was quite surprised and thrilled when she agreed to go for a drive with him after the dance one night. He'd only driven a short way from the dance and then he'd parked quite near a street light. Cree was surprised at that. She was used to the boys taking her a little way out of town or at least somewhere they wouldn't be disturbed, but no, here they were in a brightly lit part of the street. She almost suggested they should go somewhere else, but thinking they could always move on later, decided not to say anything. It was only the third time they had been alone, and so she was more than happy to go when he had finally asked, and thought it better not to be too pushy.

The subject of his father came up again.

'You must have a fairly good relationship with him though.'

'Yair, I s'pose so. Yair, pretty good I s'pose, altho' we need to keep a little bit of distance. We get on O.K. then.'

'Does he ever get really mad at you?'

'Yair, sometimes. Like the time I brought home a funny report from school.'

'What was that about?'

'I had a teacher called Elliot. We didn't get along at all. I thought he was a pretty good advert for contraception. He was a real prick of a teacher. At least I thought he was till the last week of the year.'

'Actually, my father said that about Mr. Woodley.'

'What?'

'That thing about contraception.'

'Who's Mr. Woodley?'

'He owns the local garage. You'll meet him one day.'

'Oh. Right.'

'O.K. Tell me about the last week of school. What happened then?'

'Actually, it all started early in the year. There was a cricket match going on out on the oval and I was watching it out the window. You could see right down the wicket, you know, right behind the bowler and the bowler hit the batsman on the pads, you know, right in front of the stumps. The whole team appealed and at the same time I jumped up and flung my arms up and yelled — Howsat? The whole class roared. He didn't think that was very funny and yet he didn't give me a detention or anything. He should have I s'pose, but somehow, I got away with it. Come to think about it, I s'pose he'd've had trouble keeping a straight face when he told the other teachers.'

'Yes, I imagine it would have caused a bit of a giggle.'

'We had bits of differences through the year, but when he failed me in English in the final exam, you know, the subject you have to pass, I got really pissed off.'

'What'd you do?' She wanted to keep him talking.

'I told him what I thought of him. I said, you did that on purpose. I said — Just because you don't like me doesn't mean my work's no good. We knew he was leaving and I said I was glad he wouldn't be there next year and I reckoned we'd be better off when he left. And do you know what he did?'

'No, what?'

'He said — Stand up Chapman, and I thought here it

comes, and he goes — Keep going Chapman. And I goes — What? And he said it again, he goes — Keep going, don't stop now, what else do you think? I got a hell of a shock, but then I thought, what the hell, he's leaving so I won't have him next year and I kept going.'

'You did? What else did you say?'

'I said — you're a hopeless teacher. We'll be better off with someone else, and he kept encouraging me, rolling his hands over and over like a footy umpire calling play on, and he kept saying louder, louder, and I kept going, telling him he couldn't teach a kindergarten and all that sort of thing and finally I said and your hair looks like last weeks' lettuce.'

'What?'

'Well, it did. It was shocking. Always flopping everywhere.'

Cree burst out laughing at that. Chapman went on,

'He laughed at that too. The whole class laughed. I suppose it was funny really. It took several minutes before anyone, even Elliot, could speak. And do you know what he did then?' He didn't wait for Cree to answer. She was still giggling.

'He was sitting at his table at the front of the class. It was on a raised platform and he stood up and said — Chapman you've done well but I want you to learn something from this. I want you to realise that nothing you can say can hurt me or bother me in any way unless I let it. He stressed that 'unless I let it' bit. Then he said, now, *I* won't let it bother *me*, he stressed the I and the me, but it is vital that you always remember an outburst like that can be devastating to some people. That was a strong statement, you really let your feelings out. I can handle that, but that sort of blast can really hurt. Some people will not be able to handle it. Then he goes — sit down now and keep that in mind. I want you to always remember that. Funny thing, suddenly I started to like him.'

'Actually, he sounds like a really great guy, but I can understand your father being a bit cranky about all that.'

'Oh, that's not what he got mad about.'

'It's not?'

'No, it was the report Elliot had written.'

'What'd it say?'

'In it he'd put — your son would do well to find some other form of entertainment.' Creewell doubled up with laughter at that. 'I think my old man got a bit pissed off at that 'cos he said, if that's what your teacher thinks you might as well leave school. I don't think he was serious, but I jumped at it and I goes, Good, I will then, and that was that. I think he thought I'd come home on the farm, but I didn't want to do that. I did it for a while but then I got a job with a stock agent.'

Cree was leaning back in the front seat listening to all this, fascinated. Although she would much rather be in the back seat fooling around, she felt it was strange that somehow, she was content to just listen.

'How did you get the job?'

'It was funny how I did that. I was at a sheep sale and I was eardropping on two agents talking.'

'It's eavesdropping.'

'What is?'

'When you are listening in on someone else's conversation.'

'Oh.'

'It's eavesdropping, not eardropping.'

'Oh, well, ...er....yair... O.K.... that then, I was doing that, and one of 'em said — I could do with a young bloke to work at the moment, but it's hard to get someone good and reliable, and I just walked up and said — I heard that, will I do Mr. Watkins? Like, it was just an impulse. Didn't stop to think or anything, just walked right up and said it.'

'How'd he react to that?'

'He knew who I was and he stood and looked and said — You cheeky young bugger, and I goes — yes I know but do I get the job? The men both laughed, then Mr. Watkins said — O.K., start on Monday, be at the office at six and don't be late. I thought — shit, that's as bad as farming. I didn't know where his office was but I thought I'd better ask Dad instead of asking him. So I said — right-oh Mr. Watkins I'll be there. I was so pleased with myself. Like, I didn't even ask how much he would pay me or anything.'

'And?'

'I worked there a few months. They took the mickey out of me for a while, but it was all pretty harmless.'

'What 'd they do?'

'Who?'

'The men. How'd they take the mickey out of you?'

'Oh, that, er, well the first time was at a clearing sale. You know how they hold things up while the auctioneer sells it? Well, here I was, holding up this grotty piece of old horse harness and Mr. Watkins was taking bids from everywhere. Hell's bells, I thought, this stuff's worth about a dollar if that, and he was up to thirty. The crowd was giggling a bit and I was looking around a bit mystified and when he got to forty dollars he said — Sold — to the holder!! The old bastard had set me up, I was the only one there who didn't know what was going on.'

'The bugger. What'd you do?'

'Well they all had a bit of a laugh and that was O.K.

Fortunately, I had a quick reply, I just said I only bought it for you, so you can catch a filly. Everyone had a good laugh. It went down all right in the finish.'

'What else did he do?'

'The next time it was a bit embarrassing. The sale went on for quite a while and one thing you learn very quickly is that there are no toilets at a clearing sale. You make sure you go just before you go to the sale. I'd asked him what to do a couple of times and he said just hold on. Towards the end I had to go so he said — Go down to the end of the row behind that old tank. I didn't hesitate. I just strolled down there and I had a real good stream going when suddenly there were people everywhere and he was saying, — now we'll sell this old tank. The bastard had brought the sale right down to where I was. It's just as well I can take a bit of crap.'

'It's a wonder you didn't tell him to shove his job.'

'I bloody near did but then I thought, you bastard, I'll show him so I just kept right on. Actually, I've only just now seen the funny side of that. I suppose it was O.K. Just a bit of harmless fun really, but I thought — you'll keep. I got him back a couple of times later and then we sort of understood each other.' Cree was still giggling, but finally managed to ask,

'How did you get back at him?'

'Oh, that. The day after the tank episode was the sheep sale and it was a bit hot and dusty and by the end of the sale everyone was a bit buggered and we still had sheep to count out and he was a bit further down the yards and he yelled out to me — Can you count the sheep out of pen B 6 ? and I goes, — too right. See there's a bit of an art in counting sheep as they run past, you get one or two then a rush of three or four in a bunch, then one or two more and then another rush and it's easy to lose track. There were still quite a few men around and I said quietly to them — he thinks I can't count sheep; you watch this. I called out ready, here they come and then I called out, there's one, there's another one, there's three, there's two more, and there's four more. It was a bit late in the day for that sort of a joke but all the men laughed so he couldn't really go crook. They all knew about the tank thing from the day before. It doesn't take long for stories like that to get round in the bush. Farmers are like anyone else, they like to share a good joke, so they all knew I was getting a bit of my own back.'

'You really are a bit of a character, aren't you?'

'Oh, well, I do like to have a bit of fun.'

'What happened next?'

'When?'

'Next time you had him on.'

'Oh, yes, that was even funnier. He's got this racehorse see, actually it was quite a good horse I found out later, and we were watching this neddy train, and Watkins was big noting himself in front of a few of his racing mates. He had a stop watch and I said — can I time him? He was a bit reluctant to hand the watch over but a couple of the men said — Go on, give the kid a go, so he more or less had to. He handed the thing over with these instructions on how to work it, and I goes — It's O.K. Mr. Watkins I know how to do it. So, he goes — All right then, time him from the 600-metre post. I made a great show of holding this watch up and pressing the thing as the horse galloped past the post on the other side of the course. There were about a dozen men there and Watkins was all smiles as the neddy came round and thundered past us at the winning post. He was really pleased with the run and he turned to me and asked — What time was it? I held the watch up and shook it a bit, looked at it and said — It didn't go, it's still on nought. There was some muttering amongst the men and Watkins started to get real shitty, and I just said quietly — So I s'pose you could say he did it in no time. It got a great laugh. I think he nearly sacked me that day but with all the men laughing he more or less had to wear it.'

'You really did that?'

'Yair. Actually, I had timed the run so it was O.K. when I told him that.'

'Sounds like you had a pretty good intro to the way things worked.'

'Yair. It was pretty good really. Actually, we made a pretty good team after that. He taught me a lot of bush philosophy, and a lot of the principles of a good stock agent and he taught me how to read people a bit. He said sometimes the hype and excitement of an auction turns people's brain, then you get the situation where some fool buys something too dear then goes looking for a bigger fool to sell it to. But he tries to avoid that. I saw that happen a couple of times with other agents, but never with him. And most important he said never sell something to someone that they can't get out of if they find they need to get rid of it later. He reckons there are a lot of agents whose idea is to sell at any rate and to hell with what happens later, like, they just don't care about the client just as long as they make a sale. I've watched that since and he's dead right. My father knows all the ones you couldn't trust in the district. Farmers are like that; they tell each other what's going on.'

Cree was still sitting back in the seat, leaning against the door, her thoughts on what might have been when she was brought back to the present. She didn't think she had missed much of his harangue. He was still talking.

'One time I got into strife with his missus.'

'How did you manage to do that?'

'We'd just got back to his place after drenching some sheep for a client and as soon as we walked in, she started at him. She said — you were supposed to ring Bartlett's before you went today. They've been ringing all day trying to find you, and I didn't know where you were and he just kept walking past her without saying anything and she said, that's right, just ignore me that's typical of you these days, and when he was out of earshot I said, Yair, I've noticed he's a bit like that too, and she rounded on me and flared up. Crikey, it was a bit scary. I'd never seen a woman flare up like that.'

'What did she say?'

'She said, now just a minute young man… I can say things like that but you can't.'

'That would've set you back on your heels.'

'It sure did. But only for a few seconds and then she was real nice as always and said would I like a cup of tea. They always drank tea, never coffee. She always made it in a tea-pot, never used tea bags. I tell you what, I was always pretty careful not to over step the line after that. We talked about various people while Mr. Watkins was in his office. She knew pretty well all their clients and she was just as insightful — is that a word?'

'I don't know but I s'pose you can use it 'cos I know what you mean.'

'Well I reckon she was just as, er, that word I just used, as he was. You know, she'd have met most of them or talked to them on the phone. Like, the place we'd just been to, he was all right but I couldn't take to her at all and Mrs. Watkins asked how I got on with her.'

'Oh, that would've been a bit ticklish.'

'Yes, it was a bit. I wasn't sure how much to say after the previous rebuke and she sensed that so she said — come on, you can say it this time and I said I didn't know how to handle her and she was a bit fiery and I was bloody glad I wasn't married to her.'

'Did you actually say bloody'?

'Yair, I did. Deliberately. I thought I would just test the water a bit more, and she said — she's one of those people who are easily offended and in fact if you don't offend her, she'll often go out of her way to make sure she gets upset somehow. I laughed when she said that, actually, we laughed together.'

Cree was fascinated by the way these stories just seemed to keep coming.

'Have you ever struck a person like that?'

'Like what? Mrs. Watkins?'

'No. A person who's easily offended.'

'Well no, not really. Sounds like a bit of a hard case, the client I mean, not Mrs. Watkins, she sounds great.'

'Oh, yair, I reckon, she's the best. We had quite a few talks, usually short ones while I was waiting for him but by crikey, she covered a lot of stuff in a short while. She was one of those people who could change the subject in mid-sentence. Sometimes you had to really concentrate to keep up.'

Marion didn't make any comment but he went on,

'I guess I mostly listened rather than talked, altho' sometimes she would egg me on a bit.' When Marion didn't comment this time either he said,

'Am I boring you?' Her mind had wandered again. Even though she found him to be great fun, she felt it was late enough.

'No, you're not boring me, not in the least, but I think it's probably time I was getting home.'

'Oh, yair I suppose it is getting late. Hang on, I need a leak first.'

Cree thought there still may be a chance for a bit of hanky-panky but still felt it was not the right time to make any sort of a move, so she said, 'I need one too but I don't think there's a tank here anywhere.' They had a bit of a laugh at that.

They both hopped out of the car. Chapman walked away a few steps but Cree left the door open and squatted in the light, right beside the car. Perhaps I can still stir him she thought. She deliberately took her time and she was still squatting when he got back in the car.

'Didn't take you long,' she said as she stood up, still facing him. She pulled her shirt up a bit, just enough to give him a little look at her bush as she pulled her slacks up and kept talking as she did to make sure he was watching. He just said,

'That's fascinating, I've never seen a girl have a pee before,' started the car and headed home. She thought, you'll see more than that before long. Just you wait till I find the right moment.

When they reached her gate she reached over, took his hand, then quickly put her arm around his neck and kissed him. Not just a little peck on the cheek, but a full passionate kiss, full on the mouth. She held the kiss for a few seconds, then broke away, thinking, I'd better not hold on too long, I might scare him off.

'Thanks for tonight, I enjoyed it, it was great,' she said it as she slipped out of the car.

She walked to the gate hoping he would follow but he didn't, just sat there till she went in the gate. She turned and waved, still hoping, but no, he drove off.

Chapter Fifteen

Ben

Her parents would be in bed by now, probably well asleep. They were used to her odd hours and gave her a pretty free reign, never waited up or anything. She headed inside and went straight for the cupboard where her father kept his booze, grabbed a bottle of Johnny Walker and took a big gulp straight from the bottle. It burnt all the way down. She'd done this before but only rarely. It wasn't for the taste; it was for the effect. She waited till the burning eased then took another large mouthful. She debated waiting and having another but decided against it. Usually a couple of big swigs was enough. She replaced the top and went to bed and lay waiting for the booze to have its' effect. Soon, completely relaxed, she slid her hand between her legs. It was not as good as the real thing but it was a reasonable substitute.

She kept thinking maybe next time I'll ask him, then if he doesn't want to at least we'll talk about it. She was still playing with herself when she heard her brother come in.

Ben was four years older than her. As he passed her door she called,

'Ben.'

'Ah sis, you're awake.'

'Yes, and bloody frustrated.' They had a very close relationship, just about as perfect as any brother and sister could have. They talked about anything, joked about anything, shared everything. No subject was taboo between them. It was their mother's influence more than their father's. They had always done things with her when they were small. She was usually the one to take them to netball, football, swimming, cricket and all those things that kids need to be taken to. Their father was away a lot with his job and was rarely available to do the taxiing to and fro to parties and dancing lessons and the like, he just never seemed to be around when these things were on. The weekends were always hectic but she never complained. She was always there for them and it was not surprising that all this caring rubbed off on them. They were always there for each other. When Ben turned eighteen, he had taken over the taxi role a bit and often drove Cree to some of these activities, become a sort of surrogate father. All her friends thought he was fantastic and told her how fortunate she was to have such a great brother, but she didn't need them to tell her that, it went without saying, she would do anything for him just as he would for her. Some of her mates were quite forthright about how they would love to get him alone for a while, but they accepted they were all a bit too young for him. Three or four years seemed a lot at that age, but it didn't stop one or two of them from putting out feelers in his direction. So far, he hadn't taken any of them up but, although they didn't know it, he had been very tempted a couple of times and it was probably only a matter of time till he would be tempted enough to follow up one invitation or other. A couple of them had even asked Cree to ask him but she hadn't. She simply said, if you want him, you ask him, but even then, she knew sooner or later she would ask for Milly. Milly was her special friend and she would love it if she and Ben got together. Maybe one day she would ask.

'How come that? Did you miss out?'

'Yes, I bloody well did, and I really wanted him too.'

'You must have been a bit slow; you don't usually miss out. How come? You weren't with that bloody Clifton Dexter, were you? Or is it Dexter Clifton, I can never remember which way round it is.'

'No, not him. I tried it with him once but he didn't set the world on fire.'

'What, couldn't he even get it up?'

'Oh, he got it up all right but I was only just starting to enjoy it and it was all over. No, it wasn't him. It was a new boy in town. Chapman's his name. Don't know the first bit. I've been with him before and we just sat and talked, but I thought tonight it might lead to something, but it didn't. We sat in the car for about two hours, two bloody hours, in the front seat mind you and he didn't even try to kiss me or anything. Didn't even touch me. Why would that be? God it makes me horny just thinking what it might have been like.'

'How come you didn't start something?'

'It's funny, with most of the other boys I would but I fancy this one a bit and I didn't want to scare him off. Why do you think he didn't start anything?'

This was the sort of conversation they could and often did have. No fears, no secrets, frankness and openness was always there between them. Even as they talked her hand was still between her legs, not moving much, but she made no attempt to hide what she was doing. He was used to her doing things like that and simply sat on the end of the bed and talked. It was quite a normal thing between them.

'How old is he?'

'I don't know really, he's probably twenty-one or twenty-two.'

'Well that's probably it then.'

'It doesn't matter to me, so why should it matter to him?'

'Three or four years makes a difference to some guys. It does a bit to me, that's why I don't do anything with your friends, even though one or two are pretty tempting.'

'Which ones?'

'Well, just one or two.'

'Yair, but which ones? You'll have to tell me now. Come on, tell.'

'Well, Thelma for one.'

'I tell you what, you picked the right one there. You wouldn't have to ask her twice. She's really got the hots for you. Come on who else?'

'Maybe Caroline.'

'Ah, her too, and she's on the pill. Thelma isn't. You'd have to be a bit careful with her, but you'd have no worries with Caroline. Are you going to ask them?'

'Maybe one day.'

'Thel is a bit reserved. She holds back a bit, just can't let herself go. We keep telling her to go on the pill, makes a hell of a difference when you know you're safe. Caroline and I found that out, we started at about the same time. You'd love it with Caroline, she really lets herself go. And Milly, what about Milly?'

'No, not Milly, she's too much like a sister.'

'Oh, that's a bit sad. She's the one that asked me to ask you. She's the keenest of them all.' The disappointment in her voice told Ben a whole lot. He hadn't thought about it much but quite suddenly he realised the girls had talked about him, and equally just as suddenly he realised that his sister wanted him to start looking at her friends a bit more closely.

'Milly did? Oh, did she now? Well maybe I'll have to think about that.'

It wasn't a yes but Cree knew the idea was well planted. Maybe it would happen one day. Ben was sitting on the end of Marion's bed. Her hand was still between her legs and she had parted them a little and was still stroking herself when she asked,

'Did you have some tonight?'

'Too right.'

'Lucky you, lucky her.' Her hand was moving a little further and a little quicker.

'Gawd you must be in a state, I'll leave you to it.' He kissed her cheek, and said goodnight. His footsteps were hardly at the end of the passage when her first orgasm started.

Chapter Sixteen

Jane

A few days later Mrs. Jamieson invited Scott inside for the first time. She showed no sign of any bad effects of the binge she had had. It was a cold, wintery day. One of those dark, dismal, depressing days. The cold wind was blowing at the back door as he knocked. As soon as she came to the door he said, 'Not staying today, too bloody cold, just thought I'd call to see if you wanted anything.' Her reply was short and simple as she flung the door open,

'Get in here. It's time I invited you in.' He entered with some apprehension, not knowing what he might find, half expecting a mess. He was pleasantly surprised when she led him up the passage way. The door to the room he had seen the night he put her to bed was closed. She led him into a small dingy room which was obviously the room she used as her kitchen and it was spotless. Everything was nice and neat and clean and tidy. The only problem he had was seeing in the half darkness. Visibility was probably only about forty per cent, like many of those old weather-board houses. The minimal light came from one small window.

'Now you see why I haven't invited you in before. I don't have much to offer.'

He looked at her as she stood there looking sort of forlorn. For the first time he stepped up and put his arms around her. It was an impulsive move, he didn't stop to think, just stepped up and did it. It seemed a natural thing to do. She responded, returning the hug. They stood thus for a few seconds and then he said,

'I didn't come to judge where you live, I came to see you.'

After a few moments she said in that quiet way he become used to,

'Thank you.' Just a simple, quiet, 'Thank you.'

Mrs. Jamieson made coffee in two large mugs and they took them into the adjoining lounge room which to Scott seemed even darker. Immediately he felt he would love to knock a large hole in the wall, put in a big window and let some real light in. A whole lot of light. His mind went back to the small bedroom which had been his as a young boy and to the day his father had a carpenter in and they had put in an extra window. It had made the room seem so much bigger and the effect of being able to see the whole room as one unit was incredible. He thought about saying something while they made some small talk as they often did. Maybe he could offer to do it, or somehow arrange to have it done. However, he felt that this was not the time, then later, decided, maybe it was as good a time as any. Their relationship had developed over the months to a point where they could talk openly about most things, be frank with each other, without the need of the tact which is usually associated with a developing friendship so he blurted it out.

'You know what I'd like to do to this room?'

'No, what?'

'I'd like to put a big window in that wall there and let some real light in.'

He wondered how she would react. His heart was beating a little harder when he realised he may have overstepped the limit of their relationship. There were times when their roles seemed to reverse and he became the older one, the more mature, the one to make the decisions and she was like a little girl, so he was a bit relieved when the little girl in her responded,

'But wouldn't that make it hot in summer?'

'We could use blinds or outside awnings or something in summer and then open them up in winter. I reckon the sun would come right in here. It'd be fantastic, that winter sun in the afternoon'd really warm this whole room.'

'Would it really?'

'Yair. Dad did that to my room when I was a kid. It was terrific the difference it made. We could get a window from a house wrecker or something. Maybe I could do it, or I could get someone and I could help. Wouldn't cost much then.' Nothing more was said about it at the time but he could see he had started a train of thought.

'Well, maybe,' was all the response he got.

Chapter Seventeen

Marion and Chapman

Marion and Chapman were quite often together, sometimes going for a drive or just sitting in the car in the street, or on a seat in front of the shops. She wondered why Chapman never made any move to kiss her or even hold her hand or even touch her in any way. She thought of a few possibilities. She knew he wasn't shy. Maybe he's gay, or he could be just an old-fashioned puritan, one of those who thinks you should wait till you are married. She'd heard they exist but she'd never met a boy like that. Sometimes her mind would wander as she imagined them on the back seat. She hoped he would ask her soon, she was ready and willing, very willing. She loved meeting new guys. Usually she couldn't wait to get her hands in their pants, and usually if they didn't ask her, she was pretty quick to ask them. Somehow it was different with Chapman. She fancied him but something told her to wait.

It seemed appropriate. She knew they would make love

eventually and no doubt it would be better for the wait. Horny and all as she was, she knew there was no hurry. She could wait. But still she wondered why he didn't ask. One time they'd been sitting in car for an hour and he hadn't even tried to kiss her. Her daydreaming had taken her far away, well not all that far really, just into the back seat. She brought herself back to the present.

The real reason he didn't try to start anything was none of these things she'd imagined.

Chapman thought the world of Cree and he realised she expected him to try to get physical with her. Gawd knows she had dropped enough hints, but the simple fact was, he wanted to find his way slowly with all these new people. Didn't want to be regarded as a go getter who would go to bed with just anyone.

There was a code of conduct between the girls. Don't butt in. Cree saw him first so Cree knew she wouldn't have any competition. Cree had had it off with quite a lot of the boys and wasn't backward in asking. She couldn't understand that Chapman came from a different place, had a different set of values. Sex for him was regarded a little more seriously. Not just a good night out. He'd only been with a couple of girls, and with both it was fairly lasting and pretty traumatic when it ended, so he was in no hurry to get involved with anyone. He knew, however, that sooner or later he was going to ask Cree to get a bit serious. He seemed completely oblivious when sometimes she stopped listening.

She wondered if maybe he'd heard stories about her. It

was no secret that she was very co-operative but also the boys all knew she would only have sex with the ones she fancied. Rumour had it that she had also fancied one or two of the older, married men too. One time when her attention wandered, he asked,

'Am I boring you?'

'No, not at all. Actually, I might shock you if I told you what I was thinking.'

He had a fair idea but he left it at that.

Chapter Eighteen

The Meeting

Scott came to the meeting quite early. He sat at the back so he wouldn't be noticed and when Cree walked in, she seemed to be with Chapman, a young bloke he'd seen at the dances but had never really met. Cree said hello to him as she came in, then sat with Chapman towards the front of the room. Chapman had only come to the meeting because Cree had asked him. The subject hadn't really interested him very much and when he had heard the speaker for a few minutes it interested him even less. When this man spoke, he hardly opened his mouth. Only his lips moved. His teeth hardly parted. Chapman couldn't remember seeing anyone quite like it before. He supposed maybe he had but he couldn't remember noticing it. With this joker it was so obvious Chapman felt like calling out — open your bloody mouth when you speak then maybe we could understand you. He almost said it. He was like that. Speaking up when he would have been well advised not to. Got him in trouble sometimes but often it cleared the air too. The trouble he had was know-ing which time was which. Actually Mr. Watkins had been good about that. Tried to educate him in the art of timing. Once he'd been pretty blunt with a client and Watkins over-heard him. The client had some very ordinary cattle. Not very well bred at all. Two or three people had said that and Chapman had seen it too but while the others had chosen to say nothing, Chapman had one day said without thinking — I reckon you ought to sell all these and start again. Watkins had said — Don't ever say things like that to my clients again. While you may well be right, and I know sometimes a little less tact now can often save a problem later, blokes don't like to hear that sort of thing coming from a young smart-arse. He'd always kept that in mind and decided this was one of those *little less* moments.

He looked around the room — Am I alone in this? It pissed him off so much that he couldn't concentrate on the message the speaker was trying to get across. He just kept staring at those immobile teeth thinking it was just as well they were a good set of molars. Chapman's thoughts wan-dered. They ought to make this joker Minister for paper bags or cardboard boxes or something. What a great time a psy-chiatrist would have with this bloke. No doubt he would have some incredible explanation for it. Not that it would do either of them much good. He smiled at the thought, one egghead analysing another.

He thought it amazing that a Government department would send a man like this all the way up from the city, no doubt a reasonably expensive exercise. Fancy me coming to a meeting like this. Only half interested in the subject in the first place.

Creating an area to be fenced off to save the habitat of the nimble footed numbat and the hairy nosed green tree frog or some such bloody obscure species. What earthly use will they be to society anyway? And then to find a clown as the main speaker. Perhaps this whole thing is a joke. Maybe they are putting me on. Or even trying to pull the legs of the whole town. He had a flash of people waving banners in the main street, collecting funds and carrying on a treat. I wonder if these supposedly endangered things really exist anyway?

He remembered a holiday he'd had at his uncles' place when he was about sixteen. The government had provided quite a bit of money for a program to save some obscure little frog, and they had a display in the local hall, with this egg-head from some equally obscure Government Department, proudly showing some of these endangered species which he'd found in a creek up in the hills behind the town, claim-ing to have found the last living examples of this bloody frog, and the look on his face when one of Chapman's cousins said,

'There's millions of them things in the creek at our place.' How many wasted dollars of public money was that?

He wished he'd gone to the pub.

'What about you Chapman?' The question jolted him back to the present. He remembered his school teacher, Elliot say-ing once — Chapman, you've got the attention span of a flea.

'Me, what?'

'How about being part of the team?' The question came from one of the ladies who ran the local milk bar. Chapman had often been there to buy his fish and chips. Sometimes they had chatted a bit. Chapman was surprised she knew his name, and even more surprised to find her asking him something. Cree nudged him. She knew he hadn't been listening.

'They want a group to do some preliminary work.'

Searching for a way out he decided to come right out and say it.

'I don't think I'd be much good at that,' and then he thought he'd better make it pretty clear in case someone asked him again later so he added,

'And besides I've got a sore finger.'

There was a bit of shuffling and a few giggles around the room. One or two tongues clicked. Cree kicked him in the ankle, quite hard. Mercifully they found three or four volunteers fairly easily and the meeting ended fairly soon after. The last bit was a bit of a blur for Chapman and he was more than pleased when he could get up and go. He was standing outside with Cree silently vowing, 'Never again' when Cree's father walked past and, without breaking his stride said,

'You weren't much bloody help in their young fella' and then, 'Let's go Marion.' Chapman had only met Bob Creewell once before and he thought he'd better steer clear of him for a while. The pub was still open so he wandered in. Scott was sitting at the bar with his back to the door so he didn't see Chapman come in. He was telling a couple of his mates and the barman about the meeting, and had just finished the bit about the bloke with the sore finger when he looked up and saw Chapman's reflection in the mirror above the bar. Chapman had heard enough to know Scott was talking about him and was beginning to get annoyed until Scott turned and said,

'Here he is now,' and then directly to Chapman,

'Do you want a beer? I reckon you earned one in there. Give this bloke a beer Jock.' The ice was broken in a second. Scott offered his hand,

'Scott.'

Chapman shook the outstretched hand,

'Chapman.'

Chapter Nineteen

Scott and Chapman

Scott and Chapman became good mates quite quickly and they often could be found together around town and sometimes in the pub.

They had a few things in common, some common interests, one of which, Scott found, was cricket. Scott had been playing in the local team. Most weeks they seemed to be struggling to find a full team as is often the case in small country towns. One night, after a few beers and a bit of chat Scott had a sudden thought.

'Hey, now there's a thing. Do you play cricket?'

'Well, I usually play back home but I didn't get started this year. I knew I wouldn't be playing the whole season so I just didn't start.'

'There's only about three games left this year, but I reckon if you wanted to, we could use a regular to fill in. We won't make the finals or anything, but we have a lot of fun.'

'Aw I don't know, well.... maybe.'

'Why not come down on Saturday. We're half way through a match, we're batting this week. They made two hundred and fifteen last week. We'll struggle to get that many, especially seeing we'll be batting one short.'

'How come that?'

'Well, it's quite a story. One bloke we had was a fruit picker, you know, just passing through the place and he was playing for us. Quite a good cricketer he was too, but last week we found that wasn't the only thing he was good at.'

'Oh, what was he up to?'

'Up to his nuts I reckon. Seems he was visiting the wife of one of the Italian veggie growers about a mile out of town when the husband wasn't about if you get my drift. Apparently, she made him welcome a few times but then last week the veggie grower came home when he wasn't expected. And he wasn't alone, He'd brought a mate with him. Rumour has it that they met our mate as he was coming out the door. The husband just said something like — you've got twenty-four hours to get out of town, and when you go don't ever come back. Guess how many hours he had left when he went?'

'Well, I imagine he went pretty quick.'

'You're right about that. He was gone in about an hour. Apparently, he went back to his digs, paid his bill and was heading for the gate when his landlady said, Ah, ha. — they caught up with you, did they? and he said what do you mean? and she said everybody knew they 'd catch you sooner or later, but he wasn't waiting round for any small talk, he was off like a shot, straight out to the orchard to collect what was owing to him, then away. He won't be here to bat on Saturday.'

'Sounds like a few people knew about it.'

'Oh, yair, a few. The silly bugger. He was lucky he didn't get carved up properly. You don't mess with those Italian guys. They don't do things by halves. Silly twit. Still she is rather nice, but I can't see me risking my balls for it. I've heard too many stories about those fellers which seem to end up involving blood on the streets. No, I've got more sense than that.........Well, anyway, come down on Sat'd'y.'

'Yeah, okay, I might just do that. Where are you playing?'

'Down at the oval at the end of Tyler Street. It's called the Tyler Street oval would you believe. You know, in behind the trees.'

'Is there an oval there? Crikey, I've driven past there and not seen it.'

'Yeah. You go through the trees and on about half a k. Can't miss it. I'll ask the captain if there's a spot. Do you bat or bowl?'

'A bit of both. I usually opened the bowling back home, batted in the middle order.'

'Sounds like you might be a handy bloke. See ya Sat'd'y.'

Chapman wasn't sure he wanted to get involved but thought it wouldn't hurt to go and see their form. If he did decide to play it'd only be for a few weeks and it would be a chance to meet some locals.

He spent Saturday morning checking out some fishing spots he'd been told about, once again, by a bloke in the pub. Where else do you get local knowledge in a country town? The local pub is the place you will always meet someone who knows someone who knows the answer to any question a new chum might have, or for that matter anything a local may want to know. Country people are always very ready to swap stories and show their knowledge. Unfortunately, things sometimes tend to become exaggerated and quite often a little distorted, and the longer one stays the more one has to sift through the information and to try to retain that which may be useful. It is up to the listener to sort out the facts from the pub talk. The directions he'd been given were fairly explicit. You'll find a good fishing spot about ten k's out along the creek. You'll come to a sweeping bend and just after that you'll see a black gate on a track into the bush. It's always open. Follow that track in to the creek, there's plenty of good fishing there.

After driving along, the creek for about half an hour, looking for, but not finding, the illusive 'black gate just past a bend in the road' he decided to turn back and head to the pub for a counter lunch. Consequently, it was mid-afternoon by the time he left for the cricket.

He found the ground all right, tucked in behind the trees and it was immediately obvious why he hadn't known it was there. It was completely hidden from the road. Scott was just taking the pads off when Chapman arrived.

'How's it going?'

'Bloody well run out. I never get run out. I was going all right too.'

'How many to get?'

'We need another twenty-five.'

'How many wickets left?'

'Three, but one of them's Jock.'

'Who's Jock?'

'You know, the barman at the pub.' He nodded towards the portly bloke sitting on the seat with a stubby in his hand. It was immediately obvious that Jock's batting prowess would be fairly limited.

'I suppose that was a bit of a rough comment on him but we don't usually expect much of him with the bat, or in the field either I suppose. Anyway, he makes up the numbers so we're thankful for that. There was a loud appeal. Scott and Chapman both swung round in time to see the umpire shaking his head. The players sitting, waiting, relaxed a little, but the tension was mounting. Chapman could easily pick the recognised batsman of the two at the crease. The guy with the red cap was obviously a fairly capable bat. The other chap he could see had a limited ability and it was quite clear to Chapman that the red capped bloke was the one who would have to get the runs. Chapman asked,

'How many's the bloke in the red cap?'

'Ah that's Ben. Cree's brother. Been in for a fair while. Must be about forty by now.' Ben clouted a four soon followed by a three. Cheers from the fence soon changed to Ohs as the other batsman's stumps went flying. Still eighteen to get. The next batsman edged a ball past slip, ran two and was run out by about three yards trying for a third. That brought Jock to the crease. Jock seemed to have the idea that you shouldn't do things by halves and you should swing the bat as hard as you could so that if by some strange quirk of fate, the bat and the ball should happen to be in the same place at the same time, the ball would travel a long way. The first ball he faced missed his bat by quite a considerable distance, however he managed to make some contact with the second and the ball sliced off the blade over the wicket-keepers' head and they ran three. This was probably not a good idea because it left Jock spluttering and having to face the first ball of the next over. Still fifteen to get but the whole team knew even two or three would have been too many. The three he had just scored equalled his top score for the season. The bowler figured he only had to put the ball on the stumps and Jock would do the rest. He was quite right too. It took the bowler only two balls to find the stumps.

They went to the pub after the game. As they approached the pub Scott once again saw Ned in action.

Chapter Twenty

Larkin

Learning to live in a small town was quite a process for Larkin. He breezed down the main street, window down, radio blaring and pulled up with a screech in front of the Post Office as he had done a few times since he'd moved here two weeks ago. There were two or three people standing around. They seemed to be watching him. No-one spoke. Typical small town he thought. He went into the little shop next to the Post Office and bought a paper and a packet of cigarettes. He dropped the empty packet on the ground as he got into his car. He spun the wheels as he took off and as he went, saw in the mirror a small boy carefully pick up the packet and put it in his pocket. That's odd, he thought. Why would he do that?

Larkin was to learn a lot in the next few days. He'd rung his mates back in the city, 'You know, there isn't a cop in this town, you can park anywhere and tear up the street at any speed, no way of getting caught. This is the place for me.' Larkin roared up the main street and skidded to a stop in front of the pub just near Scott and Chapman. They'd seen him about the town once or twice and had not been impressed with what they saw. A man appeared beside his car. An ordinary looking bloke, wearing an old jumper and track suit pants. He put his hand on the door of Larkin's car before Larkin could open it. Scott had told Chapman about Ned. About the altercation in the street which Ned had settled in a few seconds, and about one or two other things he'd heard.

Scott said, 'That's Ned.'

'Who?'

'Ned. You know, I told you about him.'

'Oh, yair. I remember.'

Ned spoke directly to Larkin,

'We've decided to let you stay in town for a few more days, you know, just to give you another chance at fitting in. Your form so far hasn't been too good, but we'll give you another chance.'

'What? But I like it here, and I've got a job and all that. Anyway, who the hell do you think you are telling me if I can stay in the town or not?'

Scott and Chapman watched as Ned allowed Larkin to get out of his car. A couple more men appeared, and a lady came out of a shop. Next a man on a bike stopped behind the car. Ned spoke again in a quiet, calm voice,

'We don't have a policeman in this town as you've obviously noticed. We don't need one. The locals keep all the order that's needed. Now think about what I said.... We've decided you can stay a few more days, just to see how you go. Do I make myself clear?' By this time there were about eight people standing close by, watching. Larkin looked around them. He'd seen only a couple of them before. Certainly, had never seen the man who was doing the talking. He was, in fact, the only one who had spoken.

Larkin began to take notice. He'd never heard of anything like this and he'd begun to feel just a little bit uneasy. Especially seeing a couple of the bystanders were women. Somehow that made it just that bit more serious. These people were trying him out so he thought he would brush it off, bluff his way past. Show these people he could look after himself. He took two steps towards Ned. Ned didn't move. Larkin stopped. He had to stop. Ned was blocking the way between his car and the next. They stood, eyeball to eyeball. After a pause, Ned said,

'Now just get back in your car and go away, and think about what I said. We'll see how you are in a few days.'

Larkin looked around the people standing about. They were all just doing that, standing around, but they were all watching, waiting for his reaction. He thought it might be as well to listen, and after a few more moments silence, he decided he'd better listen.

'A few days, Okay?'

As he drove sedately away, he realised they had been watching him, and conferring about him and deciding what to do about him, and this was the decision. He also recognised the significance of the — we don't need a policeman statement.

As they went into the pub Scott said,

'See what I mean?'

'About what?'

'About Ned's influence in the town.'

'Oh... yair.'

Larkin thought about it for a day or two, then he decided it was for the best if he left. He just packed up and left without saying anything to anyone. No-one was surprised, in fact most people were glad to see him go.

Chapter Twenty-One

Jane and Scott

Scott continued to visit Jane every few days. They would chat, sometimes for only a few minutes, sometimes for quite a long while. The window in the lounge room wasn't discussed again. Scott felt the idea was still there but it was not likely to happen. It was during one of these longer visits, Scott sensed Jane was un-easy about something. He knew her well enough by now to say what he was thinking. Their relationship had grown to be one of old friends who could say anything to each other, open up their deepest thoughts, so when Jane took so long to speak her piece Scott knew something different was happening in her life. Finally, he couldn't stand it, so he blurted out, 'Come on. What's eating you? You've been like a cat on hot bricks all day. What is it?'

'I've decided to move on. You know, sell up and go away.'

Scott was shocked. This was a real bombshell. The last thing he expected to hear. He sat silent for a while, thinking, remembering the last time someone had said that to him.

Remembering how devastated he'd been when his mother had said something like that. He sat trying to get his head around the idea that she would leave. This woman who'd become a sort of mother substitute, now she was going to leave, just as his mother had. He looked at her, then out the small window. He felt the tears coming. Then after quite a long silence, he said, 'I don't want you to leave. I've grown so used to you being here. We've had so much together. I don't want you to leave.' His voice trailed off. He covered his mouth with his hand, trying, not very successfully, to hide his emotions. He composed himself, and asked,

'When will you go?'

'I've sold the house. They take it over in three weeks.'

Scott was devastated that she had done all this and not said anything to him. Then, he thought, why should she? It was really none of his business. Then he repeated the question,

'Where will you go?'

'I'm going to stay with Alec and Evelyn for a while, and I'm not sure after that.'

Scott knew there was no point in continuing the conversation. He stood, said he'd like to see her before she went and left quickly, before he lost control. He didn't want her to see him in a state. Jane, for her part, was quite shocked. She hadn't expected a reaction like that.

He stayed away 'til a few days before she was due to go.

'Just thought I'd call and see if you want help to pack or anything.' He tried to keep the mood light, but it was quite a struggle. She said,

'No, I'll be O.K. thanks. Alec has organised people to pack and all that.'

'Well, I guess this is goodbye then. Please write. I'll go now. I couldn't stand to see you drive away, so I won't come back before you go.' He hugged her for a second, then took off before he completely lost control.

Jane stood and stared after him, thinking, wondering what she had done to him. She realised then what she meant to him. Scott drove down to the cricket ground and just sat in the car.

The clouds dissipated a little and the sun elbowed its way through the gaps and sent cheerful shafts of light down on the oval for a few minutes, then it clouded over again.

Scott felt it was like a sign. One minute all was bright and cheery and then it all became dark with heavy black clouds. He felt exactly the same as he had the day his mother had left. Like a part of him had suddenly been torn away with gut wrenching force. He felt like bawling his eyes out but somehow composed himself. He couldn't believe that the two women who'd been such an integral part of his life would leave him, desert him. He drove back to his rooms, laid on the bed and then it all welled up inside and he burst into tears.

Chapter Twenty-Two

The Drum

Chapman had only been able to find some part time work so he was often at a bit of a loose end. It rained quite heavily the day before. Rain means stop work for concreters. Harry had told Scott there would be nothing to do for at least three days, so Scott and Chapman headed off to Chapman's parents' place. Scott hadn't met the parents so he was a bit apprehensive about the visit. Chapman had told him he and his father had a mutual, unwritten understanding that they keep just the right distance between them. Things had been a lot better since Chapman had left home. The distance was about right.

It was about a three-hour drive to Chapman's home. They arrived about lunch time. Chapman's father, Wilson, was talking to another man as they pulled up. They caught the last of the conversation. Wilson was saying,

'Bloody hell, Jack you're hopeless. You come here and ask my advice, then you say you reckon you'll do the opposite.

You'd already made up your mind before you came. I don't know why I bother. You're just wasting my bloody time.'

'Ah, I don't know Wilson. It's always good to get a second opinion. You know, helps clarify the thoughts.'

Wilson threw up his hands.

'Ah, piss off, you silly bugger.'

'I think I will. Thanks for your help Wilson.' He winked at the two boys, got in his car and drove off. Wilson came over.

'Shit, sometimes that prick is a pain in the arse.' He held out his hand,

'You must be Scott. How are yer?' They shook hands and headed to the house. Inside, Chapman's mother was setting plates on the table. Scott saw before him a woman of striking beauty. An incredibly beautiful woman. A strong woman with broad shoulders and a broad smile to match. Chapman said,

'Mum, this is Scott. She came over to Scott, took both his hands in hers, looked directly into his eyes and said, 'Ah, I'm so glad to meet you at last. Kelly has often mentioned you.'

Scott was taken by surprise on two counts, first by the striking appearance of this woman. Chapman hadn't really spoken about her much. Scott couldn't take his eyes off her wide, twinkling, sparkling eyes, and dark shoulder length hair. Her whole face was beaming. She exuded charm, and vitality. Her whole being seemed to be vibrant. She seemed far too young to be Chapman's mother. The other surprise was her calling Chapman, Kelly. Scott's first reaction was — Who the hell's Kelly? Nobody had ever called him anything other than Chapman. That's all they knew. Nobody knew his first name.

She was still standing in front of him, holding his hands,

looking into his eyes as she said to Chapman, 'You didn't tell me he was a handsome young man Kelly.'

'Oh, leave him alone Mum, you'll embarrass him.' He was certainly right about that. Although Scott was enjoying the attention, he was beginning to feel a bit awkward in front of the others.

'Don't mind Mum. She always likes to make people welcome. What're we having to eat Mum?' Wilson chimed in,

'Yes, come on Lucy. Leave that boy alone. Let's eat.'

'Oh, we were just getting acquainted. I think he likes me.'

'Yes, I'm sure he does, but you can talk to him after.'

'Oh, all right then. Put the jug on while I dish up.' She winked at Scott and went about serving the meal.

Scott was taken by surprise by all this attention but he was starting to enjoy her flirting. It made him feel as though he did mean something to her in the short time since they had met. Chapman brought him down to earth,

'Don't mind Mum. She flirts with anything in pants. You'll get used to her.' She gave Scott a silly grin.

'I do not. I only flirt with the nice ones.'

After the meal Wilson headed out to his favourite place, the workshop.

'Lovely meal Mrs Chapman.'

'Why thank you Scott. But, call me Lucy, I'd like that.'

They could hear Chapman's father hammering in the workshop.

'Let's go see what the old man's up to. I always try to do something to help when I'm home.' They wandered out to the workshop.

'You two looking for a job?'

'I s'pose so Dad. Depends what it is though.'

'How about we load that drum of fuel and you take it up to the pump.'

'O.K. Dad. I reckon we can handle that.' Chapman backed the farm ute up to the shed.

'Which drum Dad?'

'The forty-four.'

'Dad never has learnt to talk metric.'

'Don't need to. Everyone knows what a forty-four is.'

They loaded the drum.

'Now just unload it on the channel bank, then roll it over to the pump. You know how I do it.'

This last comment was more of a statement than an instruction. A forty-four-gallon drum of fuel is quite heavy. It slides quite easily across the steel floor which makes for easy loading but the two factors together make a pretty lethal combination. If the driver tends to go a bit quick without tying the thing in the back somehow, it is inclined to slide, which it did when Chapman turned onto a bridge a little too sharply with a little too much pace. A loose forty-four-gallon drum sliding across the tray of a ute makes it very hard to keep control of the vehicle, in fact, almost impossible. The ute careered sideways, slid off the track and cannoned into the railing fence beside the gate. It smashed two rails and one headlight. That was bad enough but unfortunately the drum had quite a head of steam and the side of ute did nothing to stop it. It went off the tray, landed on the channel bank and before the boys could get to it, slowly eased its way into the water. Chapman backed the ute off the fence and turned for home.

'I think you're about to see why my old man and I don't always get on.'

They drove up to the shed. Wilson came out.

'You were pretty quick. Get it unloaded okay?'

'Well, we unloaded it okay but it's not quite where you wanted it.'

'Oh, well that's all right. I'll fix it later. Where'd you put it?'

'Well, actually it's in the channel. It sorta slid off the back when we were going over the bridge.'

'Shit son. Didn't you tie it to the tray?'

Then he spotted the broken head light. Chapman saw him looking.

'Oh, then there's that too. I sort of lost control and ran into the fence.'

'Bloody hell boy. How the hell can you make such a mess. He walked around for a few seconds, quietly fuming.

'Jesus Christ. I give you one job to do and somehow you manage to create four others.'

Wilson walked around for a couple of minutes, then, 'Right, get the tractor and a couple of chains, and those two planks.'

Wilson sent Chapman into the channel with the chain and after a bit of a struggle he managed to get the chain around the drum. Wilson hooked the chain to the tractor and slowly dragged the drum up on to the bank. Chapman clambered out of the water. Mud up to his knees.

'Hold her there till I get the ute backed up.'

'O.K. Dad.'

The three of them rolled the drum up the planks and on to the tray.

Scott had watched Wilson and Kelly. He was amazed how well they co-ordinated. Each seemed to know what the other was going to do next. Seemed to know what the other wanted. Even though Wilson was obviously in charge of the operation Scott could see him defer to Kelly every so often.

'Right, now chain the bastard on this time.'

They did that. Chapman's boots squelched as he drove but it wasn't till they had unloaded the drum that he took them off. As he washed them and his legs in the channel he said,

'I thought I'd better wait till we were out of range before I stopped to do this. I don't think the old man was in any mood to be hanging around.'

'You know, I watched you two. You work well together. Why it is you say you don't get on? Like, I can understand him being just a trifle annoyed about the whole thing, but when he settled down you got on real good.'

'A trifle annoyed is the understatement of the year. I was thankful you were here. Christ he would have blown his top. He's never hit me, but there's been times when he's gone awful close. I reckon today would've been one of 'em.'

'Nah, there's no way in the world he'd ever do that.'

'Ah, yair, I suppose you're right. Actually, I reckon one of the main reasons he's often shitty with me is 'cos I didn't stay home here on the farm. I s'pose when my two older brothers went off doing other things, he reckoned I'd be the one to stay. He never said it but deep down I think he's still angry at me for leaving.'

'What'd they do?'

'Who?'

'Your brothers.'

'Oh, one went to uni. Did Ag. Science. So, I s'pose he's still got some connection to farming. My oldest brother took on journalism. He's working for a newspaper up in Queensland. He'll never come home to the farm, but the other one just might one day. Probably a long way off yet though.'

They drove up to a gate.

'We'll go through here and I'll show you where we used to swim, that's if you ever get to open the bloody gate.'

They went through some trees and came to a creek. There was only a narrow trickle of running water, but it looked clean and inviting. The stream meandered over some tree roots and a few stones then widened into quite a large pool.

'What a fantastic place to swim, and plenty of shade all around.'

'Yair. Great. Crikey we spent a lot of time here in summer. Sometimes the water'd stop running but the holes never dried up. Always enough to swim in.'

They sat in the ute under the shade of a big old grey box tree.

Suddenly, out of the blue Scott said, 'Gee I like your mother. She's fantastic. She's really with it.'

'Yair. Everybody loves Mum. She does really well to stay out here. On her own most of the time. She must get awful lonely at times but she copes with a smile most of the time.

She loves it when we have visitors. Sometimes she has to keep the peace between Dad and me.'

'She go out much?'

'Not often. Goes into town for the bingo sometimes.'

'Where? Archerville?'

'No, Bates Hill. It's closer. We never went to Archerville much. They might come more often now though. Now that I'm working there. You ever play bingo?'

'No.'

'I tried it once. Found it pretty boring after half an hour, but Mum likes to go every so often. She meets the local women and has a good old chat. I think that's why half of them go.'

Chapter Twenty-Three

Lucy Chapman

Scott found Chapman's mother easy to talk to. He was still shy with girls his own age but usually coped well with older women. Chapman and his father were out fixing the bridge Chapman had knocked down and had, at Lucy's insistence, left Scott and her to chat. They talked about all sorts of things and eventually the conversation turned to the farm.

'One day we'll sell the farm. I doubt any of the boys will want to take it on, besides I think they'll be better off doing something else. There's not much money in farming these days.'

'What'll you do?'

'When?'

'If you sell the farm.'

'Oh, I don't know. I think I'd be quite happy moving in to town. Archerville would be good, I think. It's big enough to find things to do, and yet not too big. I'd hate to live in a big town.'

'How would Mr. Chapman cope with town life?'

'Not very well for a start but I reckon he'd adapt eventually.

Actually, he doesn't realise it yet, but if the boys aren't coming home, the sooner we make the move the better for all of us. At least that's what I reckon, but don't you go telling him I said that.' She gave him a grin and a wink.

'That's just between us.' Scott felt sort of privileged to have her say these things to him. It felt as if they were sharing a sort of bond between them.

'Don't worry. I think I know when to speak and when to shut up. I'm not likely to say well it sounds like you'll be moving to town soon, or anything like that.'

'Good, I think we understand each other. I'm glad we had this little talk. Makes me feel close. I do love some company.'

Scott rang his boss and found he had to be back for work next morning so they had to leave after lunch. When they went to leave Mrs. Chapman gave Scott a big hug and to Scott's surprise kissed him full on the lips and held on for a few seconds.

'Come back soon. I've really enjoyed having you stay. You'll be welcome any time.'

They drove in silence for a while. It finally got the better of Scott.

'Does your mother do that to everyone?'

'What?'

'Flirt like that.'

'Not everyone. You seemed to be a bit of a hit. Sort of a bit special.'

'Doesn't your father care?'

'I don't know really. We've never talked about it. She's always been like that. We don't take any notice. I s'pose if Dad didn't like it, he would've said something by now.'

'Do you think she means anything by it?'

'Why, did she get you going a bit did she?'

'Well, I sort of wondered.'

'Don't worry, you're not the first to get ideas. Sometimes I think she's fair dinkum, but then, ah, I don't know. I think it's usually just a bit of fun. Actually, she did seem to take to you a bit more than usual. Maybe one day you'll find out.' Scott was quite amazed to hear Chapman talk so casually about his mother. He had to admit that farewell kiss did get him going a bit.

Chapter Twenty-Four

The Roadblock

Chapman was one of those casual types, always good for a laugh and often quite unpredictable. They travelled on for quite a distance and as often happens, they came to a road gang where half a dozen men were repairing a bridge. They slowed to the appropriate speed and were almost past when Chapman noticed a very big, red headed chap leaning on the inevitable shovel, obviously not very interested in the job. Chapman said,

'Watch me stir this bloke.'

Scott held his breath as Chapman leaned out the window and yelled,

'I bet if you didn't have that shovel to lean on, you'd fall over you lazy big Irish clown.' This provoked the expected reaction. The bristles rose on the back of the shovelman's neck. Chapman laughed and sped off. Still giggling,

'Did you see the look on his face?'

Chapman turned his attention back to the road, something

he would have been well advised to do earlier because not more than a hundred yards up the road were more road-works with a man in yellow overalls holding up a stop sign as a large truck turned around completely blocking the road. Chapman's face was something to behold as he looked in the mirror to see the big red headed, and by now very red-faced fellow charging up the road. Yellow overalls said,

'Won't be long mate.'

Chapman regained his composure quite quickly, and casually asked,

'Is it clear past the truck?'

'Yes' was the reply and then the look on the flagman's face was even more incredible as Chapman took off spraying gravel everywhere. Only then did he hear shovelman yelling,

'Stop that bastard, stop him!!'

The men on that road gang still talk about the day the two young fellers drove around the roadblock, missed the truck by a whisker, squeezed between the tree and the fence, then skidded back on to the road, waved to the flagman at the other end and drove off without a scratch. It took a while for Scott to settle down after that, but he gradually saw the funny side of it.

Chapter Twenty-Five

Brad

Scott and Chapman and Cree became good mates and were often together around the town, sometimes at the pub or just eating fish and chips in the car, or on the grass or on the seat in front of the shop. The boys were to learn a lot about Cree over the coming weeks. Scott regarded her as a good friend but Chapman was getting quite fond of her, felt maybe they could get something going between them.

Cree was always a cheeky chick. Always full on and full of fun and never backward in saying what she thought. She showed them something of her real persona one night at the pub.

'You just watch him. I bet he takes Melinda home, pretends he's crook or something, then comes back and races that other chick off. You just watch. I bet he does.'

'Has he done that before?' Lena asked.

'Course he has. He's known for it. The bastard did it to me.'

'How'd you know?'

'My mates told me. Never spoken to him since. He's just a sleaze.'

'Who is he?'

'His name's Brad. Works over at Bates Hill somewhere. Doesn't come here all that often. Just as well. All the locals know what he's like.'

'Did ya front him about it?'

'Na, I didn't think he was worth the bother. Sides, I thought he could find out how things worked for himself. We'll see in a little while if he's learned anything.'

Scott, Chapman, Cree and Lena were sitting at a table in the corner away from the bar. Lena hadn't been in Archerville very long. She was one of the many young people who gravitated to town looking for work or for various other reasons. Because she was a local, Cree seemed to attract a lot of the new comers. Lena was the latest of these and Cree had taken a liking to her. The party had been going for some time. Just a few of the locals celebrating someone's birthday. They didn't need much of an excuse to have a night out.

'When was it?' asked Scott.

'Oh, it was just after he moved here. 'Bout a year ago.'

'Crikey that's amazing. Why would a bloke new to the town do a stupid thing like that?'

'Dunno really. Tho' I think it's because he came from the city. I guess he could do that sort of thing down there and get away with it 'cos the girls wouldn't know each other and they'd never find out.'

They all listened to the story. Lena said, 'But that's not how it works in the bush?'

'That's right. He didn't know how it worked in small towns. You know how we talk about that sort of thing.'

Scott and Chapman drifted off to the other end of the bar. It seemed to them that Cree wanted to talk some girl talk with Lena, and they were right. Cree wanted to make sure Lena didn't get caught the way she had been.

'How's he get away with it?'

'He only does it occasionally. It's always with someone who doesn't know. Why he would do it to Melinda I don't know. She's real nice. Probably she told him she wouldn't let him shag her.'

'What?'

'Oh, don't worry, he's not backward asking about that. That's what he did the one and only time I went out with him.'

'What? He asked you for a shag during the evening?'

'Yair. He asked while we were dancing.'

'Bloody hell, that's unbelievable.'

'The funny part was I might've if he'd waited till we were parked somewhere or something. I was starting to feel a bit horny but when he said that I turned off. Right off. Straight away.'

'What'd he say?'

'He just came right out and said something like — 'how do you reckon we're going?' and I said — 'what do you mean?' and he said — 'do you reckon we'll get friendly later?' and I said — like, how do you mean?' I knew bloody well what he meant but I wanted him to spell it out. I knew as soon as he said that I wasn't gunna but I wanted to make him look silly. Like, he gave me the shits. All in a matter of a few seconds.'

'What'd he finally say?'

'He said — 'you know, a bit of a tumble in the back seat' and I said — 'what sort of a tumble? and he said — 'you know, pants off and all that sort of a tumble.'

'And ...?' Lena asked,

'I looked him straight in the eye and said — 'never in a million years' and he soon pissed off and chased Josie. She was new to the town then. Didn't know hardly anyone. After a while he came back and reckoned, he was feeling a bit crook. Said he'd been outside spewing and all that perhaps if I didn't mind, he'd like to take me home so he could go home to bed. All the time he'd been outside with Josie.'

'And did he take you home then?'

'Yair, I was ready to go. I'd had enough of it all, so I let him take me home. I found out the full story later in the week. I even talked to Josie about it. She was all apologies but I didn't feel cranky at her. She didn't know he'd brought me.'

'Josie seems nice.'

'Oh, yair, she is. We're good mates now. We often have a laugh about it. She'll be here later; you can ask her all about our Brad. She reckons he was a lousy shag anyway.'

'You mean she did it with him?'

'Oh, yair, I reckon. She reckons she was pretty randy that night and a bit pissed and when he asked, she was more than willing.'

'And it wasn't too good?'

'Nah. Apparently, he only lasted a couple of minutes. She said she was just starting to get worked up and it was all over. Needless to say, he hasn't had a second chance.'

They watched, and sure enough it wasn't long before Brad and Melinda headed for the door.

Scott and Chapman came back to the table with fresh drinks.

'You two finished your little heart to heart?'

'Sort of. I've just told Lena all about our friend Brad. He's just gone out with Melinda. He probably asked her and she said no so he probably went and asked that new girl.'

'And you reckon she said yes?' said Chapman.

'Fair chance. Otherwise why would he whiz Melinda home early. She was having a good time too. I wish I'd had a chance to tell her.'

'You wouldn't?'

'Too right I would. I'd fix the bastard and he knows it too. Don't worry, I'll tell her first time I see her.'

'Will you?'

'That's if I'm right. Too right I will. Bugger him. It's not a very nice thing to do. That's why not many of the local girls'll have anything to do with him.'

Cree was starting to get worked up. The more she thought about it the angrier she became. She went on,

'Let's watch her. If she goes out, we'll follow her. The bastard knows better than to come back in. 'Specially when I'm here. He would've made some arrangement so he didn't have to come in.'

'Do you reckon?'

'Shit yair. In fact, better still, let's go and talk to her. Get in first before she goes out.'

Lena had a bit of devilment in her, similar to Cree. They had soon found they had things in common and this bit of devil was one, so Lena was quick to follow Cree's lead. Cree stopped at the bar and got more drinks. She asked Jock,

'What's that new girl over there drinking?'

'Bundy and coke.'

'Okay, I'll have one of those too.'

The new girl was sitting alone. Lena and Cree breezed up. Cree put the bundy in front of the new girl.

'Hi, I'm Cree and this is Lena. Mind if we join you?'

'Well... I ...er, was just about to leave actually.'

'Ah, come on, you've got time for one more.'

'Well I haven't really. My boyfriend is coming to pick me up. He's probably out the front now.'

'Well, why don't you whiz out and tell him to come in. We'd like to meet him too.' Cree knew she was right and was warming to the project. She was enjoying the prospect of stuffing Brad's little plan. The new girl was beginning to fidget a little.

'Or, do you want us to go out and get him? I'll bet he'd love to have drink with us. Come on what do you say to that idea?'

'No, I can't really. I should go.'

'Well, at least have the drink I bought you. He can wait a minute. Then we can go out with you and tell him it's our fault. We kept you. We insisted you have a drink with us.'

Lena chimed in,

'Yeah, that sounds pretty cool to me. I bet he won't mind really.'

'Oh, well all right then.' She took the drink.

'What'd you buy me anyway?'

'Same as you've been drinking.' She took a sip.

'How'd ya know what I was drinking?'

'A good barman always knows what everyone's drinking. Jock's the best.'

'Oh, yes, of course.'

Cree decided to go slowly, even gently for the girl's sake.

'You're new in town. Staying long?'

'I dunno yet. I'm hoping to get a job of some sort, so I can stay.'

Cree changed her tack. The girl seemed nice and a bit innocent. She decided to come straight out and say it.

'It's Brad out there isn't it?' The girl looked up quickly, startled.

'How did you know that'?

'We've been watching. Not much escapes us.'

'I probably should tell you to mind your own business.'

'Ah, but you see, in a strange sort of way it is our business.'

'How the hell can it be. It's my business who I go out with.'

'You seem to be an all right kid. Let me tell you a story, then you'll see what I mean.' She was just up to the 'I'll wait outside bit' when Josie burst in. She'd obviously been drinking somewhere. She flounced into the bar, spotted Cree and came straight over.

'Guess who I saw waiting outside with the engine running? Eh, guess who? You won't need two guesses, I bet.' Cree nodded towards the new girl and winked at Josie. Josie was at her belligerent best, not caring what she said or who heard. 'Yes, it's our mutual friend Brad. He's got a bloody cheek coming here again. You'd think he'd get the message.' She had obviously twigged that he was up to his old trick. She'd also twigged that maybe this was the girl in question. She wasn't about to let up,

'I bet the rotten bastard has conned some chick to race out and go off with him.' Then, pretending she had only just noticed the other girl,

'Well, lo and behold, it's not you is it?' The new girl blushed. Cree said,

'We were just getting to talk about that when you came in. Maybe you said it all for us.' Josie sat next to the other girl, spoke directly to her,

'Oh, shit. I hope I haven't spoiled your night. You go with him if you want. But I reckon we could save you making a mistake. At least we reckon it would be a mistake. What's your name anyway?'

'Edith.'

Josie kept on,

'Well, Edith, I s'pose you're old enough to make up your own mind about that.'

'About what?'

'Whether it'd be a mistake or not.'

'Actually, I'm starting to think it might've been. I'm glad you lot told me. Thank you.'

They sat talking for a few minutes till Edith said,

'Well, I s'pose I should go out and tell him.'

Cree was still in the mood for a bit of devilment,

'Yair, let's all go,' and without waiting for any confirmation, jumped up and led the charge.

Brad saw them coming and very quickly drove off, leaving them laughing.

Chapter Twenty-Six

The Corner Shop

A few days later Chapman met Cree in the street. They wandered about, chatting as they often did, just filling in time together, as friends do. As they passed a little corner shop Chapman said, 'I'll just duck in and get a paper.'

He wandered into the little shop. As he opened the door a little bell, tied to the door, tinkled. He stood and looked at it for a second, hadn't seen one of those for a long time.

'Cute isn't it?' came a voice, a woman's voice from a very small lady who was almost invisible behind a display rack of magazines and various greeting cards.

'I know it's old fashioned, but I like it. Better than them new- fangled things what go bip, bip. My sister's got one of them things in her shop, but it's always giving trouble. Often has to get her husband to fix it. Me, I like the tried and true type. No bother with it. Always works. That's the trouble these days. Everyone's trying to save time or money or something. What's time? That's what I always ask. Now what did you want?'

'Just the Australian please.' He picked up a copy.

'I like the Sun myself. That Australian is too big. Fair covers half the kitchen table. My husband, he won't read it neither. Says it's nearly all ads. Then I s'pose, so's the Sun. That's the trouble these days, always someone trying to sell ya something. They even come in here. In my own shop if you please. Had a bloke in here the other day trying to sell me one of them new-fangled cash registers. I told him I was all right with what I had thanks very much. This old cash drawer lasted many a year and I reckon it'll go many a year yet. Probably see me out, and anyway if it packs it in, well I'll just go out and get another one 'zactly the same as this. That's if you can get one. That's the trouble these days, they don't make them old fashioned things that really work.'

She took his money. Put it in the drawer.

'See...simple.'

A lady entered. The bell tinkled.

'Hello. I hope you're not going to try and sell me something.'

The lady looked puzzled.

'It's O.K. just a little joke. This gentleman and I were just saying,'

Chapman rolled his eyes as he passed the new customer. He walked out just as she started again,

'That's the trouble these days...'

The whole time he'd been in the shop she'd hardly drawn breath. He was walking along shaking his head and staring back at the little paper shop. Cree grinned at him. She knew the story. She'd been in that shop many a time.

Chapter Twenty-Seven

Woodley

They wandered down the street with no particular destination in mind but Cree steered them towards a car repair garage.

'This is Woodley's garage. You remember the joker we saw in the car park.'

'Ah, yair. The one with the battered old car.'

'Let's go in here. I want to see something.'

Woodley didn't have many friends in town so it was no surprise that when he was seen walking down the street sporting a fantastic black eye it caused quite a few giggles. The story had circulated round the town very quickly. Cree had heard part of the tale but Chapman was unaware that there had been quite a bit of excitement at the pub a couple of days before, so Chapman was quite surprised when walking past Woodley's garage Cree had said, 'Let's go in here, I want to check something out.'

'I thought you hated that bloke.'

'Yes, I do. Like most of the town, 'specially after what he did to Sally Perkins, but I just want to see something.'

'What did he do to her?'

'Well, actually it's what he tried to do. He came off second best then, same as he did on Sunday.'

'You're talking in riddles.'

'Yair, I know. Don't worry I'll tell you all about it later. Right now, I want to go in here.' They went in and Cree marched straight up to the counter. It was a minute or so before Woodley appeared. Chapman got quite a shock. He'd seen some dandy black eyes in his time but Woodley had one which would take a prize anywhere. Cree was unfazed. He was about to see what a cheeky bitch she could be.

'My word Mr. Woodley that's quite a bad eye you've got there. Did you walk into a door or something?'

He looked straight at her. 'What do you want?'

'I want a.... My goodness that's a bad eye. Have you been to the doctor? You really should have some treatment for it.'

'Are you quite finished?'

'Well, really Mr. Woodley. I'm only concerned for your wellbeing.'

'Yes, I'm sure you are. Now you've had a good look, piss off and don't come back to my shop. I've had enough of you.'

'Oh really Mr. Woodley. I'm surprised... Oh, well, I'll be off then.' She walked calmly out of the shop leaving Chapman staring after her until Woodley's 'You too' brought him back to reality. He caught up to her. She'd heard some of the story of how Woodley got the black eye but so far hadn't got around to telling Chapman. It was obvious to Chapman that Woodley didn't like Cree. His curiosity was aroused.

'What was that all about? That joker doesn't like you, does he?'

'Not even a little bit, not even the tinchiest little bit, not after the thing with Sally.'

'I'm getting keen to hear that story.'

'Oh, you will, you will. Don't worry, the whole town knows it, it's no secret. That's part of the reason everyone thinks the black eye story is a bit of a giggle.'

Chapman's mind was racing. What the hell could it be? Surely, he didn't bash her up or try to rape her or something.

Scott drove up and parked just in front of them and they automatically piled into his car. He didn't start the car or anything. They just liked to be together, the three of them. Cree was dead keen to hear the full story of the pub fight so Chapman knew the Sally episode would have to wait.

'You know the story Scott. What really happened?'

'When?'

'On Sunday, when Woodley clobbered old Johansen.'

'Oh that. I wasn't there but apparently Woodley and Johansen had been in the pub for a while and old Johansen was a bit pissed and he started to get a bit cranky like he does and somehow things got a bit heated and the upshot of it all was they finished up out the back and Woodley belted him up. It wasn't really a fight so much as a bashing, see, Johansen's got a bit of arthritis and a dicky hip. Everyone knows about that and he can be a bit obnoxious at times, and quite sour but the locals usually just ignore that. You know, just leave him be. Apparently, it got to Woodley and that was the outcome. It shouldn't have happened. Some of the blokes tried to stop Woodley. They knew Old Johansen would be no match. It seems it only lasted a couple of minutes then the blokes stopped it. They had to drive Johansen home. He was a bit battered but he's okay.'

'Then how the hell did he get the black eye?' Chapman asked.

'That's the good bit. I'm coming to that.'

Cree piped up,

'Yes, this is the bit I want to hear.'

'It happened the next day. I was in the pub at the time. Woodley was there when young Bully came in. You know, Johansen's son.'

Cree looked at Chapman. She didn't think Chapman knew Bully Johansen.

'You haven't met Bully, yet have you?'

'No, I don't think so.'

'Oh, well, you will.'

'I think I know the bloke you mean though. Solid joker. Not all that tall. Reddish hair. Only young. Only a kid really.'

'Yair, that's him.' Cree went on,

'He's a bit of a rough nut but he's decent enough. I like him all right. I'd sooner he was my friend than my enemy tho.' He looks after his mates.' Scott nodded agreement to Cree's description, then continued,

'Well, he came in. He's only sixteen and not supposed to be drinking but they usually let him have one or two. He came up to the bar and ordered a beer, said g'day to me and a couple of others then he spotted Woodley up the other end of the bar. There was suddenly a hush in the bar. You could see Bully's hackles rise. He said, you know, loud and clear, everyone could hear — you reckon you're as good as you were yesterd'y? I reckon if there'd been a mouse running around you would have heard it. Absolute dead silence. Woodley, just as arrogant as ever said — Yair I reckon I am and Bully says Right, out the back. Of course, no one tried to stop it this time. They all reckoned Bully could look after himself and by Christ he could too. He belted shit out of Woodley. Woodley hardly landed a blow. Nobody stopped it either. I think they were all enjoying seeing Woodley get thumped. Woodley is a few centimetres taller than Bully and a bit heavier, and probably twenty years older too, but that didn't stop Bully. You could see he was furious but he stayed cool and just kept picking Woodley off. Just one hit at a time. I guess he had a real reason and it showed. By Christ he was wild. It was an incredible performance. I actually wanted to clap, but of course you just don't do that at a pub fight.'

Chapman hadn't seen much pub brawling so he was intrigued by the whole scenario.

'Must've been a hell of a whack to give him that shiner.'

'Well, that's the interesting thing. It wasn't just one hit. It was several well aimed blows. He concentrated on it. You could see every so often he'd land a punch right on target. I reckon he's been in a fight or two.'

'How long did it go on for?' It was Cree asking this time.

'Oh, not long. Pub fights don't usually last very long. When Bully knew he had him beaten he started talking.

Saying things like next time you take on an old man crippled up with arthritis stop and think what might be around the corner, it might be someone like me.'

'How did it finish?'

'Well that was another funny thing. Jocks' wife came out and the two stepped apart. You could see she was angry and everyone knew you don't mess with her when she's like that.'

'What happened?'

'She just said righto you lot, out, now. And you two, is it over? Bully said it is for me unless he wants some more and she looked at Woodley an' he didn't answer for a while, an' then he said I s'pose so an' she said I s'pose so what? an' he said I s'pose it's over, an' she said right shake hands and she waited. Bully put out his hand and it took Woodley a few seconds to respond. He knew that would mean an end to it, that he would look a bit silly for a while but he had to admit defeat, so he shook Bully's hand and Jock's missus said right you're both out for a week so they had to go, but Bully said I just need one or two to settle down and she said right a couple of drinks and then go.'

'What about Woodley?'

'Oh, yair, he didn't hang around. His eye was almost closed already so he pissed off pretty quick. Bully stayed. He hardly had a mark on him. The only thing that showed he'd been in a fight was his knuckles. He'd taken the skin off a couple of 'em. About an hour later Jock's missus came in to the bar and saw him still there and said I thought I told you to go and Bully said just on my second one now. He'd had about five or six. Jock was slipping them to him but eventually he had to go. I tell you what, it made for a very interesting hour or so.'

Chapman's car was parked in front of the takeaway. They bought chips and sat in the car. Chapman was dying with curiosity. He wanted to hear the story about Sally.

'Why does everyone hate Woodley?' He thought — Surely, I'll get the answer now, it's been mentioned often enough, this Sally thing.

Cree started the tale. 'When he first came to town, he bought the garage and my father got him to fix a starter motor off this car he was fixing up for me and when he went to pick it up Woodley wouldn't let him take it away without paying. Dad was just a wee bit pissed off. He'd never been refused credit in town in his life. Dad didn't have a cheque book or enough cash so he had to go and borrow it. A lousy forty dollars. So that's why my dad doesn't like him.'

'I've heard similar stories,' Scott chimed in,

Cree continued, 'And when it's his turn to pay he's always hard to get money out of. Somehow he wants everyone to pay him but he reckons it's okay if he's late.'

Cree was talking between mouthfuls of chips,

'And at first he wouldn't guarantee his work. You know how it works. You get a bloke to do a job and something goes wrong you take it back and he fixes it. Even if you've paid the bill. My dad says it's unwritten law. But Woodley would make people pay again. He's learnt different now, but he upset quite a few people and the memories are still there.'

'Why do you reckon he's like that?'

'My dad reckons it's 'cos when he came here, he had no

idea how country people lived. He was used to the dog eat dog ways in the city and took a while to adjust. Like, country people support each other and trust each other, at least you soon find out if there's someone you can't trust or rely on. Those sort don't usually last long. My dad's surprised Woodley has lasted here as long as he has.'

'How long's he been here?'

Cree thought for a minute,

'About five years I think, something like that. Probably 'cos he hasn't got much opposition helps.'

'What happened to Sally?'

Scott was all ears. 'Yair, I'd love to hear about that.'

'Well, oh yair, that. It all happened before you guys came to town. It was actually only about six months after he started in the garage. I was walking past the garage when Sally came rushing out. She was in tears. Apparently she had taken her car to him for a service and a couple of other little jobs and when she went to pick it up he demanded payment and she'd said, like, how much and he said let's call it three hundred and fifty which was an outrageous price and she said I'm not paying that much and he said, okay then, the car stays here till you do. That's when I saw her. We could see him through the door. He'd put her car on the hoist, and was taking the back wheels off. Do you know what the bastard did?'

Both Chapman and Scott were leaning forward, intent, hanging on each word. Cree was really getting into her stride. She loved telling this story. Each time she told it she seemed to find some way to add a few embellishments but the basic part didn't change. Without waiting for them to answer she went on, knowing she had a captive audience.

'The rotten mongrel threw the wheels in the boot and raised the hoist to about head high. Poor Sally was distraught. Then the bastard waved to us and went into his office. You know Sally. She's only little. He thought it was a bit of a giggle I reckon but he hadn't reckoned on what fiery little bitch he had taken on.'

The boys were all ears. Cree went on, 'I'd only known her about a year. Met her when she first came to town. We hit it off as soon as we met. Somehow we just clicked and became real good mates.'

Chapman knew Sally and liked her a lot. He figured she would have been about eighteen when all this happened.

'When she calmed down a bit, she told me the tale. Then she said what'll I do and I was just as wild as she was by this time and I thought it best to go away from there and take some time to think. This all happened on the Wednesday. I saw her again next day and she said I've got a plan; I'll fix the bastard. At least my uncle has got a plan, and I said, your uncle? Like, it was a question and she said yair. You wait till you meet him. He doesn't stand for any nonsense, and I said what's he going to do? And she said you'll see. Meet me there at five tomorrow. Don't be late, it'll be worth watching. She wouldn't say anymore so I had to just wait, and believe me it was worth the wait.'

It was killing both the fellers, but Cree took her time in the telling. She was enjoying herself.

'I got there early and waited down the street a bit. I

couldn't imagine what they had in mind and I tell you what, I would never have thought of doing what they did.'

'And what was that?' Chapman urged her on.

'At about five past five the bloke that works there left and suddenly, from somewhere these people appeared. I hadn't seen them come but they must've been over the road, watching. There were three men and in amongst them was Sally. She beckoned to me so I shot over there and as we walked, she said this is her Uncle Max and I can't remember the others names. Uncle Max said Hi without breaking his stride. Straightaway I could see what Sally meant about the no nonsense bit. We charged into the garage. Sally's car was still up on the hoist. Max banged his fist on the counter and Woodley came rushing out, starting to complain but when he saw this little group with Sally beside them, he stopped in his tracks. The two guys with them were big fellers. They both had on black tee shirts. Made 'em look pretty menacing I can tell you. I was sure glad they were on our side. One of them strolled over and pulled down the roller door, then came back and stood half way across the shop. Max said quietly, Miss Perkins here reckons you are trying to overcharge her for a job on her car. Woodley tried to go back in to his office but somehow the other guy was standing in front of the door. He moved like a panther, bloody hell he was quick. I guess he'd anticipated Woodley would head for cover so he was more than ready. Max said okay what have you got to say to that?'

Scott was intrigued,

'This is fascinating. Keep going.'

'Well, Woodley said something like I don't think it is excessive and Max said — show me the bill and Woodley produced the bill. His hands shook a bit when he handed it over and Max said — it looks excessive to me, how about you trim it down a bit and Woodley said how much and Max said — you decide and Woodley said — how about I knock thirty dollars off and Max said — well that's a start, what say you knock a hundred off that would be fair I reckon. In fact, let's say, make it an even two hundred. Woodley jacked up, said that's not enough. I won't accept that and Max said — oh I think you will and I'll tell you something else. Today you'll get paid and we'll drive that car away and that'll be the end of this whole sorry saga. At the same time the bloke from the front of the shop had gone over to the hoist and was trying to get it to go down and Woodley yelled — get away from that hoist and so the guy picked up a bottle of oil in one hand and a big heavy spanner in the other. He walked over and stood beside that big glass showcase, you know, the one that's got all the books and photos in it. He just stood there rubbing his foot up and down the glass, and holding the spanner up about shoulder high. The message was quite clear. Woodley's eyes darted from one to the other. Sally and I were standing back watching all this, but he never looked at us once. He knew he had no choice so he said — all right, two hundred then. Max turned to Sally and said — is that satisfactory Miss Perkins? Sally just nodded. Max held out his hand to her and said — give me two hundred dollars so I can pay your bill. Poor Sally was so nervous she had trouble getting the money out of her purse. For a start I didn't think she had that much on her but I should've known Max would've made sure of that. Sally told me after they had agreed that that was the amount she would pay. Max took the money turned back to Woodley and said — right, there's you money, now count it, adjust your bill and give me a receipt.'

Here Cree stopped for a minute to draw breath, relishing the fact she had a captive audience. The boys waited patiently for her to continue. She soon started again,

'It seemed to me that that would be the end of the matter but there was still more to come. Woodley's hands were shaking while he fixed the bill and Max made him give it to Sally and said — is that satisfactory Miss Perkins and she nodded again. As soon as he handed it over Max said right now let's get this car on the road. Woodley let the hoist down a bit and they got the wheels out but his hands were shaking so bad when he tried to do up the nuts on the wheels that one of the guys said he'd better do it and took the wheel brace from Woodley and finished the job. Then Max tried to start the car but the battery was dead. Absolutely flat. Not even a click. They lifted the bonnet and it then became obvious why Woodley had been so agitated. There was no battery. Max said — well fancy that. He'd been pretty calm till then. He rounded on Woodley, took two paces and grabbed him by the front of the shirt. You slimy little bastard. You were making sure of it weren't ya. Where's the bloody battery? I ought to make you put a new one in. Woodley was shit scared by this time and he said okay, okay I'll put a new one in, but Max had settled down a bit by then and he said, no, no, on second thoughts, no, that would be a bit dishonest on our part and we wouldn't want that would we? Well, come on, get the bloody battery and hurry up about it. And Woodley said, I can't, I took it home. And Max said, Oh, did you now? Well then perhaps you'd better put a new one in. They put the battery in and finally drove the car away. You know, the whole thing only took about half an hour. I was amazed. We seemed to be in there for ages. Sally couldn't trust herself to speak but by hell I could so as we left, I couldn't resist saying something so I said — thank you Mr. Woodley. See you later Mr. Woodley. So now you might have some idea of why Woodley doesn't like me.'

Chapter Twenty-Eight

Old Jack

The three of them had been sitting in Scott's car for some time. Not long after Cree had finished telling the story about Woodley, old Jack, the local drunk, came staggering along. Weaving along he stumbled in front of the car and fell quite heavily to the footpath.

The next few minutes were to have quite an impact on the relationship between Cree and Chapman.

Cree, Scott and Chapman watched for a minute as he lay there 'til Cree said,

'Come on Scott let's go somewhere else.'

She and Scott had seen it all before. Cree didn't want any part of it, but Chapman got out of the car and went to help. Jack was trying to get to his feet mumbling,

'Just … a hand up… will ya.'

Chapman leaned down and was trying to help when Cree called,

'Just leave him be Chapman, he'll recover in a minute.'

But Chapman couldn't leave it at that. Jack mumbled again in his befuddled state he wasn't making much sense, but Chapman realised he wanted to be helped over to a seat in front of the shops. Cree urged Chapman to come, at the same time urging Scott to start the car. Scott was unable to decide, so they just sat and watched. Chapman helped old Jack stagger over to the seat. In the process Jack spewed down the front of Chapman's shirt. Chapman finally got Jack onto the seat with Jack mumbling many thanks. At least that's what Chapman thought he was saying. Finally, Chapman came back to the car,

'I think I'd better walk home. I seem to have got something on my shirt.'

Cree was furious.

Chapter Twenty-Nine

The Disagreement

A few days later Chapman saw Cree in the street and suggested they go for a drive. Cree was still angry at Chapman but she had cooled down a bit from the fury she'd felt after the incident with old Jack. She reluctantly agreed, mainly because she liked Chapman, but also because she wanted to tell him how she felt. She would have preferred to wait awhile 'til she could get a true perspective on the whole thing, but she thought, maybe best get it off her chest so they can move on. So, she went. A decision she was to regret for a long time. Not so much the going for a drive, but the repercussions were quite dramatic.

They drove for a while. Chapman sensed Cree wanted to talk so he stopped, faced her and said,

'Well, come on out with it.'

'For God's sake Chapman, stop trying to please everyone. You can't do it. Stop trying to be so nice to everybody all the time. Do something for yourself.'

'You mean about old Jack?'

'Yair. Course I mean about old Jack.'

'I was only trying to help.'

'And you didn't want to, but you still did it. Why didn't you just say you didn't want to do it?'

'Well, Miss Smarty-pants, it just so happens, I did want to help the poor bugger. He asked me and I didn't want to refuse him.'

'That's right, mister 'be nice to everyone'. You know, you don't have to hurt anyone. Mostly when you please yourself it doesn't affect other people. If it seems likely that it will you can back off. It's not being selfish.'

'Look, he asked for help and I wanted to...'

'If he can't handle it tell him to get stuffed — it's his problem if he can't handle it. I mean, he got himself in that state. It was his problem. Just look at the mess he made.'

Cree didn't know Chapman had an old uncle just like old Jack. The family stuck by him, even when it hurt. He was starting to get annoyed. He liked Cree a lot but he didn't take too kindly to her telling him how he should or shouldn't act. It didn't occur to him that she was only doing it because she fancied him.

'I do most things to please myself. Even when I do something 'nice' as you put it I only do it because it gives me pleasure.'

She wondered at that. Didn't believe him really. But, well, maybe he's not such a real softie after all. She decided to keep on now she had started.

'I'm not sure I can accept that. Is it possible you couldn't say no?'

'You doubt me?'

The tone in his voice warned her to back off a bit, her instincts said hold it there, but somehow, she couldn't stop herself now.

'Well, I do sometimes wonder.'

'Well, you can wonder all you like, it makes no bloody difference to me. I do what I choose to do and I only helped him because I chose to help him. Not because I couldn't say no. I would've told him to go to buggery if I wanted to but I choose not to.' Then after a pause,

'You don't believe me?'

His voice was quite sharp. She knew she should stop, but then some belligerent part of her make-up came to the fore and she kept on. She thought — If I stop now, I'll probably never start down this track again, besides it wouldn't hurt to stir him up a bit, so she kept on, not aggressively but quietly she said,

'Well, I'm not real sure about that.'

'Well, I hope you find time to think about it. Maybe you'll work it out. That's if it's of any real interest to you. Right now, I don't give a stuff what you think. I did before tonight, but now, suddenly I don't give a shit.'

She got quite a shock at this outburst. Wasn't expecting anything like that. He sat silent for a few seconds. Then she got a bigger shock when without another word, he started the car and headed home. He pulled up at her gate and left the motor running, waiting for her to get out. She tried to make a bit light of it,

'Ah, it looks like I might just might have overstepped the line. Just a little bit.'

'Are you going to get out?' The drive home hadn't calmed him at all. There was a lot of anger in him still. In fact, if anything he was even angrier now.

'In a minute.'

'Now would be a good time. You better go now before I get completely mad. It doesn't happen very often but when it does it's not very pleasant, and you've managed to start it.'

She knew she had made a very big mistake and felt she had better try and correct it now.

'There's no need to get so het up about such a little thing.'

'You doubted me twice and you call that a little thing. It seems we live in different worlds. Now it would be best if you get out.'

She got out but before she closed the door she tried once more, 'Hey, what's it like to have the last word?' In the midst of his anger he was still thinking quite rationally and it seemed to him that she wasn't bothered at all by this sort of confrontation. Maybe it was commonplace for her. It certainly wasn't for him. His voice was quite even when he said,

'You can have the last word if you like but you'd better make it good, 'cos it'll be a bloody long time before you get another chance.'

He waited a few seconds as she stood there, mouth open, struggling for words, but no words came.

'O.K. then... I suppose that's it then. See ya.'

She stood unmoving.
As he drove off, the tears started.

Chapter Thirty

Quentin Castlebridge

Quentin Castlebridge was the owner, editor, sales manager, proof reader, in fact the sole director and operator of a small newspaper in Chalingford, a small country town quite some distance from Archerville. He always felt it had a nice ring to it, Castlebridge from Chalingford. He'd been there many years and had built up a nice business but times had caught up with him. Things hadn't been going very well for some time. He was struggling to keep his publication afloat. He would lay awake at night, often for hours, worrying about the newspaper and also his financial affairs. He owned his house which he shared with his long suffering wife and he owned the small office where he produced the paper and all the printing presses and machinery, plus he'd managed to put away a stash in his bank account, and had a few other investments, but that was about all he had to show for many years hard work. The downturn in the rural community, high interest rates on the small loan he'd taken out some years before to prop the paper up, added to the fact that he hadn't kept up with the latest technology — his main printing press was long past it's best, in fact it was only his experience that kept the fading monster alive — and then the fact that he was up to retiring age meant it was always an effort to meet the twice a week publishing deadline. He hated asking people to advertise in the paper, knowing full well that most of the town business people only took adverts out of sympathy or loyalty to old Quentin because he had done a lot for the town over the years. Sometimes he would find himself just sitting, staring at blank pieces of paper, or blank walls with an equally blank mind. He would sit thus for quite some time, then suddenly jolt awake with no idea how long he'd been in a far-off dream-world. He would go to bed each night dead tired. Almost always he would fall very quickly into a deep sleep. This would often last only an hour or two and he would then find himself wide awake and there he would be for a major part of the night, slowly becoming conscious that his hands were clenched into tight, straining fists. Sweat would wet his pillow. He would doze a bit, off and on and seven in the morning would find him half awake, wishing some power would allow him just a bit more sleep. Even half an hour would be a help. But, no, it wasn't to be, couldn't be. It was time to rise and face another set of problems. Sally, his long-suffering wife, had long since given up trying to help and had even moved into the spare bedroom. She couldn't sleep in their bed with him tossing all night.

Things finally came to a head when he received a visit from

the editor of a group of newspapers saying they wanted to increase their sales in his town, and were offering to buy him out. He knew he could never compete. They offered him a fairly low figure for his business. They didn't want his building or printing gear, not that that was any real surprise. It was obvious to Quentin that they just wanted him out of the way. It was probably out of pity they made the offer because they knew they could run him out of business quite easily, but fortunately for him they chose to make a gentlemanly offer. Still a low price, but more than he would have received had they decided to play rough. Enough in fact to pay off the small loan he'd taken out and, added to his savings, have quite a handy sum to invest for the future. Enough really to retire on.

Take it and run, Sally had said. We'll still have the house and the newspaper building. Bugger it all, you're sixty-three. Time you thought about retiring anyway. Maybe someone'll buy the old printing gear. Yair, like who? he'd said, knowing all the while she was right. Then you can go away for a while, she'd said, you know, rest up, relax then come back and we'll find something to keep us going. So, it was decided.

It all happened quite quickly. Two weeks to be precise from that first visit to the Friday afternoon, Quentin unscrewed the board with the name of the newspaper and his name below from the old shop front door.

He slept late for the next few days, then after rising and having his usual tea and toast he would wander around like a lost child.

Sally said, 'You should go away for a while. Take time to get used to the idea of having no pressures. No commitments.'

Two weeks later he got in his car, already packed with the few basic essentials one needs when travelling. His wife kissed him and said,

'Now I don't care where you go or what you do, but I don't want to see you for at least a month. I want my man back.'

He drove aimlessly for a few days. Stopping here and there. He booked into a motel for what he planned to be a couple of days, but which stretched into a week. He spent days in that lonely room, just sleeping when he felt like it, or watching afternoon T.V. These things he'd never been able to do. He would soon tire of the T.V. and wander down the street, maybe have a couple of drinks, something to eat then back to his room — and sleep. Gradually he found his sleep patterns returning to some semblance of what a normal person would experience. He gradually came to himself. Realised just what his wife meant. 'I want my man back' she'd said. Realised what a pain he must have been to her over the last few years.

He rang her one night. Hello, he'd said. Hello, she'd said. How's it going? And he'd said, something like, I think I'm realising what you meant. I reckon I'm getting back to normal. You were right about selling you know. And she'd said, I know but don't come back till you've had a real rest up and you're ready to get on with the rest of our lives.

He was rather relieved she'd said 'our'. He'd often wondered where they were headed but at least 'our' meant she hadn't given up on him entirely. He felt better knowing she'd be there whenever he found his way home.

He moved on. He'd bought a swag. Sometimes he would just throw it out on the ground beside the car and sleep in the open, just enjoying the freedom and the crisp air, and the stars.

Chapter Thirty-One

Marjorie

So it was, sometime later, Quentin drove into Archerville.

It was a typical Sunday morning. The sun elbowed its way through the clouds. Thin, bright shafts of light shone down on Archerville, selecting various significant spots around the town. Significant spots and significant people. People occupied doing things, important or otherwise. Things which are needed to keep a town thriving.

And thriving Archerville certainly was in its' own quiet way. It was just the usual Sunday morning one might expect in any small Australian town. People mowing, or digging, or strolling to the shops, or just talking, passing the time of day, always taking time to stop and chat. And kids playing in the park, on skateboards or throwing sticks for some useless dog to fetch. Maybe not really a useless dog for it kept the young ones amused with its antics.

Feeling fresh and with the rejuvenation process well

under way, Quentin parked in the main street and was standing on the footpath with absolutely nothing on his mind, when Marjorie drove round the corner. Ned Brannigan and Bob Creewell were standing, talking, in front of the supermarket. Scott and Cree were walking past. A scrawny nondescript dog lay dozing in the shade of one of the shrubs on the footpath.

Marjorie's station-wagon came round the corner quietly enough but continued on the same curve, scraped the side door of Quentin's car and ran onto the footpath, snapping a low branch off the bush the sleepy dog had chosen for its morning rest. The car stopped, the dog yelped and took off. The car rolled back and came to rest in a normal parking position. Nobody took any notice. Quentin started to remonstrate,

'Hey, that's my car.'

Ned Brannigan stepped in front of him,

'Don't worry about it. It's only a little scratch.'

Quentin tried to push past Ned but Ned stayed put. He looked Quentin straight in the eye and said, 'I haven't seen you round here before, so I'll just ask your patience. I'd like you just to stay a while, wait here and we'll explain.'

Quentin looked about. He noticed the two young people who'd been walking past were standing, looking but pretending not to look. The girl seemed to be explaining something to the boy.

'But, bugger it all, it's my car.'

'Patience please.' Ned said this with a certain tone which

was all authority. Intrigued by all this, somehow Quentin held his cool. Ned went on,

'Just wait a minute. It's Marjorie. We'll work it out. It'll be O.K. Just leave it be.'

The car door opened and a small lady emerged, slowly, with some difficulty. Nobody made any attempt to help her, although Quentin sensed everyone was, in their own way, watching. Quentin first thought the lady had been injured in some way but then saw why she had difficulty. Her leg seemed to buckle a little as she tried to stand. She was quite unsteady on her feet. She leaned on the car for a second, got her balance, then clutched a rope which was strung along the side of the car, just above the windows, attached by a series of very sturdy, well-made brackets. Holding on to the rope, she shuffled along the side of the car. Ned strolled over. She managed to make her way to the rear of the car, looked up and appeared to see Ned for the first time,

'Ah, it's you Ned. How are you today? Still keeping well, I trust. Gee this rope's good. Don't think I could manage without it. It was very kind of you lot to put it on there for me. Did I hit something when I parked? I thought I felt a bump.'

'Na, nothing much. Just brushed that little tree. No harm done.'

She started to open the back door.

Ned asked, 'How are you today Marjorie?'

He pushed the door wide. She leaned into the back and after a bit of rummaging around pulled out a walking frame.

'Just steady me a bit Ned.' Ned took her arm. The frame

was specially made to suit. It had raised rests on the arms so she could take some weight on her elbows and had a small basket in front. She took hold of the handles of the frame, backed away,

'Leave the door Ned. It's easier when I come back.'

Quentin was intrigued. Couldn't recall seeing anything quite like this. This little dot of a woman seemed to be the centre of attention and yet people were pretending not to pay her that attention.

Marjorie shuffled around, over to where there was no kerbing. Just a slope for wheelchairs. Ned came over to Quentin at the same time motioning to Cree and Scott to come too. Ned put out his hand, a big powerful mit. He squashed Quentin's hand, as he said,

'I'm Ned. This 'ere is Cree and Scott.' He waved the same ham sized fist in their direction. Not waiting for Quentin to introduce himself he continued,

'Thanks for that. Cree'll tell you about Marjorie. Oh, and if you insist, we'll get that scratch fixed.' He turned to Cree, 'You be about for a while?'

She nodded and he headed off. He hadn't gone more than half a dozen steps when two young boys came skating along the footpath, their skateboards clicking over the joins in the cement. Click, click, click, like a train clicking over the joins in the rails. Ned stepped in front of them, held up his hand like a policeman. They screeched to a halt. Ned looked them up and down for a second, then, pointing a finger at them said, very slowly and deliberately,

'Don't... ever... do that... again.'

The boys nodded, one said,

'No, Mr. Brannigan.'

Sheepishly, they took up their boards and walked off. Ned went on his way. By this time Marjorie had made it to the footpath. She went into the Supermarket. Scott hadn't seen Marjorie before and was just as mystified as Quentin. Cree said quietly to both of them,

'Stop staring. You'll get used to Marjorie. You don't hurry to help. She hates people to make a fuss.' Then directly to Quentin,

'Oh, and don't park there next time.' She said this with all the assurance of a senior citizen. Quentin was quite taken aback by this girl's confidence. Here he was, a man old enough probably to be her grandfather and here she was telling him where to park and seeming to indicate in some way it was his fault that some woman scratched his car.

'But I was there first. And where she parked is a no parking anyway.'

'Yes, but she only parked there 'cos you're in her usual spot. That's why she hit your car. Everyone leaves that spot for her. You don't park there or the one next to it. It's her spot. Makes it easy for her to get up on the footpath. The spot next to it is usually left as a safety zone. People tend to leave it vacant. As you can see, she's not always quite right in her judgment of space.'

Scott hadn't been in town very long but he was learning a lot about the locals. He, like Quentin, was curious to hear some explanation of this episode. Why would the townspeople pander to one lady? He guessed some of it was self- preservation, but felt there must be something more to it. Quentin asked Cree, 'What is it that's special about her?'

'What do you mean?'

'Well, everybody seems to make a special effort for her.'

'It's a long story. I'll tell you both. First move your car.' Quentin understood. He moved the car. They bought coffee at a little shop and sat at a table on the footpath. Cree loved Marjorie and loved to tell this story,

'Every town has its' personalities. Actually, you've just met two of them. Ned and Marjorie. I'll tell you about Marjorie, she's a bit of a heroine around here. She was a school teacher. Her father had a farm about ten miles out. She went away to college and all that and after a few years came back to teach at school here.'

Cree's father walked up,

'You two going to be here?'

'Yes, Dad, we'll be here. Or at least I will be. Don't know about Scott.'

With those few words it was understood that Cree would be there to help Marjorie if she was needed. She would wait around 'til Marjorie came back, even if it was an hour or two, or no matter how long it was, she would wait.

'O.K. I'll be off then.'

He nodded to Quentin,

'Thanks for that, we appreciate it.'

Quentin was trying to work this thing out. He gets his car scratched and they all want to thank him. He asked Cree,

'Why do they all want to thank me?'

'They're saying thanks for not making a fuss about your car.'

'I don't really understand what this is all about.' He said it half as a statement and half as a question.

'What is it with that woman?'

'You'll understand when I tell you her story. You see, it all happened the day she and another teacher were taking some of us little kids to a sports day at Bates Hill. We went in a small bus. You know the sort. About a twenty-seater. Us kids were all laughing and singing. You can imagine the sort of thing. Imagine the racket a dozen excited eight and nine-year-old's would make. We came into smoke. It wasn't much at first, just wispy little puffs but it suddenly got real thick just as we crossed that bridge over Swan's Creek where the road starts to go into the bush. The driver pulled up and tried to back up but he couldn't see properly and Marjorie and the other teacher were trying to direct him but he ran off the side and the bus sort of bumped and bounced down the embankment. It stopped half way down. If you haven't been out there, some time you will and if you look, you'll see it's quite steep down towards the creek. The driver was knocked out. Most of the kids were alright, you know, knocked about a bit but not too bad, but a couple were hurt quite badly. You know, cuts and stuff. One kid had a broken arm. The other teacher was a bit dazed. See, all the kids had been sitting in their seats but the two teachers were standing up trying to tell the driver where the road was, that's why they got hurt a bit. When the bus stopped there was smoke everywhere, and we could see flames further up the road.'

The two men were listening, fully attentive. They'd been sitting for quite a few minutes, when Cree got up and moved to the other side of the table. Scott wondered at that but then realised she was watching the door of the Supermarket. Watching for Marjorie.

Scott said, 'Crikey, that sounds horrific.'

'It was horrific alright. Us kids were screaming and the smoke was coming in the bus. Fortunately, the bus stopped in a more or less upright position but there was a tree jamming the door. It was probably that tree that stopped it from going into the creek. Marjorie was first to recover. She somehow kicked the emergency door at the back out and started to get us kids out. Some of the kids wanted to take their bags and stuff but she just said quietly to leave them and they could get them later. You know, she talked the whole time in a calm but very sure voice. I reckon it was that as much as anything that kept us a bit calm even tho' we were scared stiff. She told us to slide down the bank and get in the water. She had to help a couple of the kids. She finally got us all down and in the edge of the creek. She said for us all to hold on to the ferns and each other. When she thought we were safe she went back and dragged the other teacher out. I don't know how she did it. You saw how small she is and the other teacher was quite a bit bigger than her. Anyhow she got her down into the water. By this time the other teacher was recovering. Marjorie spoke real sharp to her, yelled at her something like 'the kids need you' and that really woke her up. Then Marjorie took one of the older boys and somehow, they clambered back up to the bus and dragged the driver out of his seat, along to the back and out and down the bank.'

Scott and Quentin were silent as they waited for Cree to go on Quentin said, 'I can't believe all this. Is that how she hurt her leg?'

Cree said, 'That's half of it. They lost hold of the driver at the last and he kind of slithered down to us. How they did it no-one can work out to this day, 'cos, altho' he was only a little bloke he was completely out to it and couldn't help at all. By this time the fire was quite close. We could see the flames coming up right near the bus. Marjorie decided we weren't safe there so she said we all had to get over to the sand bar on the other side. There was a log, sort of half way across from the other side so she and the other teacher took us one by one over to that and we were able to get across. She made sure we were all there, even had a roll call there on the sand, told us to stay near the water and if the fire got too close we were all to hold hands and get in the shallow bit, put hankies over our mouths to breathe through if it got too smoky, and keep splashing each other. She said she might have to wait over the other side with the driver. As she got back in the water, she stopped a second, turned and called 'I love all you kids' then waded across. I've thought about it since. I reckon she didn't think she'd survive. You know, didn't think she'd get out of it. She didn't come back. The fire went all over the place. We could see the flames all over where they were. We thought she would've been burnt. The smoke came and went. We were all crying and scared and then quite suddenly the smoke cleared enough for us to see.

They were a bit further down the stream sort of half under a log. We heard a loud crash. A burning branch came down right where they were. They weren't moving. We cried and screamed and then suddenly there were men there. They had somehow got through the smoke and got to us. We were all crying and pointing to Marjorie and the driver. Some men jumped in and waded across. They dragged Marjorie and the driver back to our side. She half sat up and said, 'Are the kids all there?' and we yelled yes and then she just collapsed. It was like as if she'd done her job and could now let go. I heard one of the men say Marjorie had her leg jammed in a fork of the log so the driver couldn't slip away from her. She had to keep his head up too. She must've splashed water over them both the whole time. When they got her out on to the bank, I saw her foot. It was all twisted and bent sort of sideways. It was horrible. The doctors reckon she must have broken her ankle when she kicked the emergency door out. It must've been like that the whole time so she must've done all that more or less on one leg. Her knee was all twisted and her leg and arm and her clothes were all burnt where the burning log had fallen on her. Gawd it looked horrible.'

Scott and Quentin sat there, transfixed, waiting for Cree to continue.

'She had lots of operations but they could never really get it right. That's why she has trouble getting around. She was in hospital for ages. Her right arm and the side of her face were quite badly burned too. They fixed her face pretty well, there's only a small scar but her arm is really scarred. The doctors wanted to do more operations on both her arm and her leg or foot but she said no, she'd had enough of hospitals and wouldn't let them do any more.'

Scott and Quentin sat in a stunned silence after Cree finished the story, trying to get their minds around the whole thing. After quite a pause, Quentin said, 'I think I'm beginning to understand.'

'Now don't ever make a fuss over her. She says she only did what anyone would've done. We all know different. Superhuman was what one of the doctors said.'

'The understatement of the century I reckon,' said Quentin. He'd seen and heard a lot of stories in his time on the newspaper but was struggling to remember anything like this.

Marjorie came out of the store, shuffled her way across the footpath. Scott made to help. Cree stopped him, saying,

'Not yet. Just wait a bit. She prefers to do for herself.'

Marjorie got to her car and with some difficulty started putting her purchases in the back. Cree strolled over and started talking to her, at the same time, just quietly putting some things and the walking frame in the car, and then with the sense of being there to help if needed, moved aside just far enough as Marjorie, using the rope as support, maneuvered her way along the side of the car, got in and as she started to back out,

'Anything coming? Gee, I love this car. I'm so lucky the men adapted it for me. Makes it real easy for me to get around.'

Quentin heard all this. Tough and all as he thought he was and a bit hard bitten from experiences in life, he had to turn away to hide the emotion he felt. Here was this little dot of a woman, who'd done so much in what was probably only half an hour, saved everyone from an absolute disaster and pretty near ruined her life in the process, and here she was thankful that the people had modified her old car for her. He took a few moments to compose himself.

Marjorie continued back without waiting for Cree to answer. A car came up behind, stopped, waited for Marjorie to go then continued on. Obviously a local who'd seen Marjorie's car start to move. Quentin noted that as well. In those few minutes he understood how much they must love this woman.

Chapter Thirty-Two

Leach

Quentin wandered about the town, had lunch at the pub. He was about to leave when he heard a chorus from the main bar. There was quite a bit of laughter. He poked his nose in there. Leach, a short nuggety man with long curly hair, was holding forth, addressing the few drinkers. A captive audience. It reminded Quentin of an evangelist at a revival meeting. He'd obviously just told a great story and wasn't content to leave it at that. He kept on,

'Hey, you blokes know that woman who lives across the road from me? You know, what's her name?'

Someone in the group tentatively suggested, 'Gerda Wilkins.'

'Yeah, that's the one. By Christ, she's a strange one.'

'Didn't take you long to figure that out.'

'Shit no. I sussed her out right from the first. You know what she said. The first week I was here she came over for a chat. That was O.K. but then she said, you know, we looked at this place before we bought our place but decided against it. It's really not such a good place, you know the good ground finishes on the other side of the road. This side's not half as good as the other where our place is. Jeez, I felt like rushing to ring a real estate bloke right then. Bloody hell I thought, I'd better sell quick. As if that's not bad enough, then I find they've come from the city and only been farming for six months. That bloody woman wouldn't know shit from clay, yet she spoke as tho' she knew everything.'

By this time Quentin had got himself a drink and perched on a bar stool at the other end of the bar. He'd become intrigued by Leach and decided to hang around for a while just to see what other little gems might come out. He certainly wasn't disappointed.

Bart Leach was a rather aggressive type. Soon after he moved into the district, he made his presence felt. He and his wife bought a small farm. When the locals found out what sort of bloke he was, it seemed to all the district that it was perfect that he should move into the place next to Rex Herbert. Nobody liked Rex Herbert. He had a well-earned reputation about the place of being very hard to deal with. Pretty quick and handy with his fists. Just as likely to thump someone if he didn't agree with them. In fact, he'd done that once or twice and now people left him be. Most couldn't be bothered with him. Some were just plain scared of him, never being sure what he was likely to do, so they gave him a pretty wide berth.

The inevitable showdown came, strangely enough in the

main street, in front of the post office. Apparently, Herbert's bull had pushed through the boundary fence and got in with Leach's cows. Leach had a very good cattle dog and the dog soon persuaded the bull to go home. A few nips around the heels saw to that. The end result was the bull back in its paddock and a couple of broken wires in the fence.

Leach had collected his mail and was just getting into his ute when Herbert pulled up. Leach paused. A few people watched as Herbert walked towards Leach, saying,

'You'd better fix that fence you knocked down.'

Leach reached into the back of his ute, came out with an axe.

'I've heard a bit about you Herbert. Your bull busted it so you fix the bloody thing.' He stood his ground, holding the axe in both hands looking as though he would use it if he felt the need. Just how he would use it Herbert didn't wait to find out. He retreated rather quickly. As usually happens in small towns, the story circulated at a rapid rate.

Leach had become a regular in the pub on Saturdays. That was his drinking day. Never went there during the week but every Saturday his wife would drop him off soon after lunch and there he'd stay. Quite often till nine or ten at night. He was one of those rare types who could drink all day and yet never seem to get drunk. Never unsteady on his feet, never slurring his words or anything like that. He would just gradually get a bit louder and more assertive. Some of the locals made sure they called in during the day just to listen for a while. It was a bit of an education and a cheap form of entertainment. Despite his funny habits people warmed to him and he soon learned about the locals. People everyone liked or everyone hated, or laughed at or sympathised with. Of course, there was plenty of variety.

One such was Kingston Clovelly. Leach summed him up pretty quickly as he did most people.

Leach soon started again,

'Hey, any of youse blokes ever get caught with a shiela, by her father I mean?' No one spoke. Leach took that as a signal to keep going, not that he needed any prompting.

'I nearly got caught once. Back in my teenage years. I'd walked a girl home and we were fooling around behind a little hedge in her the driveway of her parents' house. Things hadn't developed very far when the father came home. We stood still as he put the car in the garage and walked up the drive to the back door. He stopped and proceeded to have a leak on the hedge. He didn't see us.' Clovelly listened to this story and as soon as Leach finished, he piped up,

'I had a similar experience only the father actually pissed on my leg. It was all we could do to keep quiet.'

Clovelly had done a similar thing only a couple of weeks before. Come up with what he thought was a better story. He'd never realised nobody took much heed of his ramblings. Most thought him a bit of a joke. Leach stood and waited for a silence, then faced Clovelly, put his hands on his hips. No need to call for silence then. The crowd of drinkers watched with expectant curiosity and sure enough they weren't to be disappointed. Nor did they have to wait long. Leach started,

'Gawd you're a smartarse Clovelly. That's the second time

you've tried to go one better. You always have to go one better don't ya? Don't you realise we all know it's bullshit? You're full of it aren't ya?' The crowd erupted. It seemed a funny thing how this new joker figured people out so quickly and accurately, but not only that, he then said exactly what the locals all felt and had thought for a long time but nobody had gotten around to saying it. Leach went on,

'Alright now I'll tell you all a story, an absolutely true story that I'll bet no bastard can top. Not even you Clovelly. It's the reason I left home. The district I'd lived in all me twenty-two years 'til then. See, I was pretty keen on this chick. I reckon she fancied me a bit too, but her father was a bit of a snob. You know, thought they were a bit better than the rest of us. I 'spect you've got one or two of them round here.'

There was a general nodding and indications of agreement amongst the drinkers. Quentin got another drink and settled down to listen again. He was fascinated by this bloke. Leach was one of those types who always seemed to draw a crowd of eager listeners. His wife called him the Pied Piper of where-ever he happened to be. When he had their attention he went on,

'Well, anyway her father didn't seem to like me at all.'

'Did he tell you that or did you just work it out?' asked a bloke in a tee shirt.

'Oh, he told me alright. I called round to take her out one night and he met me at the door and said — 'Don't think you're going to take my daughter out. Especially not in that old heap of crap.' He was of course referring to my old ute. It wasn't much to look at but she was reliable and it was all

I could afford and it was four — wheel drive so I always got where I was going, no matter what the roads were like. Then he said — 'Now just keep on going and don't bother coming back. I won't have my daughter going out with riff-raff.' Well, I got a bit pissed off about that but I just thought I'll do just that but if I find out she wanted to go out I could do something to make him regret he said that.'

A fly landed on the bar.

'Er, hang on. Get me a fly swat,' he said to no-one in particular. He watched the fly. A fly swat was produced from behind the bar. The fly took off. Leach watched it for a second. He went on,

'Yair, you'll keep. I reckoned she was all dressed ready to go out 'cos as I walked away, I heard her say, 'Oh dad you shouldn't talk to him like that', but that was all I heard. A couple of days later I met her in the street. She came straight up and said something like don't take my Dad too seriously, he's not usually like that, and I thought to myself — not bloody likely, I won't forget that in a hurry. Just to make sure she was a bit interested I said, what about coming for a spin now but she said she had to get back home to babysit her little sister so I reckoned that was fair enough an' we made a date for the next afternoon and we went for a drive. Not far, but I wanted to make sure she wanted to see me. I took her out a couple more times without him knowing. I really liked her. But then he found out and he came round and threatened me with all sorts of things if I tried to see her again. Called me a useless ratbag and all those sorts of things. That was the last straw. He didn't care a fig for her feelings, he only concerned himself with what people would think. It was obvious he didn't know what I was capable of.'

'And what could that be?' someone asked.

'Well, I'll tell ya.'

The fly landed on the bar again. Leach swatted it.

'There, he said. Gotcha. Now, if Noah had done that it would've saved us all a whole lot of headaches.'

When the giggling subsided, he went on, 'See, her father was building this house, just out of town. Up on a hill so the snooty bastard could look down on everybody. I'd had a plan for a while and when he let forth that last barrage, I decided I'd do it. The house had the frame up and a whole heap of tiles stacked ready on the roof. It was quite simple really. That night I went and got a bloody great cable I'd seen at the railway yard. It was a beauty. Quite long and strong. It was quite foggy so I figured no one would see me and I put the cable round part of the house frame, hitched up to my trusty old ute and pulled the bloody thing over.'

There was a silence in the bar. Someone said, 'Are you fair dinkum?'

'Too bloody right I am. It took a couple of runs to get her started, she rocked a bit at first, but once she started, she went over like a bloody great box of matches.'

Quentin looked on in total amazement. He couldn't believe what he'd just heard. He looked about the other drinkers and saw many similar looks. Then someone asked,

'How'd he react to that?'

'He was just a little peeved. Like you might say a trifle angry. He came round to my place and confronted me. He threatened me with all sorts of things, but I just stood my ground and said something like, really, I'm not sure I know what you're talking about, and that got him even angrier. He threatened to sue me and all that and I said even if I've done whatever it is you reckon, I've done it'd be no use suing me, remember I've got nothing, you told me so. Things were pretty stirred up for a few days.'

'It's a wonder he didn't set the cops after ya.'

'Wouldn't have done him much good. The copper was a good mate of mine and I don't reckon he'd 've tried very hard.'

'How'd the girl re-act?' was the next question.

'She wasn't all that impressed either. I guess blood's thicker and all that. Somehow, she wasn't all that keen to go out with me again so I left it at that. Don't suppose you can blame her. I guess it was a bit of self-preservation on her part. I don't s'pose her old man would've ever forgiven her if she kept seeing me. I s'pose it was for the best that I didn't keep after her. Mainly for her sake I stopped chasing her. I told her I was leaving town a few weeks later. I guess if she had been really keen, she'd have said right I'm coming with you. But she didn't. Probably for the best in the long run. Don't think she'd 've liked my lifestyle much.'

'How long ago was that?' was the next question, this time from one of the young blokes who with his mates were lapping up the whole story.

'That's like, twenty years ago. I wonder if he'd remember me.' He said this with a wry smile. He turned to Clovelly,

'Well, Clovelly, what do you think of that eh? Aren't you glad I wasn't chasing your daughter, eh?'

Clovelly didn't stay long after that. Decided he'd leave before Leach had another shot. Leach was by now right in his element.

'Do you have the Jehovah's around here? By crikey I soon piss them off.'

Leach had spotted Quentin earlier and without drawing breath, strolled up to him, stuck out his hand and said,

'I'm Leach.'

Quentin shook his hand,

'I'm Castlebridge.'

'Christ that's a mouthful. What's happening in your neck of the woods?'

Although Quentin didn't feel much like getting involved in this charade, he answered,

'Just passing through.'

'Stick around. This place can get quite interesting.'

Chapter Thirty-Three

The Park Bench

Quentin left the pub with Leach still holding forth.

The clouds dissipated a little and the sun elbowed its way through the gaps and sent cheerful shafts of light down on Archerville. It was as though by some divine direction it selected various targets about the town. This time it shone on a bench in the park.

Quentin took a book and a cushion, found the park bench, and settled down to read, a luxury he'd not allowed himself in many years. He leaned back, put the cushion as a head rest and dozed. He slept easily for perhaps half an hour, then gradually, as he became awake, he realised he was being watched. Two young boys were standing a few feet away. Boys aged about ten or so, with tennis racquets under their arms, dressed typically as one would expect to see boys on a Saturday afternoon, daggy shorts and the sort of shoes they might wear for running around the tennis court. Boys just standing, looking. The taller one spoke,

'Are you all right mister?'

Quentin gathered his wits, then replied,

'Yes, sure. Just having a bit of a nap.'

'We saw you sitting there. Just wanted to be sure you're O. K.'

They sauntered off. The episode made Quentin think. This town must be a good place. The story he'd heard about Marjorie, saw Leach in action in the pub, and then here were two young boys who obviously cared about a stranger. Cared enough to ask if he was O.K. and had the confidence to ask. Sure, Leach might be a bit of a rabbit, but every town has one or two of those, but this joker seemed to be a decent sort. A straight shooter.

It was unusual that he should see all these things in the space of a few hours. These incidents gave him a good feeling. A sense that this town had good vibes. The whole place seemed to be alive. His newspaper instincts told him here was a story here but it wasn't a news item. Maybe he could write the story more easily about a town other than his own home town. Could be more objective, could see the people in an uncluttered way. After all it's the people that make a town, and he knew everyone back home so well it would be hard to be objective, hard to write truthfully without offending someone.

A plan flitted in and weaved its' way around in his mind. Maybe he would write a story. A story of a small town. Here he was, sitting in a park in some town he'd only vaguely heard of before he drove into it a few hours previously. Two minutes ago, he'd had two young kids ask if he was O.K. He decided to stay around for a while, looked around, found a bed and breakfast place on the edge of town and booked a room.

Quentin spent the next few days just wandering about the town with no real plans. He rang his wife, 'Sally, I'm still here in this little town, Archerville. I like it here. I've met some of the locals. This place has quite a buzz about it.'

'That's good Q. Sounds like it's doing you some good. I like the way you sound.'

'Yair. I think I'll stay around here for a while. Actually, why don't you come over? You know, meet some people or something.'

'Maybe I will later. We'll wait a while yet.'

Quentin accepted that. He knew Sally was usually right.

Quentin was enjoying Archerville. So much so that he stayed on, a lot longer than he first planned. Actually, when he drove into Archerville that Saturday morning he hadn't any real plans. Thought he would maybe stay a day or so but somehow that short stay had drifted into weeks. Quentin got to know quite a few of the local identities. He'd become an admirer of Ned Brannigan. Liked a lot of things about him. Liked the way he went about things, the way he dealt with people, his forcefulness, drive, and the fact that he obviously loved his town and was always ready to do something to benefit the town, but more importantly the people in the town. Ned was the sort of bloke every town needs.

Chapter Thirty-Four

Ned – The Shire Office

Ned was a legend in the town. There were many stories told about Ned's escapades. Most of them true, or at least the basic story would be true. Sometimes, though there may be a little embellishment. Most of the people in Archerville liked Ned. Those who didn't had usually suffered some sort of admonishment or had a bit of an altercation with him, which they would have probably lost, or at best, come out with a draw. Ned usually won because he was usually right. Unfortunately, he often upset people because he said what he thought. Tact was not a big factor in Ned's life as Quentin saw at first hand one day when he went to the Shire Office to inquire about what rates he might expect to pay should he buy a place in town. It was about the time of year when Shire rates were due, so there were quite a few people waiting. Ned was at the front of the queue when Quentin walked in. Looks like a long wait, he thought and was about to leave when the sparks started to fly from Ned.

Ned had waited patiently. Now it was his turn. Just as the receptionist said, 'Now, Mr. Brannigan', the phone rang. Ned put his account on the desk. The girl answered the phone,

'Yes Councillor, he's not in at the moment. Can I ask him to call you?' She listened for a few seconds, took a pen and started writing, at the same time looking at Ned, she put her hand over the mouthpiece and said, 'Excuse me I won't be long,' turned back to the phone and started writing. Ned stared at her. He couldn't believe it had happened again. Twice in the space of half an hour.

What Quentin didn't know of course that Ned's previous call had been at the plumbers. He only wanted a couple of pipe fittings. Should have taken only a few minutes. He waited behind another customer. There was nobody serving. Normally there would be two or three people serving but this time there was no-one behind the counter. Ned could see them out in amongst the shelves busy serving other clients. He waited his turn. And waited. The phone rang. One of the owners, deliberately not looking at Ned and the other man, rushed to answer it. 'Yes,' he said into the phone, then yes again, then picked up a pen, started writing, said yes a few more times, then, 'Yes we can deliver that. Would tomorrow be all right?' A pause then,

'O. K. we'll do that. See you.' He put the phone down, looked at Ned and the other man and said,

'Sorry I can't serve you just yet. Be back in a minute.'

Ned lost patience.

'Look here, we were here before the bloody phone rang

and you took time to answer that. Maybe next time you'll let them wait.' The man looked a little surprised.

'But I've always got to answer the phone.'

'Well why not get an answering machine or something?'

'Oh, I couldn't do that. That wouldn't be acceptable.'

'No, well neither is me waiting while you answer the bloody phone. Stuff the phone. I'll go somewhere else.'

With that, Ned had walked out. His next call was to the Shire Office, so it was not surprising that his patience was a little frayed when the girl left him standing while she answered the phone.

He waited a few moments, decided this could take some time, then interrupted,

'Excuse me, I was here first. Could you ask him to wait please or ring back or something?'

'I'm sorry, I can't. It's one of the councillors.'

'All the more reason to ask him to wait.'

The girl became a little flustered,

'I'll try.' Then back to the phone,

'Er, Councillor, can I ring you back? I've got some people waiting at the desk.' The voice on the phone obviously persisted. The receptionist listened for a few seconds, then,

'I've got that Councillor, now if that's all, I've several people here waiting.' The caller kept on. The girl listened patiently. Then said,

'Er, Councillor, can I call you back. I'm here on my own and there are six people waiting.'

The voice came back quite loud. The girl held the phone away from her ear. It was loud enough for Ned to hear.

'Let them wait, this is important.'

That was it for Ned. He reached over and took the phone from the startled girl's hand.

The girl's eyes widened. Her mouth dropped open in disbelief. Ned started,

'Enough,' he said into the phone.

'Brannigan here. Now I heard that and I think it's you who should do the waiting. You've probably never heard of me, but that doesn't matter, what matters is I've been waiting here for about fifteen minutes, along with a few others. It's my turn and you can wait. Oh, and do you know what I'm doing here? I'm paying my bloody rates. My money that you clowns need to keep this bloody circus going.'

He paused, listening. Then went on,

'Just a minute.'

Then in an aside to the girl who was busy writing, trying to hide a smile,

'Yes, that's Brannigan with a double n.' Then back into the phone,

'Yes, Ned Brannigan, one of your ratepayers. Now, if you like you can hang on and listen to me for a few minutes, and I'll tell you a few things you're not likely to hear from anyone else, or, if that doesn't appeal, just hang up and this charming, patient girl will ring you back, eventually. Actually, you could do some good by organizing someone to come down here and help this poor girl. Let's see,' he looked around, counting,

'Now there's eight people waiting. You people must realise that rate time is a busy time.' Ned paused, waiting. There didn't seem to be anything coming from the other end, so Ned went on,

'Now, if you don't like that idea just wait a minute 'cos I've got a few more.' Then after another pause,

'O.K. Oh, and, now, don't even think of getting cranky at this girl here. She didn't give me the phone, I took it. Yair, just reached over and took it out of her hand. She's doing her best. Are you getting the message?' Then,

'O.K.' as he put the phone down. By this time the receptionist had regained her composure. Ned asked quietly, 'Which one was that?' There were incredulous looks around the office.

'Councillor McLean.'

'Ah, good. I never liked him much anyway. I guess now feelings will be a bit mutual. Now if you have any bother at all about this just give me a call. Any little problem at all, just let me know.' There were a few smiles from the other people in the queue.

As Ned walked out the next lady who came to the desk said with a grin,

'And he didn't even know which one he was talking to. Absolutely amazing.'

Quentin thought the same thing. The more he saw of Ned the more curious he became. He wondered what drove Ned and was interested to find out.

Chapter Thirty-Five

Quentin decided not to wait at the Shire office, opting instead to head for the pub for a counter meal. He parked a little way from the pub and as he walked, saw Scott and Cree sitting at a table in front of the fish and chip shop. Quentin had seen Scott and Cree a few times. They were often together, sometimes walking, sometimes driving. Quentin found that usually when he saw one the other wouldn't be far away. Cree said, 'Want some chips?'

'Er, yes please, they look good.' Quentin only stayed a few minutes, then took off as though he'd just remembered something.

Scott was thinking about Chapman.

'It was sort of odd. Him taking off like that.'

'Who, Quentin?'

'No. Chapman. He saw me in the street one day and just said he was off home for a few days and took off without any explanation. Didn't even give me time to ask when he'd be back or anything. It was sort of odd.'

'Ah well, I s'pose he had his reasons. Here you finish the chips; I've got to go.' She got up and took off quite quickly.

Scott thought that a little odd too, but he shrugged it off, and drove home.

Two or three days later he found out what was going on between Cree and Chapman.

Chapter Thirty-Six

Nora Jeffery

One of the people Quentin had met was Nora Jeffery. She was obviously one of the long-time residents of Archerville. Her husband had died a few years earlier and had left her well provided for. He'd made quite a lot of money in Real Estate in the town and district and she'd stayed in the town and was always ready to give something back to the people who'd given so much to her. Quentin had often seen her about the street and she always seemed to be talking, chatting to someone. He found later that chatting was one of the things she was very good at. He thought she might just be the one to ask.

He continued on to the pub, had lunch and as he walked to his car, ran into Nora. After a little chat he decided now was as good a time as any.

'You've known Ned a long time I think.'

'You could say that.'

'What do you reckon makes him tick?'

'Who?'

'Ned.'

'How do you mean?'

'Well, he's so full of get up and go, and he does so much for the town, yet he doesn't seem to have any family or anything.'

'Well, it's a long, sad story.'

'I'd like to hear it if you'd like to tell me.'

'Why are you asking all this?'

'As you know I'm a writer and I'm always interested in different people. You understand, and Ned's certainly different.'

'Well, you've got that bit right. But why don't you ask him?'

'I'm a bit intimidated by him. Maybe if I get to know him a bit, then I might feel I could talk to him. As it is now, I don't think I could handle it if his re-action was a bit negative.'

'O.K. I think I understand that.'

Nora went quiet for a while.

'What do you intend to do with the story?'

'I don't really know. I've just retired and I'm looking for something to do. Maybe I'll write a book. I don't know. But you can be sure if I do it'll be an honest book. I won't rubbish anyone who doesn't deserve it. People like that garage feller that every one hates would probably get a bit of a serve, but you couldn't give Ned a hard time. He's too positive, does so much good in his own offbeat way.'

'O.K. I'll hold you to that. If you do write a book, I'll hold you to that last statement. I tell you what, I can be just as blunt as Ned, you know, when I get my dander up. My husband used to say I could stun a bullock at forty paces. I hope you never see that side of me. Still I don't think you will, you seem to be on the level.'

'Well, I try.'

They strolled over to the park and sat on the same seat Quentin had sat on and dozed when the two young boys had asked if he was O.K.

'O.K. Now what do you want to know?'

'Just talk about Ned. He fascinates me. How come he's so passionate about the place?'

'Well, a lot of its frustration, some of it anger. After what he's been through he gets really cranky when he sees people wasting their lives or stuffing up in some way.'

'What do you mean, after what he's been through?'

Nora Jeffery paused, pondered, as though she still wasn't sure she should be talking about Ned. Then she figured if he didn't hear it from her he'd doubtless hear it somewhere else and at least her story would be accurate. She went on, 'Ned was brought up on a farm about five miles out of town. He married a girl from the city. She seemed quite nice at first but she changed later. They had two kids. Two girls. Beautiful girls they were. They went for a holiday and Ned took the two girls out in a boat on a small lake. The bloody boat sank and one of the girls drowned. The wife blamed Ned. The inquest found the boat was unseaworthy. I suppose you could say Ned should've checked it out but apparently it looked okay but there was a lot of rust underneath it. Anyway, his wife changed after that. She kept on about it being his fault and that. Finally, one day he came home from town and she'd gone. Just packed some bags for herself and the other girl, and took off. Ned chased every-where looking for them.'

'How old was the girl?'

'Louise was her name. She'd have been about ten I reckon. Yair, about ten.'

'Did he find her?'

'Yes, he did. After about six months, somehow, he tracked her down to a place about four hours away. Someone who knew her had seen her. Needless to say, Ned went straight there and confronted her. She talked to him for only about ten minutes. Wouldn't let him see Louise. He booked into a motel thinking maybe next day she might change her mind, but when he went round to where she was staying next morning she was gone. The landlady said it was strange. The wife had come to her late that afternoon, paid up her rent and was packed and gone in a matter of an hour.'

'Where'd she go?'

'No-one knows. He's never seen them since. Nor has any-one else.'

'What'd Ned do?'

'Well he gradually gave up. He'd tried to find her through her parents but she hadn't contacted them either. At least that's what they said. He didn't really believe them but what could he do?'

'How long after the other girl drowned was it when she left?'

'About a year. It was gut wrenching for Ned and not only Ned but everyone else as well. Everyone knew Ned. Like, he'd lived here all his life.'

'And no one's seen her since?'

'No.'

'What happened after that?'

'Well, Ned took to the bottle. The farm got very untidy and so did Ned. He'd come in to town and get drunk three or four times a week, then some of his mates used to drive him home. He'd often pass out in the car on the way. But his mates stuck by him. You know how mates do, although I reckon there were times when they were ready to give up on him.'

'How long did it last, like, I mean, he seems to be okay now.'

'It went on for about two years. Then, one time, at about five in the morning, a cold morning it was too, he came to in his car. He felt around and his hand found water. The car was half in a channel in his drive. Fortunately, he wasn't hurt. He staggered up to the house and went to bed. That's where I found him. I was driving past when I saw the car. I dragged him out of bed and proceeded to give him a good old-fashioned blast. Told him it was a wake-up call. He could've drowned, and anyway we were all sick to death of his stupidity and all that, and it was time he got his act together.'

Quentin could imagine her doing it too. He figured the message would be loud and clear and realised he was only hearing a very short version. He asked, 'And then?'

'I told him to get the tractor and pull the bloody car out and I sat and watched him. A couple of neighbours called in to help but I sent them away. Let the silly bastard suffer I said. It had the right effect. At least I like to think it was my doing. He doesn't drink much now. I guess that's why we get on so well, Ned and I. Even though I'm only a few years older than him, eight to be exact, we have a sort of unspoken understanding. He knows when I'm serious. That day gets mentioned occasionally.'

Quentin went back to his rooms. Nora had given him a lot to think about.

Chapter Thirty-Seven

Tom Fraser

Quentin needed some milk. As he entered the supermarket, he met a woman returning a trolley, 'Do you want a trolley?' she asked.

'No thanks,' he said. 'I only want one thing.'

As he moved past, he heard her say to her friend,

'Typical man.'

Still grinning, he bought the milk and as he came out, he bumped into Tom Fraser. Literally bumped into him. Quentin caught his heel on the step and stumbled just as Tom was coming in. The milk went flying. Quentin tried to catch it but couldn't and only proceeded to send it crashing to the floor.

Quentin had seen Tom about the street but had never met him. Never spoken to him but now, over a spilled carton of milk and a couple of apologies and I'm Quentin Castlebridge and I'm Tom Fraser, they shook hands. Quentin had only seen Tom from a distance, but now, close up, he saw Tom's thin featured face with a few lines and wrinkles but with very bright, alert eyes. Tom Fraser was a man a little shorter than average but he stood quite upright. Slim and dignified. Quentin thought him to be about eighty or so but felt it a little difficult to judge. While someone was mopping up the milk, they started talking, or at least Quentin started talking. Trying to get some sort of rapport going between them, Quentin was saying things like sorry for being so clumsy and I'm only passing through and I like your town and are you a local? This question he knew the answer to anyway but he felt he'd like to get to know this man and bumbled on trying to make some sort of communication. Tom wasn't helping much. As they parted, Ned Brannigan walked past and G'day Tom and G'day Ned was all that passed between them. Tom mostly kept to himself. Because of the difficult conversation, Quentin wondered if he had upset Tom. Curious about this, he debated waiting and asking Ned, thought better of it and left it at that.

Cree and Scott were coming up the street. Also coming along from the Supermarket was another couple, an older couple. Quentin stopped with the intention of speaking to Scott and Cree as the other couple drew alongside. She was a big woman with an ill-fitting dress hanging off her like an old wheat bag, and he was a small, wimpy bloke, hunched forward, his eyes down, pushing a shopping trolley with their purchases, and she was not happy.

Quentin, Scott and Cree stopped and as the couple passed by her aggravation became more apparent, her voice louder, obviously with no concern as to who could hear or what they thought as she said,

'You didn't tell me that.'

'Yes, I did. I did tell you that,' came the weak response from the man still hunched over the trolley.

'No, you didn't.' She leaned towards him. He continued on, hunched over the trolley, eyes down.

'I did. Told you yesterday.'

'Well then, next time, tell me thoroughly.'

The three onlookers stood, watching, giggling.

Quentin told Scott and Cree the story about the spilt milk and asked about Tom,

'Do you think I upset him in some way?'

Cree was first to answer. She knew Tom and was quick to tell Quentin,

'No, you wouldn't have bothered him. He's always like that. Keeps to himself a fair bit. Everyone accepts that.' Then she went on,

'No, you wouldn't have upset him. In fact, I don't think you could upset him. He's just a real nice man who everyone likes.'

'Not like Woodley,' suggested Quentin. He'd heard a few stories. Cree grinned,

'No, not like Mr. Woodley.'

Quentin went to his car and drove off.

Chapter Thirty-Eight

The Falling Out

Cree and Scott bought some chips and were sitting in Scott's car, chatting, when Chapman pulled up a bit further down the street. He jumped out and was heading towards Scott's car, but when he spotted Cree sitting beside Scott, he altered direction, waved to Scott and kept walking. Scott hadn't seen Chapman for a few days, in fact, nobody had seen him much. He'd gone home for a while after the confrontation with Cree. Kept his distance. To say he was angry was to put it mildly, so he'd gone away to think about what had happened. Scott was glad to see Chapman and was looking forward to a chat, but then, when Chapman veered away, he was quite surprised. He hadn't heard about their disagreement. He turned to Cree,

'What the hell was that about?' Cree was silent, then after a while,

'We had a falling out.'

'What, you and Chapman?'

'Yes.' He looked at Cree then and saw she was close to tears.

Scott was staring, amazed at this turn of events. Amazed that Cree and Chapman could have anything to argue about, and even more amazed to see Cree, the one who was always so self- assured and usually happy go lucky, almost in tears. He was struggling to get his head around the whole thing. Although at first, he thought it was really none of his business, Scott wanted to know all about it. Then he thought, maybe it is my business. His two best mates here in town and they'd had an argument. He wanted to get it sorted. He waited for Cree to say something, but when nothing was forthcoming, he said,

'Well, come on. Let's hear it.'

Cree was still silent. He tried again,

'Come on, out with it. We're not going home 'til you tell me, and that's all about it. I'm not having my two best mates fighting without I try to fix it up. So, you might as well start and get on with it.'

Gradually Cree told Scott the story. Told him about talking about old Jack. Told him about doubting Chapman and Chapman's response. Told him how in the finish Chapman had gone off in a very angry frame of mind. Told him about how Chapman had said there was not going to be anything between them.

'Oh, Gawd Scott I've been a silly bitch. I know I should've stopped but somehow, I kept on. All the time making it worse.'

Then after a pause,

'I really fancy him you know.'

Their friendship was such that they could talk about anything. Cree had become like a sister to Scott. The sister he
never had and always longed for. They had somehow come
to an understanding, without actually talking about it, that
they would only ever be friends. Nothing more than that, so
they could tell each other what they were feeling.

'Yes, I know you fancy him, that's why I can't get my head
around the fact that you had a fight. You're right. You have
been a silly bitch.'

They sat in silence for a while, each with their own
thoughts, Cree thinking she wished she hadn't done that and
Scott thinking what he could do to get them together again.
He thought of a book he'd read once about a 'go-between', a
friend in the middle. Somehow, he felt he could be that person. Somehow sort these silly pair out. Somehow.

Scott started the car,

'All right. I'm glad you told me. At least I've heard one
side of it.'

'What're you gunna do?'

'I don't know, but one thing's certain. I'm gunna sort you
silly pair of buggers out.' This was a part of Scott that Cree
hadn't seen.

'Well, at least I'll talk to him, for a start.'

Chapman wasn't like that. Not that Scott had seen. He
was usually fairly placid and care-free. Scott wondered how
he was going to handle it. Thought it best to think for a while.
Sometimes a little time thinking made it easier to see a possible way to go.

It was a couple of days before Scott caught up with Chapman. As things had been before, Scott usually knew where Chapman would be, where he could find him, but since the altercation with Cree, Chapman had become a bit elusive, so Scott went to his place and waited. And waited. It was a couple of hours before Chapman showed up. Chapman said,

'I know I've been avoiding you a bit. But something came up.'

'I know. Cree told me about it.'

'Ah, did she now.'

'Yes, she did. Now let's go inside, make a cup of coffee and you can tell me your side of it.' Chapman paused, then,

'O.K. Let's do that.'

Chapman made coffee. They sat in silence for a short while, each waiting for the other to start. Finally, Scott broke the silence,

'Well, come on, let's hear it.'

'I s'pose she told you what it was all about.'

'Yair, she told me her version, now I want to hear yours.'

Chapman was quiet for a bit then he opened up.

'She doubted me. Questioned what I was about. Questioned my ideas. I only helped old Jack 'cos I've got an old uncle like that.'

'You have? I didn't know that…. I don't s'pose Cree knew it either.'

'No, I know. It's not the sort of thing ya go talking about much. The family just put up with him 'cos he's family. I saw old Jack lying there, friendless. Just like my uncle, so I helped him up. You saw that. I just did it 'cos I thought of my poor uncle, and here was a man, similar, really, who needed help.'

Scott understood that, but realised Cree wouldn't have understood. Chapman went on,

'Gawd she made my mad. Probably if she'd just made a comment it would have soon passed, but she kept on, making it worse. The more she went on the madder I got.'

'That ties in with what she told me.'

'It sorta felt like she was telling me my family didn't matter.'

'Yair, but can't you see, she didn't know about your family. All she was on about was you and old Jack.'

'Yair, I know you're right. But the whole thing gave me the shits.'

'You wanna know what else she said.'

Chapman was quiet. Thinking.

'Well, I'll tell you anyway. She said she knew she should've stopped but somehow, she couldn't help herself. You know what else she said?'

'No, what?'

'She said. Gawd Scott I've been a silly bitch.' He thought of leaving it at that but then he blurted out,

'And she said, you know, I really fancy him.' Then after a pause,

'That's why I'm here.' Scott waited a while so that could sink in, then went on,

'I've always known that. She didn't have to tell me 'cos it's been so bloody obvious, well, to me anyway it's been bloody obvious.'

That struck a real chord with Chapman. Scott thought maybe he'd said too much but was quite relieved when Chapman said,

'You know I've wanted to go and talk to her, but after what I'd said I felt I couldn't.'

'Like, what d' ya mean, what you'd said?'

'I said something like I don't care what she thinks and it'll be a long time before I talk to her again. Something like that.'

'Yair, she told me that too.'

'Gees Scott, I feel like crap about the whole thing.'

Scott heard the emotion in Chapman's voice and now he felt there was a real hope that he could get them together again.

He understood how Chapman felt he couldn't make the first step.

Scott was starting to see a way to get his two friends back on a sensible track. He left Chapman then and went straight around to Marion's place. Marion answered the door and after Hi Scott and Hi Cree, Scott said,

'Right, now, there'll be no argument about this. Come, now. Come on, in the car.' He waited while she hesitated.

'Come on. Now.'

Cree had not seen this side of Scott before. Usually he was a fairly placid, easy going sort of bloke, but today it was a different Scott. A strong, no nonsense Scott.

'O.K. Wait 'til I change into my slacks.'

Scott looked at her. She was wearing a daggy old pair of track-suit pants, with an equally daggy old t-shirt to match.

'You'll do like that. Come on.' Cree sensed what Scott had in mind and began to have some doubts. She felt a bit like a shy kid again. Then she made up her mind. She called to her mother,

'Just going out with Scott for a while,' and headed out to the car.

'Where're we going?'

'You know bloody well where we're going. I'm going to sort you pair out.'

Cree was both nervous and excited and a little scared when they got to Chapman's place. She said, 'I'll wait here.'

'Like buggery you will. Come on.' He pulled her reluctant form from the car, led her to the door, bashed on it, and called out as he pushed the door open,

'I've brought someone to see you.' Chapman had seen them coming so he'd had a few seconds warning, but was still a little apprehensive when Scott burst in. Then there she was. His dream girl. The one he'd fancied for so long, standing there in her old knock-about clothes, daggy, baggy tracksuit pants and an equally daggy tee shirt, looking very uncertain. This girl who usually exuded confidence, but today here she was standing there looking very unsure but even so still meeting his gaze. To Chapman she looked beautiful. Absolutely beautiful. They stood thus for a few seconds. Scott had brought a bottle of wine. He found some glasses, opened the wine and set it and the glasses on the table. He looked around. Neither Cree nor Chapman had moved. They were still just standing, neither prepared to make the first move, 'til Scott in an inspirational, unplanned move stepped up, took Cree's hand then Chapman's placed them together and said,

'I now pronounce you to be friends again.' That broke the awkward silence.

'Right you pair, I've done my bit, now you bloody well sort

it out. This crap has gone on too long.' Still they didn't make a move. Just stood, unmoving.

'Shit. Looks like I'll have to do everything. O.K. my decision, Cree you go first. Come on, let's hear it.'

'What?'

'Let's hear what you said to me. Come on.'

That was what finally did it. Quietly and evenly Cree said,

'I'm sorry Chapman. I was a silly little bitch.' Chapman quickly responded,

'No, it's me should be sorry. I shouldn't have gone off like that.'

As Scott headed out the door, he said,

'See ya.'

They hardly noticed him leave.

Cree was the first to move. She slid her arms around Chapman and he responded, immediately.

They kissed then. Their first real kiss. Cree thought — Gawd, how long I've wanted this.

She rested her head on his shoulder,

'Let's just forget the last few days. You know. Just sort of start again.'

'Sounds great to me.'

They stood. Arms around each other for quite some time, 'til Cree felt Chapman's erection, pressing against her.

Suddenly her old cheeky self-returned. She pushed herself against him, rolling her hips from side to side. After a few minutes he led her to his bedroom. She stood, waiting.

He slowly undressed her and pushed her nude body on to the bed as he took his clothes off.

Afterwards he said, 'You know. I'm always going to see
you in those daggy old clothes. I'll remember you like that
before I think of you in those pretty dresses and stuff you
wear to the dance and that.'

Chapter Thirty-Nine

Quentin

Quentin rang Sally, told her he was ready to come home. 'Well, you certainly sound a lot more positive. If you feel you'd like to come home I'll be very glad to see you.'

'Mind you I really like this place. I'd like you to see it. I'll bring you over here one day. See what you think of it.'

A plan was forming in his mind. Maybe they could shift and live here. Or maybe they could buy a place here and just come here sometimes. Perhaps just stay a week or two, like a holiday house. Yeah. That could work. Thought he'd suggest it to Sally. Best have her come here for a visit first tho'. Hell, she mightn't like it here. I'll have to do some thinking about it all.

Sally greeted him at the door, wrapped her arms around him,

'God, I'm glad you're home. I've been so worried you mightn't come back.'

'You silly twit. Of course, I was always coming back. The

only thing that worried me was that you mightn't want me back.'

She burst into tears at that. Tears of relief after all that pent-up anxiety, she was at last able to let herself go. They ate the meal Sally had cooked. Each one trying to tell the other all that had happened. They talked like they hadn't talked in years, then when they headed for bed each was a little tentative. They were sort of shy with each other. It was like they were having their first intimate time. They finally got their clothes off and jumping in to bed, they made wild, passionate love. Like a pair of teenagers. Love making like they hadn't done in years. When he finally rolled off her and lay exhausted beside her, she said, 'Wow, and I thought we were past all that.'

Chapter Forty

The drug house

Nora met Ned outside the Post Office. Not a planned meeting, just one which happened, but one which she would have arranged sooner or later.

'Ned, I need a word. Why not call round later this morning if you can manage it? It's a matter of some importance.'

'O.K. I'll do that.' Ned could see something was troubling her so he made a couple of phone calls, rearranged his plans and an hour later they were sitting in her kitchen drinking hot coffee. They'd done this often and she liked to make the coffee just the way Ned liked it. Hot and strong. He'd always drunk it like that, ever since he gave up the booze. He waited 'til she was ready to talk. He didn't have to wait long.

'The reason I wanted to talk to you is this. There's drugs starting to get about the town.'

'Oh. I hadn't heard of that.'

'There's a new family moved into that old weatherboard house in Carney Street. You know, the one that's been empty since Carmel Milson's father died. Apparently, the Milson's sold it to this mob.'

'And.?'

'They've got two kids, boys, at school and they've been trying to get some of the local kids interested. Apparently, the father picks his two boys up from school then just drives a little way down the street and waits. He only does it on Tuesdays and Fridays. It seems a couple of boys have been seen to go up to the car and get something from him. It looked as if they gave him money and he gave them a parcel.'

'Who told you this?'

'Carmel Milson. Her daughter saw it.'

'Who is this joker?'

'His name's Sudwick. Don't know the first bit. He's small and looks like a creep and a weasel. I've seen him down the street. Apparently, he hasn't got a job or anything.'

'Do you know where they came from?'

'No, but I reckon Arthur might know. He handled the sale. Or maybe the Milsons, you know, it might've been on the contract or something.'

Ned was deep in thought. After a while Nora asked,

'What do you think Ned?'

'Well, I'm just thinking if we found out where they came from, we could check 'em out. Find out a bit about 'em, so when we confront 'em we have all our facts. Don't want to go off half-cocked. There's always the possibility they're not doing anything wrong, though by what you've told me that seems unlikely.' Then, after another pause,

'What do you reckon?'

'Well, it's something that's got to be stopped before it gets out of hand. That's why I told you.'

'Yeah, I think you're right.'

Nora's concern was, as always, for other people. In this case her concern was not only for the kids of the town and their parents but also, and more particularly for her grand-children. There were four of them and they were at that vulnerable age.

Nora knew she didn't need to stress the urgency. She knew Ned would do something and fairly quickly.

She was right about that.

Ned went round to see Carmel Milson.

He found her at home and in his usual manner came straight to the point.

'Nora tells me you have some suspicions about those new people in your father's house.'

'Yes, Ned. Mind you they're only suspicions, but I don't much like the look of it.'

'Go on. I'm listening.'

'Well, apparently their two boys have been saying things at school.'

'Like what?'

'Things like they've been asking the boys and a couple of the girls too, things like have they ever tried smoking and then have they ever tried pot and that sort of thing, and tell-ing them it's a real buzz and that.'

'What else?'

'They've said they can get some if any of the kids want to try it.'

'Have any of them tried it do you reckon?'

'I'm not sure, but I think a couple of the boys might have.'

Ned thought for a minute. Then, 'Where did this crew come from?'

'They came from the city. Somewhere in the Northern suburbs. They were very vague when we asked them. We thought it was probably just that city thing, you know, not like the country where everyone knows someone in every other town and likes to make some sort of connection. But now I think it was more like they were hiding something. Didn't want anyone checking 'em out.'

'Would Arthur know do you reckon?'

'I doubt it. I mean, he's just an agent. He doesn't have to know their business. They told him they were renting in the city and wanted to get out of the rat race. I doubt they would've given him an address or anything.'

'Hmm. Seems they might've covered their tracks pretty well, and sounds as tho' they had a good reason.'

Carmel was concerned, not only about the potential damage these people may do in the town, but also, she was concerned that they had brought this element into the town.

'We feel a bit sort of guilty that we've been the ones to bring this lot into the town, course we had no idea they were like this.'

'Don't feel like that. It's not your fault. People who go about blaming others are not worth bothering about. They spend their time searching for someone to blame when there's a problem. Instead of getting on and fixing the problem. It achieves sweet F.A. Why or how it happened is not the important issue here. The important question is what to do about it.'

Ned left, leaving Carmel feeling a bit better about her part in the matter, but also leaving her curious to see what Ned would do. She'd known Ned a long time and had no doubts about him being the right bloke in this sort of situation.

Things moved quite quickly after that. That evening Ned had a visit from Val Jorgensen. She and Ned made a good pair. While Ned was usually quite blunt and straight to the point, he was never likely to become physically violent. The same couldn't be said for Val Jorgensen. She was also usually quite blunt and straight to the point also but had been known to make her opinions known in a physical way. She was not a huge woman, but a bit bigger than average. And a lot stronger. A powerful woman. She had worked on the farm all her life and could keep up with and even better a lot of men with a crow-bar or sledge hammer when the need arose. A lot of the men in the local fire brigade reckon she was as good as two men when it came to belting out a fire with a wet bag or running with a full knapsack on her back. Tough as nails. When her husband died, people who knew her had no doubt that she would keep the farm going. And she had, raising her three boys and working long hours she had shown many other farmers a thing or two.

The story of a confrontation she'd had with a neighbour when her bull had pushed through the boundary fence was often told. It had become part of the town's history. The neighbour was new to the district. He was in fact new to farming and country life and hadn't yet learned how things worked up the bush. It had come to a head at the cattle sale. Val was standing talking to a couple of men when the neighbour approached, yelling at her as he came,

'You and your bloody bull. Why don't you keep it in your place?' The other men stood back. Val stood her ground and quite calmly said, 'You knew my bull was there, yet you put those heifers in the paddock right next to him. He was only looking for a little bit of fluff, same as you do sometimes, I bet.'

The neighbour was quite worked up before she said that but that set him right off. He moved towards her and raised his fist. They had stopped the sale, not only because of the noise and the distraction but also because everyone knew Val and all were interested to see the outcome. None of the locals moved to intervene. They knew better. Knew she could handle him. Not only that, they knew she wouldn't have thanked anyone who did.

'By God if you were a man, I'd thump you. Just as well you're a woman.'

She stood her ground, put her hands on her hips and with a slight toss of her head said in an even tone,

'Oh, don't let that stop you Jack.'

He looked around, saw a lot of wry smiles, uttered a few profanities, turned and left.

The story was told many, many times. The way Val got out of her car and headed up the path

Ned could see Val obviously had something on her mind.

She strode up the path and calling as she came,

'You there Ned?'

Ned opened the door,

'Come in Val. Looks like you've got something on your mind.'

'Too bloody right I have.'

'Well, go on, spit it out.'

'Did you know there's drugs about the town?'

'Actually, I just heard about it today as a matter of fact. Nora told me. I had no idea.'

'Well, what do you reckon we should do about it?'

'Well, really, I just started thinking what to do. What do you think?'

'Well, I'm all for going around there and sorting them out.'

Never one to beat about the bush our Val. Ned smiled then asked,

'I take it you're talking about those new people in Milson's place.'

'That's right. Sleasy little bastard he is.'

'I don't think I've seen him, but by the little I've heard that describes him pretty well. Tell me what you know.'

'Apparently their sons talk about it at school. One of them asked one of my boys if he might be interested in smoking some 'stuff' he called it. I've always been very definite with my boys about that sort of thing. Don't mind them having a drink or two but drugs are definitely out. That kid doesn't know how lucky he was my boy didn't thump him.'

Ned pondered a moment or two. Already a plan was forming.

'Well, I think you're right about going round to see them, but I don't think the sorting out bit will be necessary. Well not at first anyway. We'll see how they react when we show them how this town works.'

Ned outlined a plan. He was aware of Carmel's comment that Sudwick only does it on Tuesday and Friday. The next Tuesday Ned put his plan into action.

Sudwick as usual picked his boys up and drove a little way down the street. Ned was parked across the street. A couple of boys walking towards the car stopped when Ned caught their eye and pointed, directing them to go back down the street. Ned's signal left them in no doubt. They turned, retreated a short distance stopped and looked back at Ned. Ned got out of his car and the boys took off. They knew Ned well enough to know you really didn't need to be told twice.

The next few minutes were like a well-rehearsed manoeuvre from an old silent movie. Val had been waiting a bit further along the street. As Ned approached Sudwick's car, she drove up and pulled her car in on an angle immediately in front of Sudwick's vehicle. Sudwick started to get out of his car then saw Ned coming across the street. He jumped back in and was trying to start the car when Ned reached the door. Ned was too quick. He wrenched the door open, reached in and grabbed the keys. Sudwick realised he'd been sprung, took one look at the big brawny fist clenching the keys, and decided it might be prudent to just sit and listen. Val was standing next to Ned in a second. Ned held the car door open.

'Get out here and listen. We've got something to say to you. First of all, we've been hearing some stuff about you. Stuff we don't like. Stuff like you've been trying to sell drugs to the kids around town. Do you deny it?'

'Well, I don't see that it's any of your business what I do.'

Ned asked again,

'Do you deny it?'

Sudwick didn't speak. With Ned standing in front of him and Val to one side, he was very conscious of being between two very formidable characters. He thought it may be better to listen.

Ned went on, 'I take it that you don't deny it. Your silence pretty much confirms what we've been told. I don't want to hear anything from you. Now you just listen. What I've got to say I'll say only once. You pack up all the stuff you've got, take it home and keep it home. If we hear another word around that you've been trying your sleazy tricks again, you'll have to answer to a few of us. Not just us two, the locals stick together you know. This is just a simple warning. Next time it could get rough. In fact, you're damn lucky to get away with just this warning. If you're going to stay in this town, you'd better smarten up your ideas.'

Ned turned his attention to the two boys cowering in the back of the car.

'Now you two get this straight. One more step out of line and you'll get the same treatment.'

Sudwick tried to intervene.

'You can't speak to my boys like that. I won't stand for it.'

Ned was getting a bit worked up by now, and he bristled at that. Val thought he was going to thump Sudwick. She quite relished the prospect. Knew if Ned started, she would have a bit of the action too. What she saw was a pathetic little creep. She realised if Ned started there wouldn't be much for her to do.

'You're not really in a position to argue. Now just get back in the car and go.'

Sudwick got in the car, backed up and drove off.

Val was first to speak,

'Just what was needed Ned. Hopefully that'll put an end to that. If he's got any brains at all it should be. I tell you what those two boys were pissing themselves. I reckon they got the message.'

The confrontation had the desired effect. And very quickly too.

Chapter Forty-One

Mrs Sudwick

Sudwick headed home. He was silent. Mrs. Sudwick took a while to get the story. Finally, the boys told her. We were scared to death they told her. That man looked big and strong and he was very angry. Even the woman who was there looked frightening. Then Tom, the older boy, said, 'We don't want to go to school tomorrow. Two of the boys from my form heard it all. He'd told them to go but I saw them stop not far away. I reckon the whole school'll know about it tomorrow.'

Mrs. Sudwick's mind was racing. She sat for a minute, thinking. How best to proceed. Her first thought was how to protect her boys. Maybe she could confront Ned. She'd seen him about the town. Knew who he was, and could well imagine how the sight of him in angry mode would frighten the boys. She was a meek sort, always prepared to sit back and say nothing. Through fear, mainly, she always held back.

Being a small thin wispy woman, she had never confronted her husband. Somehow, she lacked the necessary fortitude or courage, call it by whatever name suits, to speak up. She sent the boys to their room with strict instructions not to come out till she said so. Strange how a crisis creates a strength.

Sudwick was sitting at the kitchen table deep in thought when she entered. Now she let go. All that pent-up anger, simmering for a long time, burst forth in a torrent. Once she started there was no stopping her. He sat there staring, eyes down, fixed on an empty coffee mug which he'd drunk from half an hour ago, before he'd set out for the school.

'Perhaps now you'll stop and think about what you've been doing. How many kids you've set off in a bad direction? How many young lives you could've ruined with your sleazy little tricks?'

'I've only given them what they wanted. No-one forced them to buy the stuff. No-one made them smoke it. They only did it 'cos they wanted to. Anyway, a smoke occasionally never did anyone any harm.'

'That's your opinion. What about what it might lead to? What about that then? What about that kid that's in gaol in the city? Certainly, did him no good.'

'Yair, but that wasn't my fault.'

'I reckon it was. He wouldn't have got into trouble if you hadn't started him on the grass. And now look where we are in this town. Only been here two months and now the whole town'll know what you're up to. You got away with it in the city but country people are different. Everybody knows what's going on in a small town like this. You're a bloody disgrace. I hoped we could make a go of here, you know, start afresh, but you've certainly stuffed that up. Now I expect you'll want us to pack up and move on.'

'Well, it might be the best thing to do.'

'Well, I'm not going.' Then after a pause –

'And neither are the boys.'

She stood, hands on hips, silent for a few seconds, then turned and started preparing the evening meal. He'd not seen her in this state before. Usually she just accepted what he said but this time things were different.

This crisis certainly did create a strength in her. A powerful force she'd never shown before, not to herself and certainly not to him. He realised he'd have to tread carefully. She stood, looking out the window, clenching her fists. Then she looked at him, sitting there, head in hands, staring at nothing. Then she snapped. All that bottled up anger suddenly burst out. She picked up a saucepan and smashed it across his ear. He jumped up and cowered, holding his bleeding ear. Physically she would not have had a chance against him but suddenly she looked formidable to him, especially since he was not operating from a position of strength, quite the contrary and when in that situation there's nothing quite as frightening as an angry woman.

'What the hell was that for?'

She let forth more strongly than before, even fiercely now,

'Maybe it'll take something like that to wake you up. You're right. It might be the best to pack up and move on but I've got news for you. It'll be you that'll be packing up and moving on, but you'll be doing it on your own and taking all that shit with you. I meant what I said. Me and the boys'll be staying here.'

She was burning her bridges and she knew it but she wasn't turning back now.

'I've put up with a lot of crap from you over the years but now it stops. Now piss off and don't come back for a couple of hours, me and the boys have got some talking to do.'

She started to tell the boys. Tom interrupted her.

'You don't have to tell us much Ma. We heard most of it. In fact, I reckon half the town heard it.'

She sat then and began laughing.

'Can I could count on you two?'

'Course you can Ma. Good on you. We're glad you finally stood up to him. We hope he goes and doesn't come back.'

'How long have you two felt like that?'

Jamie, the younger boy spoke for the first time,

'Since forever Ma. We never wanted to be involved in it but he made us do it. I've always been scared something like this might happen. Geez I loved it when you clouted him with that saucepan. I reckon we should hang it on the wall. It'll be good for a laugh.'

She realised then that the boys had been afraid of their father. Something which had never occurred to her. Afraid to the extent that they obeyed him even though they didn't want anything to do with the drug thing. She started to laugh again and this time the boys joined in. It was like a party.

Both boys hugged her. She went on preparing the meal. Sudwick drove down the road to the creek and sat there thinking, wondering where this was all leading. Sometimes when she got a bit annoyed, she'd question his actions but he would always shut her up pretty quickly, telling her he knew what he was doing and she better leave all the important things to him. She'd never stood up to him like she'd done this time. She usually backed down. Somehow, he knew she wasn't going to back down this time. This time it was for keeps. She cooked a large pot of stew and she and the boys were sitting, eating and hardly looked up when he came back. He came in looking rather like an errant schoolboy, knowing he'd gone badly wrong. He helped himself to some stew and took it to the other room. He listened to them talking and laughing and never in his whole life had he felt so alone, so not wanted. He realised he'd never be part of his family again.

He slept that night in the caravan. Stayed there 'til mid-morning. When he finally emerged and walked sheepishly in to the kitchen she was waiting for him.

'Sit down there,' she ordered. Then she started, 'Right. This is how it's gunna be. Me and the boys'll stay here. The house is paid for but I want you to sign it over to us. You know, get our names on that title thing that they have so it's ours. You can keep the big car and the caravan. Then you can put a fair chunk of that money you've been stashing away in my bank account.'

He stirred at that last bit, 'Hey, hang about. That money's mine. I worked for that.'

'Then you'll just have to go and work some more. Maybe get a proper job and earn some honest money.'

'Most of that is honest money. I never got much from that other stuff.'

'Well, then you'll have no trouble getting some more then. I tell you what, you'd better do it my way or I'll dob you in. I could tell them a thing or two.'

'You wouldn't?' He let the question hang in the air.

'Just don't try me out. Now, how soon can you do that legal thing?'

Sudwick couldn't believe this was the same woman. The woman he'd been married to for many years and who'd never say a thing out of place, never stand up to him about anything and yet here she was, laying down the law, making all the decisions which would affect his future, his future and that of his family. Suddenly she'd changed from a meek little nobody to an unassailable force. Suddenly she was in control.

He spent a couple of days moping around the house. Painful days. Neither his wife nor the boys paid him much attention, then when he knew she wasn't going to relent he packed the van and left.

The story had spread quite quickly. Some accounts reasonably accurate, some with quite a bit of embellishment, but none the less the end to the story always ended the same, that Ned and Val had given that Sudwick a fair roasting.

Mrs. Sudwick took the boys back to school the day after he left. They went first to Tom's classroom. Mrs. Sudwick spoke to the teacher,

'My name's Doreen Sudwick and my son has something he'd like to say to the class. Go on Tom.'

Tom began to mumble nervously at first. Not making much sense. His mother stopped him.

'Start again Tom, only louder.'

Tom took in a deep breath and as if inspired by his mother's strength, started again much louder and stronger, 'I'm sorry for what I was doing. I knew it was wrong but I was made to do it. It won't happen again. My father's gone away, so now I can start being me. I hope we can all be friends.' With that he took his books and sat down, not at the back where he usually sat but right there in the front row. She took Jamie to his room and he made a similar speech.

After that the boys became accepted by their peers. They were included in those groups which form around the school yard at lunch time and after school. School life for the boys became a good experience, so much so that they were always keen to get to school. They were always ready, waiting in the car when Mrs. Sudwick came out.

Chapter Forty-Two

The Progress Association

Several of the townspeople were somewhat displeased with the efforts of the council. Archerville was only a small centre in the Shire and the people felt they were a bit neglected. Felt they needed more attention. Several of the locals got their heads together and decided it was time the town had a progress association.

Some felt there was a need for a multi-purpose building and this was foremost in the minds of those who called a meeting. Quite a good crowd turned up as would be expected in any small town. Some came with serious intent, some just for something to do and some just curious, but all listened when Cr. Isherwood called the meeting to order. Cr. Isherwood was a new councillor from the other side of the Shire who didn't really know any of the locals, nor did any of the locals know him. However, he proved to be quite a good chairman. He simply asked for any speakers.

Bob Creewell was first to his feet, and in a brief speech

outlined what several people felt was a need in the town. Three of four of the locals had often talked about this idea. It was because of these discussions that the meeting had been called. Bob outlined what they had talked about.

'We need a hall which can be used for Scouts, Guides, cards, films, maybe a concert or two and even a museum of stuff from around the district.'

'What sort of stuff?' came a question.

'Just ordinary stuff that represents what the district is about. When people see we are fair dinkum they'll donate things. Scratch around in the shed and find suitable stuff. Just ordinary things. Say, things like old tools and that, or what about a water-bag. Most people today have an esky, probably never seen a water-bag and yet that's all we ever had. Things like that. Even war stuff.'

'Have you thought of maybe renovating the old Mechanics Institute?' asked a man called Polwarth.

'That's exactly what we have been thinking. I know it has been a bit neglected but old brick buildings like that were built to last.'

After various speakers it seemed to Cr. Isherwood that enough interest was shown, so he called for nominations for a president.

Ned Brannigan rose. Bob thought he was about to nominate someone but nothing was further from Ned's mind. He had decided the thing was going to go ahead and that was all that concerned him and was about to leave. He'd taken a few steps towards the door when Bob spoke up,

'Don't go Ned.' Then to the chairman,

'I'd like to nominate Ned.'

Ned stopped then. There was a silence for a few moments, and when Cr. Isherwood asked Ned if he would stand for the position, Ned said,

'Never occurred to me. Like, I'll help where I can but I don't think they'll want me as president. Might upset too many people. I'm not always the most tactful joker you know.'

Cr. Isherwood didn't know then but in the space of a minute or two he recognized that this was the man for the job.

'Do you accept nomination Ned?'

After a pause,

'Yair, well, yair alright, unless someone else'll volunteer or somethin'.'

Another pause. Then,

'Actually, yair, alright but I tell you what — I expect everyone to do their bit — If I ask you to do something, I expect you to do it. No pithy excuses or any crap. We'll just get on with things.'

Cr. Isherwood then pompously declared Ned president. Ned came to the front and sat down.

'Now I think we should elect a committee of say ten or a dozen of you people.'

Ned spoke up,

'We don't need a committee. Committees are a waste of bloody time. All these people here are interested. They'll all do their bit. We don't need names on a piece of paper.'

Isherwood was again taken by surprise. But then, he didn't know Ned.

'How much money will the council give us?' Ned asked.

'Hang on, not so fast. This is only an advisory committee really.'

'Like buggery. If I'm to be president it'll be to get things done. Not procrastinate like the bloody council usually does. I couldn't be bothered with any bloody advisory committee, wouldn't waste my time.' He addressed the councillor directly, and something stirred in Isherwood's mind. Something had been niggling at him as soon as Ned's name was mentioned. Eventually the penny dropped. This was the joker who'd given McLean a blast on the phone. One way or other the whole council chambers had heard about that. He started to understand Ned. Ned went on, 'The obvious thing the town needs is an all-purpose building. That's what this meeting was called for as I understand it and if I'm going to be President that's what we'll have. That and a shelter for the kids at the bus stop at the school. The bloody useless council knows all about those things but chooses to do nothing. O.K.?' Then he addressed the meeting, 'What's it to be? Do we 'advise' or do we just get on with it and get things done?' Ned sat down then. Bob Creewell was again first to speak. He said quietly, 'I'm with Ned. I think we should just get on with it. If the council sees we're fair dinkum they'll have to back us.'

There were various other comments, all in the affirmative, all very positive. A comment was heard to the effect that if the council won't give us funds, we'll have to raise our own. So, it was decided. They would just get on with it. Cr. Isherwood had no option but to agree.

The locals went about the job of cleaning up the old hall

with endless enthusiasm. People with a couple of hours to spare would wander down and do something towards the project.

Marion busied herself with a bit of fundraising. She organised the inevitable raffle. She'd been cheeky enough to ask the local motor-bike dealer and had got a very good deal on a new bike for first prize and then the butcher donated a hundred dollars' worth of meat. One or two other prizes were donated and Marion or one of her parents, or Scott or Chapman were often seen selling tickets in front of the supermarket. When the Council did see that they were fair dinkum, they had, at Cr. Isherwood's insistence, made money available for the project.

Work went on every day whether Ned was there or not. Tradesmen volunteered their skills. It was all go, go, go. In the next few weeks the whole floor was replaced, several windows also, doors which had been hanging loose were re-hung. Curtains were made and hung. Display shelves and cupboards were made and arranged in order in the various rooms. Everything painted. In short, a flurry of non-stop activity.

All the while donations were appearing for the museum. Ned asked Nora Jeffery to co-ordinate the display which she did with efficiency, labelling and cataloguing each gift. Nora kept the war relics separate. Displayed them in a room of their own.

Chapter Forty-Three

The Museum

Quentin Castlebridge had heard about the project and decided it would be a good time to take Sally to Archerville. Have her meet some of the locals and see what happens in the town. The first thing Quentin wanted her to see was the Hall. They went down there and were met by Scott and Cree who proceeded to fill them in on all that had happened, and show them around. Quentin was amazed at the transformation of the old building. He remembered it as a bit of a derelict old place, but now, here it was, all done up and looking fantastic. Sally was very impressed, not only with the Hall but also with Scott and Cree. She thought they made a great couple; thought they were a couple in the sense of partners until Quentin told her otherwise. No, he'd said, they were just good mates. Quentin wasn't aware of the development of the romance between Cree and Chapman. Since the 'sorting out' Scott had done they were hardly ever apart. Then they met Ned. Sally was intrigued by Ned.

Quentin had told her about him, described him and his ways. Sally soon saw why Quentin had been fascinated with this man. Ned was just walking around, directing, without any fuss. Just making sure things were as he wanted, but at the same time ready to listen to suggestions.

The date had been set for an official opening, and everything had been done with only a minimum of time to spare but despite the last rush everything seemed to be in readiness. They had asked the local Member of Parliament to come, make a speech and cut a ribbon and that's where the problem started.

The first indication that there was a problem came the day before the date set for the opening when people cleaning and tidying heard Ned on the phone in his office. As usual, Ned had the door open. He could easily be heard. Quentin and Sally were there helping to tidy up.

In the next few hours and the next day, they saw what a force Ned was. Saw what a man can do if set a task and was hell-bent on seeing things through. They heard Ned on the phone, and like all the others present, stopped to listen.

'But bugger it all, you said you'd be here at three to open this place.' Silence followed as Ned listened. Then, 'I don't care a fig about your estimates committee or whatever it is, this thing's been arranged for weeks. You're our local member. You said you'd be here and now you're welshing on the deal.' Silence again, then, eventually after the conversation lasted quite a few minutes, it ended with Ned saying,

'The invitation is withdrawn. We'll open it ourselves.'

All present heard enough of Ned's end of the story to get the gist of the matter. After a pause Ned came out and explained what had happened, then he outlined his idea of the next move. Various comments were made and suggestions offered. Quentin listened, fascinated. An idea was forming in his mind. Tossing around in his mind. Then he knew what he wanted to do. He would write a short play about what happened. Or maybe a film script. Yes, he thought, that would be better. A film script. The more he thought about the idea the keener he became. The basis of the play was there right in front of him. What he saw and heard there in the Hall that afternoon would make a great story. The whole plan got even better after the events of the rest of the day and the next. He, of course, witnessed the end result of Ned's plan the next afternoon. The rest of what occurred between the phone confrontation with the local M.P. and the actual opening he found out after talking at some length to Ned and one or two others. He told Ned of his plans and Ned, being Ned, just said, 'Go ahead. Do what you like. I'm only interested making sure this thing's a success.'

So, Quentin wrote:

The New Museum.

A short play about the opening of a renovated building in a small country town, to be used by the locals as a meeting place and a museum.

Act One.

Players.

Ned — Man about fifty. Strong, well-built man, handy-
man about town, usually dressed in work clothes.
Tom — Short, slim man, about eighty.
Nora — Middle aged lady.
Jefferson — An older man.
Extras — Several school age children and other young
people.
Voices on phone.

The hall was the old Mechanics Institute. A brick building
with two columns in the front and an arch over a heavy
wooden door.
Camera films from the street. Signs up, opening Sunday,
new local and war museum. etc
Camera then enters the hall.
Pans around. Shows books, old tools, framed pictures,
rifles, gas masks etc. in show cases. Several people moving around tidying, sweeping etc. Camera closes in on
Ned, looking his usual untidy self, talking on phone in
office inside hall.

Ned — But you said you'd be here tomorrow at three.

Voice — Yes, I know. Look, I'm really sorry about this,
but they've called a special meeting of the estimates

committee and I really have to be there. Now what I propose is that we move the opening forward to say ten o'clock in the morning. Could you phone the members of your committee and get them there then? They're the important ones.

Ned — But people are coming from miles around, some even from Sydney and Melbourne. This thing's been arranged for ages. What about them?

Voice — Well that'll be a pity but when you explain, I'm sure they'll understand.

Ned — How the hell do you expect me to explain it to them when I don't even understand it myself? You're our local M.P. We're relying on you. What about your commitment to us? We were first. Eh, what about that then?

Voice — Well, this sort of thing happens all the time in politics. You get used to it after a while.

Ned — [getting angry] — Well, you may get used to it but I won't. This thing's been arranged for weeks, I don't give a shit about your bloody estimates or whatever it is.

Voice — Well, I'm sorry, but that's just how it is. Look, surely you can get most of those that count there in the morning.

Close up of Ned, holding phone away from his ear, looking at ceiling. People out in hall become aware of Ned getting angry, stop and look at open office door.

Voice — Are you still there?

Ned — voice gradually rising — Yes, I'm still here. I'm not sure why, but yes, I'm still here. I'm just doing some thinking... O.K. I tell you what I'll do. I'll make sure everything's ready for you at ten, the door unlocked and all that.

Voice — Ah, that's better. I knew you'd see my way. You'll see, it'll be O.K.

Ned [rising to his feet and gesticulating] — I haven't finished yet. I'll make sure the door is unlocked at ten, I'll even tie a bit of hay band across it, and leave a pair of scissors there so you can cut it. But be aware you'll be the only one there, 'cos I'm bloody sure I'm not gunna try and change the arrangements we've had for about three months just to suit you. Politician or no bloody politician. We'll open it ourselves, at three o'clock. I'll just get some of the locals, have some impromptu speeches from the old timers and that. Come to think of it, that might be even better than having an M.P. there who doesn't care two hoots.

Voice — Hey now, steady on. That's not how it is.

Ned — Well, that's how it sounds to me. Tell you what, why don't you leave a copy of your speech and I'll try and get someone to read it out. I'm bloody sure it won't be me, but I might find someone willing, though you can be sure I won't try very hard.

Voice — I'm sorry you feel like that, but that's how being the local member works.

Ned — I thought a local member was exactly that. We asked you weeks ago. It's up to you. Don't bother to ring back. We're opening it at three whether you're here or not. Suit your bloody self. In fact, no, don't suit yourself, don't come. The invitation is withdrawn as of now. We'll make some other arrangements. Thanks for bloody nothing. I'm off now. I've got things to do.

Ned puts phone down muttering.

- Bloody politicians. Useless, the lot of 'em.

He walks out into the body of the hall, where about ten people are standing around.

Ned — [calls to everyone] Gather round everyone, I've got something interesting to tell you. I s'pose you heard most of that. Our esteemed local member won't be performing the opening tomorrow.

Jefferson — [a thin, balding man with big horn-rimmed glasses, wearing white shirt and tie. Looks a little out of place — everyone else dressed for working bee.]

This man was an invention of Quentin 's. He just added him to make the play flow.

Jefferson — How could that happen?

Ned — He just rang and informed me he wants to change the opening time to ten in the morning. Says he suddenly has to be back in the city for a meeting.

Lady — What did you say to that?

Ned — I just told him to please himself. He can come at ten if he wants but he'll be the only one here. I told him I'd arrange for the door to be unlocked and he can do what he likes but we're having the opening at three as arranged whether he's here or not. I told him not to bother ringing back. Then I told him not to bother coming at all and then I told him the invitation was withdrawn.

Jefferson — Hey, I think that's a bit that's a bit rich, after all he is our local M.P. I don't think you should treat an M.P. like that.

Ned — I can and I did. And what's more, I'd do it again. He wanted to treat us like garbage so I just gave him some back. O.K., now, this is what I propose. We'll have a few of our old war vets to speak and we'll get one or two of them to cut the ribbon. I'm quite sure that's how they would have done it in the war. Far better than some bloody politician who's probably never even been here anyway and certainly hasn't done anything towards the project.

Jefferson — I really must protest. I don't like this at all.

Ned — Well, you people elected me president for this job, and while I'm president that's how we'll do it. Now if you don't think that's right, then you'd better get someone else to do it.

Ned stands staring at Jefferson. Waiting. Jefferson mumbles but says nothing. Looks at the floor.

Ned — O.K. Are we all agreed?

General nodding and someone says — Good on ya Ned.
People continue sweeping etc.
Camera outside building as people come out.

Ned — O.K. I'll see you all tomorrow. We'll fire up the barby at twelve-ish. See you all then.

People disperse. Jefferson pauses as if to speak but then changes his mind and walks off. Ned returns to his office, pulls out phone book. Scans book. Dials.

Ned [on phone] — Hello, I'm trying to contact Alf Quanchi the President of Legacy over there.

Voice — Yair, you've got him. This is Quanchi.

Ned — I'm Ned Brannigan. We haven't met or anything, but I've got a favour to ask.

Quanchi — O.K. let's hear it.

Ned — Well. we've put together a war museum over here. It's not real big or very flash or anything, but we're rather proud of it and I'll tell you what's happened.......

Camera draws back. Shows Ned talking. Music over for a few seconds. Gradually Ned becomes audible.

Ned — ...in the finish I told him not to come, the invitation was withdrawn.

Quanchi — I can see you don't mess about.

Ned — Well, he got my goat. He really pissed me off, letting us down like that. Anyway, you can see I'm in a bit of a spot and I wondered if you might like to come and be one of the speakers, and maybe cut the ribbon or something. Someone local'd be better than that useless politician.

Quanchi — Well, I'd love to but I'm wondering why you're asking me when you've got a far more qualified and more eloquent bloke at your place.

Ned [pauses] — I have? Have I? Er, well... er. I thought I'd ask old Jim Wellings or maybe Maggie McInnes or Norm Peters to just say a few words but I think they're probably past making speeches.

Quanchi — Yair, I'd agree with that, but that's not who I mean. I'm talking about Tom Fraser.

Ned — What? Old Tom, I've never heard him speak.

Quanchi — Well, I have and believe me you won't forget it when you do. I've only heard him once. It was at a reunion in Sydney. He spoke for about twenty minutes, without notes. The audience was absolutely dead silent. Not a murmur. Some had been drinking a bit too. There wasn't even a cough. I tell you it was a time I won't ever forget.

Ned — But I didn't know he was in the war.

Quanchi — Not many do. He flew spitfires. He was a top pilot. Got shot down over Germany and spent a year in prison camp.

Ned — Well I never knew that.

Quanchi — He's a very private bloke. That's part of the reason he came to Archerville, you know, so he could, you know, be himself, stay out of the spotlight and all that. The fewer people know what he did in the war the better as far as he's concerned. You can tell him I mentioned his name but I want you to reassure him if he doesn't want to come out and speak you won't mention this to anyone. Your absolute discretion is important. To both him and me. Like you said, we haven't met or anything but I think I can rely on you to keep your trap shut if he rejects your request.

Ned — Well, of course. This has taken me by surprise, but I know when to keep my mouth shut.

Quanchi — Good. He'd prefer it like that.

Ned — Yair, I can understand that. Actually, he always keeps to himself. I don't reckon anyone in town would know that about him.

Quanchi — Ah, actually one or two do.

Ned — Should I ring him or just go out there?

Quanchi — Probably just go out and see him.

Music over last of conversation. Camera draws back as
Ned hangs up.

Act Two

Ned gets into his battered old car and drives along country road. Enters country lane which leads to Tom Fraser's
cottage. A little old weatherboard with a neatly kept garden. Tom appears from shed, wiping his hands-on piece
of cloth. Tom is 80 years old, slim, medium height, but
still stands straight. Is wearing old work clothes and a
battered hat.
He pauses with a curious expression, and watches Ned
get out.

Ned leans against his car — How are you Tom?

Tom — O.K. thanks Ned.

Ned — I've just learned something.

Tom — Oh, yair. And what was that?

Ned — I've just been talking to Alf Quanchi and he tells
me you're an R.S. L. man.

Tom — Oh yair.

Ned — I guess you're aware of what we've been doing down at the hall.

Tom — Yair. I've been noticing some activity down there.

Ned — I didn't know you were in the war or I'd have asked you if you'd like to be involved, so I'm sorry about that, however I hope it's not too late. Now I'll tell you what has happened this morning.

Tom — Oh yair.

Ned — Our esteemed local M. P. was supposed to come and open the museum tomorrow afternoon and he rang me this morning to say he couldn't come in the afternoon and could we change the opening to ten in the morning.

Tom — Oh, yair.

Ned — Yair, that's right. I told him we'd do it at three with or without him and then one thing led to another and I finished up telling him not to come at all. Now, the reason I'm here. Alf Quanchi, who I haven't met incidentally, suggested I ask you to speak. Now, he said not to say anything to anyone till I spoke to you and I'll understand if you'd rather not and I'll go away and not mention this to anyone, but after hearing the little bit from Alf I'd very much like you to speak and maybe even cut the ribbon. [Ned waves his arms etc.] Jeez that feller got my goat. This thing's been arranged for months. People are coming from miles away and he wanted us to change the whole thing just to suit him.

Tom — I get the feeling you're a bit annoyed with him.

Ned stops and looks then starts to grin. They both grin.

Tom — Well, I don't know. I've been away from all that stuff for a long time now.

Ned — Tell you what. How about this. Let's get in the car now and I'll take you down there and you can see what we've done and then you can say yes or no. What do you reckon?

Tom — Well, I s'pose it wouldn't hurt to have a look.

They get in Ned's car. Drive. The place is now empty. No-one about. Ned unlocks the door. They enter the hall. Camera shows the two men walking around the building. Tom stands staring at a gas mask, stands motionless with his hand over his mouth, shaking his head, visibly affected.
A few seconds of flashback of streets with people running, all wearing or clutching gas masks. Bombs exploding. Dust and smoke.
Tom walks on around the room, not speaking, still shaking his head.

They walk to the door. Ned has the sense not to speak.

Tom heads for the door — I'd like to go now.

They drive back to Tom's place in silence. Pull up at the house.
Camera on Tom and Ned in front seat. Tom staring ahead, pondering. Slowly opens car door. Ned is watching Tom. Tom gets out, leans in the open door and says -

O.K. Ned, I'll do it. I'll be there at three.

Ned [nods understandingly, pauses] then says — Thank you Tom.

Nothing further said. Tom walks to the house, slowly, head bowed. Ned drives off.

Act Three

Next day.

Barbeque cooking in front of hall. Ned eating and talking to Nora and Bob Creewell.

Ned — You know, our esteemed member's not coming. I reckon we'll do just as well without him. You two have been involved all the way with this thing so I'll tell you what happened after we left here yesterday.

There's been a bit of a development. I rang Alf Quanchi, he's president of Legacy for the district and he told me we had a very good speaker right here. A man eminently qualified. I've asked him to speak.

Man — Well, come on, who is it?

Ned [pauses, then speaks] — I think I'll wait. You'll know him when you see him.
Anyway, I went and saw him yesterday and he's agreed to speak. I'm sure you'll find he'll do a good job. He's well qualified I can assure you.
O.K. now let's eat.

Barbecue continues.

Two hours later.

Scene — Front of hall. Crowd, maybe a hundred people gathered. Ribbon tied between pillars in front of hall. Lectern with microphone set up on front portico. Five or six boys, tousled hair, shirts out etc., are running about beside the hall, kicking a football, yelling to one another. Several girls are sitting on the grass, talking and laughing. Ned is watching the road. A car pulls up. Ned watches as Tom Fraser gets out.
Ned calls for order. Boys begrudgingly stop their game

and disinterestedly make their way to the front of the hall. Girls similarly bored do the same.

Two men in the crowd confer.

1st man — Who's this joker?

2nd man — It's Tom Fraser. He's that old feller who's got that little place down on the river.

1st man — Oh, jeez. You're right. But he's a real loner. Quiet sort of joker.

2nd man — Yair, always walks away when there's a crowd. Never smiles much.

Camera back on Ned. Then on Tom.

Tom, dressed in full uniform, slowly makes his way forward with all the dignity which comes with age. The crowd steps aside. With each step Tom stands straighter, walks with more purpose. As he reaches the steps, people start to clap. Tom pauses as he reaches the top of the steps. Salutes. Ned indicates a chair. Tom sits. Two people already seated. One a very elderly man in a suit, the other an older woman.

1st man — Crikey, look at that uniform. And all those ribbons. He must've been in the war.

Ned [speaks into microphone, only parts of his speech are audible as camera pans around] — pleased to welcome you all here... We are proud of our efforts here... lots of people have put lots of energy... some have travelled great distances...

Ned [indicates those seated] — Our special guests today are all locals who you all know. Maggie McInnes, better known in 1943 as Sister Margaret Brown who served in the hospitals in New Guinea and Singapore and on the troop ships with the wounded, and Norm Peters, better known Captain Peters who served in the Kokoda campaign and on the Burma railway and somehow survived.

Later I'm going to ask them to cut the ribbon here to open this museum. However, before I do that, I'm going to introduce our special guest speaker. Some of you may have heard the story of how our local Member reneged on our deal. I only found out yesterday that Tom Fraser was an R.S.L. man so I've asked him to speak today.

Ned looks around the crowd for a few seconds then continues — I guess we don't really know Tom Fraser. I only found out yesterday what he did in the war. You see, he was there. He was a fighter pilot with the Royal Australian Air Force. Took part in the battle of Britain. Flew sorties over Europe. Was shot down and spent a year in prison camp in Germany. Escaped from there and went straight back into battle. He has agreed to speak today. Friends, I give you Squadron Leader Tom Fraser.

Tom steps forward, without notes, ignores the microphone and starts to speak in a strong voice, easily heard at the back of the crowd.
Some boys are still fidgeting and talking at the back.

Tom — I want to tell you people some things today which are very important parts of our Australian history. I want to tell what some people did so that we may be free. Free to walk the streets, free to make speeches, free to play our sports and do our own thing. Men and women fought and died so that you could have that freedom.

I think the most important subjects that should be taught in the schools today are the English language and Australian history. The schools today tend not to teach Australian history, so it's quite understandable that the younger generations don't know the danger this country faced during the war.

Those of you who would rebel, strike, fight, cheat, steal, brawl, snivel, whinge — remember this. Men and women have fought and died, or suffered untold injury, many suffered for the rest of their lives. All that, so you could be free.

Now, I have a message to all Australians.

Imagine where we would be today if Japan had won World War Two?

Camera pans around the crowd. Music over Tom speaking.
Crowd very attentive. Young people listening, enthralled.
Camera back to Tom speaking -

Now I would like all you people to stop and ask yourselves — What can I do to make Australia a better place? To show my thanks to them. [Pauses] then –
Thank you for listening, and thank you for the privilege of being part of today.
Tom sits.
The applause starts slowly then builds 'til everyone is standing, clapping.

Ned resumes the mike.
The clapping gradually stops.

Ned — By crikey I'm glad that politician reneged. I think he did the town a favour. Thank you, Tom. And after today I ask you all to respect Tom's privacy, after all that's one of the main reasons he came here to live. He's done his bit and has earnt the right to do his own thing.

Ned continues — Now I'd like to ask Maggie and Norm to cut the ribbon here.

Maggie and Norm cut the ribbon.

Ned — Good. Thanks to you both. Now let's fire the barby up again and enjoy the rest of it.

Camera closes on Tom and Ned, eating.

Tom — You know Ned, I think I needed to do that.

An elderly lady approaches them and says,

-Thanks Tom, you've done a great thing for us all today.

Camera draws back and everything fades.

It hadn't taken Quentin long to write the play. Everything was there in front of him. Fresh in his mind. When he'd finished and polished it a bit, he showed Ned. Ned took it home. A couple of days later, they met in the street,

'I think you've done a pretty good job with this thing. Now tell me, what the hell do you plan to do with it?'

'Well, first, I wanted to see your re-action. Now you've seen it and read it and you haven't jumped up and down and said it's crap, I thought I'd show Nora. I'd value her opinion as much as anyone's. If it's O.K. with you, I'll do that.'

'Oh yair, and.?' Ned left the question unasked, but Quentin knew he wanted an answer.

'Then if it's O.K. with you two, I thought maybe I'd print

a few copies for anyone who wanted one. I've still got all my printing gear. Maybe we could even sell them for a few dollars and put the money into the Hall funds. Or something like that. I'd be open to suggestions. Yair, something like that.' He waited a few seconds, then,

'Does that sound stupid or anything?'

'No, not stupid at all. See what Nora thinks.' Then,

'Maybe show Bob too. Yair, show Bob. I reckon he'd like to see it. And, most important, better show Tom. Now there's a thing, best show Tom first and by hell if he objects then that's the total end of it. Completely finished. O.K.? Yair, that's the best plan.' Ned thought for a while, then,

'Be very careful how you approach Tom. I don't want him to be upset in any way. What he did that day was a big effort. Come to think about it, I think I'd better come with you when you go to see him.'

'Yair, O.K. Ned. Yair, I think you're right.'

They went out to Tom's place a couple of days later.

'Tom, I don't want to bother you again but we've got a request.'

'Oh. And what might that be?'

'Well, this here's Quentin and he's a bit of a scribe. You know a scribbler. I think you met him the day of the opening.'

'Yair, I met a lot of people that day.'

'Well, Quentin here's written a play about the whole thing. Sort of a summary. Particularly about the last couple of days when that M.P. let us down and that, and your speech and all that.'

'And.?'

Quentin hadn't said much more than G'day. Thought it best to leave the talking to Ned. Ned went on, 'Well, we wondered if you would like to read it, and maybe if you thought it O.K., we could print a few copies and maybe sell them or something. You know, put the money into the funds or something.'

Tom was quiet for a while. Ned knew to wait. Then,

'How would you get it printed?'

'Quentin here had a newspaper. You know, used to print and distribute a paper and he's still got all the printing gear. He'd soon knock it out.' Another pause,

'O.K. Ned, I'll have a look at it.'

'Thanks Tom. Oh, and it goes without saying Tom, if you don't approve the matter ends there.'

'O.K. Ned. Thanks Ned.'

Quentin said,

'Thanks Tom. We appreciate it.' He knew the ways of country people. Knew not to say any more than that. Not to labour the point. Ned had said it all, any more would not be necessary, in fact he knew if he started talking, he could ruin the whole thing.

They left a copy with Tom. As they drove back Ned said,

'I'm feeling fairly good about that. I think it might be O.K.'

'Yair, I hope so. That's why I didn't say much. Thought it best to leave it to you.'

'Yair. Probably was.'

Tom rang Ned a couple of days later.

'Ned, I've read this play that Quentin wrote and I think it's quite good. I'm not sure I want to be, sort of, the centre of attention, though.'

'Well, I didn't either really but I think Quentin was just telling it like he saw it.'

'Yair, I s'pose so.'

'Then I thought, really, I s'pose it's about the whole picture of, sort of, getting the show on the road. Us individuals are only part of the thing.'

Ned waited. Tom thought about that, then said,

'Well, I s'pose you're right. Tell him to go ahead with it.'

'Thanks Tom. I'm not sure where he'll go with it, but I guess if it sells a few copies it'll be a few dollars in the kitty. He said he'd give any profits to the museum.'

The museum effort had quite a big effect on the town and its people. The museum was only open three days a week but there were always plenty of volunteers there to handle any inquiries. Quentin had printed some copies of his play on his old printing machinery and it was quite popular and was selling quite well. Most of the local families had bought a copy as had a lot of visitors. The whole exercise had had a big impact on Tom Fraser. After the opening, he was seen more regularly around the street, just chatting to various people, and what's more, people wanted to chat to him. He had changed almost overnight from being mostly reclusive to being more open and approachable, and he was enjoying it.

He met Ned in the street one day, and after a bit of chit chat, he said,

'You know, Ned. That day at the museum was a good day for me. In fact, I think of it as the best thing that's happened for me in a long time.'

'We're all glad too, Tom. Been good for us all. Yair, Tom, been good for us all.'

Chapter Forty-Four

Ned's School Address

Rose Attwill was fairly new to the school, new to the district in fact. She was only a little woman. Even though she was about thirty, she looked more like one of the students, but they had quickly learned you don't mess with her. They all called her Miss, and in the short time she'd been there she had gained their respect. They liked her a lot.

She'd asked Ned to address the older children. Probably had she been about town a little longer she wouldn't have done it. They were mostly teenagers and Rose liked to present different people, different ideas to her charges. Keep them thinking, and interested in the learning process.

She was always on the lookout for new ideas, new people, and being new to the town, didn't realise the kids were joking when they suggested Ned would be a good one to speak to them. Ross Wilson, the head master, was a bit of an old fuddy-duddy.

By the time he heard about it, it was too late. She'd asked Ned, he'd said yes and he was due to arrive in half an hour.

Ross called her to his office.

'I hear you've asked Ned Brannigan to speak to the older students?'

'Yes, I have.'

'How did you manage to do that?'

'Well, the students suggested it and when I spoke to him, he jumped at it. I think he'll be very good.'

'Well, I don't. You'll just have to ring him and put him off somehow. I don't know what you were thinking asking him. I can't imagine him having anything useful to pass on. Oh, and in future you'd better confer with me before you ask anyone to speak here. Now go to it and ring him.'

'Might be a little difficult.'

'And why might that be?'

She walked to the window, beckoned him over and pointed.

Ned was out in the playground talking to group of children, while they were having lunch.

'He's already here, so it's all too late, it's going to happen. I guess we'll just have to hold our breath and hope.'

Ross Wilson exhaled. Looked down his nose. Twiddled his thumbs. After quite a long pause he asked

'Did you give him a subject?'

'Yes, I did.'

'Dare I ask…?'

'I had great success at my last school when I asked one of the older people in the community to address the students on the theme, 'Where am I going?' I told Ned I wanted him to speak on that. He seemed to be very pleased I'd asked him, and very pleased with the topic.'

'Oh, well, what's done and all that. I suppose you're right… we'll just have to hold our breath. Mind you I want you to be in the room the whole time and you make very sure you stop him if the thing gets off on the wrong tack. On your head be it. Do I make myself clear?'

'Oh, yes, very clear.'

Rose breezed out of the office. She was a little uneasy but not really concerned, she knew she could handle the situation.

Ned was standing in the corridor with a folder of notes under his arm. He'd been standing, watching these young 'uns as he liked to call them. Rose was pleased to see he was dressed very neatly, not like she'd seen him several times in the street. She asked him,

'Are you Okay with this?'

Ned looked at her for a few seconds, and in that short time realised Rose was a bit apprehensive.

'Don't worry young lady. I've been looking forward to this ever since you asked me. I've got plenty to tell them.'

'Mind if I stay?'

'Please do. I may teach you something too.'

His tone was kind, not patronising, just down to earth, plain, as Ned always was.

Ned stood beside Rose in front of her students. A room filled with about forty-five noisy teenagers. As he looked at those kids his thoughts went to Louise, his little girl. He wondered how she had been at this age. Thought of all the things he would have loved to tell her but was denied the opportunity. Today however, at least he would be able to pass something on to these kids. He was brought back to the present when he heard Rose saying,

'Our guest speaker today is Mr. Ned Brannigan.' There was a little titter at the back of the room. It came from a couple of girls, girls who had thought it a bit of a joke to ask Ned in the first place. The next few minutes were to change their thinking.

'I think most of know who Mr. Brannigan is, so I'll let him get on with it.' With that Rose walked to the back of the room, sat at an empty desk and waited. Ned placed his folder of notes on the desk and started,

'Today's subject is 'Where am I going?' Or more accurately — 'Where are you going?' I want to show you all today that at some time in your life you must decide where you are going. You have a choice, and it's important for you to make that choice and then take responsibility for that decision. And always keep in mind that you can change the direction you have taken. You can't change direction if you are standing still. Sometimes you can't see the right way until you start. So, get on with it. Don't mess about, just get on with it. If you find you've made a mistake, stop, adjust, and have another shot. Show me the man or woman who never made a mistake and I'll show you a failure. It's not possible to get it right every time.' Ned paused. Every eye was on him. This opening had only taken a minute or so but straightaway he had their attention. They were absolutely absorbed.

He went on — 'I want to talk about opinion. How important it is to distinguish between fact and opinion. Yesterday it rained. The people who wanted to play golf said — This weather's awful. The farmer said — This weather is beautiful. The fact is — it was raining, the rest is opinion.'

At that moment Ross Wilson walked along the corridor. His curiosity had got the better of him. Rose beckoned to him. He came quietly in the back door and sat next to Rose.

'How's it going?'

'Brilliantly. He's fantastic. He's won them already.'

Ned by this time was getting right into his stride.

'Next I want to talk about focus. Decide what you need to know and what you don't. Don't fill your mind with extraneous guff. See if you can focus on the important things, the good parts of a person, not their faults. Try to let those faults go past. If they are really bad and you start thinking someone ought to tell him or her about that, remember *you* are someone and it's your responsibility as a friend to simply say — I think you're going the wrong way. If you don't feel you can do it alone, take someone with you. There's no need to make a big deal out of it. It may only take a simple sentence or two. Then it's up to the person to decide whether to listen or not.'

By this time there was dead silence in the room. Some were taking notes. Even the two girls who were giggling at the start were listening, hanging on every word. Ross Wilson looked at Rose, nodded and said quietly -

'You know, I think you got it right. Well done.'

Ned went on -

'It's like being part of a team. You need to help each other. Some may need a lot of help, but it's usually worth it in the finish. I'll tell you a story. I haven't talked about this since I left school myself, but I've often thought about it. There was one wimpy kid in my form. A boy. He was always untidy, you know shoe laces undone and all that, and he never had his homework done, never played with the rest of us, you know, that sort of kid. I can see him now. That kid needed help, needed a friend. I could've been that to him. So, could any of us. But we didn't. We just let the poor bugger suffer. He was important to someone. Nobody is unimportant. Everyone is important to someone, maybe his mother or his sister, she was quite a bit younger, but she was headed the same way. They left the area during the year, I've no idea what happened to them. I always wish I could have that time again. Go back there for a short while and just him give a little help.'

The room was still very quiet. Not even a cough. Even Wilson stayed, listening intently. After a short silence Ned started again -

'This team work thing is important. It can be very effective. You can all be part of it. Your teacher, Miss Rose is part of it, so too, is Mr. Wilson. You can all help each other. I read a poem once, and the first two lines went something like –

Do you know what it means to be losing the fight,
When a lift just in time would put everything right?

It was a few verses, and the last couple of lines were -

Did you give him a word, did you show him the road,
Or did you just let him get on with his load.

I can't remember the rest of it or who wrote it, but I certainly remember the message.'

Ned waited quite a few seconds, then said quietly — 'Do you know such a kid? Maybe there's one in this school. Think about what it must be like to be that kid. If it occurs to you that that someone should help that kid, always remember — you are someone. If it was your brother or sister, would you pass him by or would you give him or her a little lift up, show that kid he's not alone.'

Ned paused for a while. Rose was becoming worried that Ned had lost his thread, but no. It wasn't long before he started again.

'Ever thought about starting a big brother, big sister plan? That's where each big kid looks after a small kid. You know kind of adopts the younger one, 'specially at the start of the year when all the little ones are all new. Just supports the new one 'til he or she gets along Okay. You kids can organise that. You don't need a teacher to start it. If you think it's a good idea just get on with it, just do it. You just need to get a list of all the little ones and get others to select one to look after. It's particularly important at the start of the year.'

Ned could see the idea had struck a chord with one or two. He left it at that. Then went on,

'Now, I'll give you some homework. Australia is a fantastic country. I hope you'll grow to love it like I do and I want you to read a poem which expresses a love of Australia perfectly. It's called, My Country, and it's written by Dorothea Mackellar.'

He turned to the whiteboard, found a felt pen, and asked for a volunteer. Several hands went up but Ned looked around the room and said,

'I want someone who's never been up here in front of the class.'

He chose one very shy little girl, walked over and put out his hand to her. Rose was horrified. It was little Miriam, the quietest, meekest little kid in the class. A kid with mis-shaped teeth and ill-fitting glasses which sat cockeyed on her nose. A girl who Rose had wanted to help but wasn't sure how to help. A girl who'd never said a word in class, but then she was amazed when little Miriam took Ned's hand and followed him to the front of the room. Ned gave her the pen and said, 'Now I want you to write this. Write My Country.' He waited while little Miriam wrote, or started to write, in small letters, very small letters. Ned stopped her, asking,

'What's your name?'

'Miriam,' in a quiet little voice.

'Louder Miriam.'

'Miriam,' she said a little louder.

'Louder Miriam, so the whole room can hear you. Yell it out.'

So, Miriam yelled, 'My name's Miriam.' Rose was worried at first but then realised it was just the right thing for the little girl.

'O.K. now Miriam, write big. Like you yelled just now.'

So, Miriam wrote My Country in large letters. Bold letters.

'Now write by Dorothea.' Ned spelled it for her.

'Now Mackellar.' Ned looked at Rose for a second and when he turned to spell it found that Miriam had already written it, and what's more had spelt it correctly. Ned noted the looks of surprise on both Rose and Ross Wilson.

'Well done Miriam.' He turned to the class,

'Didn't she do well?' The class clapped. 'Now give me a thumbs up.'

She did that with a cheeky grin. He felt that was enough for Miriam,

'Well done young lady. Now sit down and always remember you can say I am Miriam and think — there's only one of me.' Then to the whole class,

'I want you all to write that down. The stuff Miriam has written.'

Notebooks were quickly opened and pens produced.

'And another poem I'd like you all to read is a message of inspiration from a father to his son, but it applies equally to girls as well as boys. It's called — If, by Rudyard Kipling. You'll find both of those down at the library.'

Ned paused once again for a few seconds while they wrote. Then went on, 'Oh, and another thing. I've got a bit to say about bullying. Whenever bullying happens there is usually a third or maybe more kids present. If it's going to be stopped it's up to that third kid to speak up. After a while you usually find the bully is weak as whatever, underneath. If someone stands up to them, they usually crumble.

Remember, you could be that third person who could help the kid that's being bullied.'

Ned paused then finished, saying,

'Look after each other. The mates you make at school will be your mates forever. Thank you for listening.'

Ned sat down. Not once had he referred to his notes. The abrupt ending caught them all by surprise. After a few seconds silence, one boy, Ned recognised him as the older Sudwick boy, stood and started clapping. Soon they all followed.

Ned left quite quickly. Just went to the door, said thank you, waved to them and left.

He knew he'd done a good job with his talk but felt he just had to get away. The thoughts he'd had about Louise had started a trail. A trail he'd been down many times, especially when he used to drink heavily. At home he took a bottle of Johnny Walker which he always had on hand. He rarely drank these days but just occasionally he'd have a quiet nip. Took the bottle and a vegemite glass and sat at a table in his back yard, as he often did, staring at the creek and feeling very, very despondent. He felt like getting drunk as he used to do but after two or three mouthfuls the feeling left him. So, he just sat, brooding.

This was how Nora found him. She came around the back as she often did, saw him sitting there. Just sitting. He no doubt heard her but he didn't look up. Nora went inside, found a glass, came out, poured herself a drink and sat. He didn't move or even acknowledge her. Nor did she acknowledge him. She recognised the signs. She knew him better than anyone. There was no need for her to speak. She knew he'd been to address the kids at school and quickly realised what he was thinking. Probably if anyone other than Nora had come, they would have tried to jolly him out of this morose mood, but Nora knew better.

They sat thus, in silence 'til Nora saw a few tears running down Ned's cheek. She stood up then, held her hands out to him, 'Come on now Ned. Time, we went inside. The mozzies are starting.' He stood up and followed her inside. She indicated the sofa and he sat, and she sat beside him, put her arms around him and just held him. Nora was probably the only person, anywhere, who could have handled the situation.

'Turn and face me Ned.' Nora's voice was calm and quite composed. He turned as she had asked. As usual, he did what she said.

There had never been any communication of a sexual nature between them, but that day Nora knew it was going to be different. Thought maybe there could be. She had thought about it occasionally before but hadn't dwelt on it much. She felt the age difference was significant. Today she started thinking it may not matter much. She knew it would be up to her to start things, if, indeed, anything was going to start.

She held him close for a few minutes. She made a decision.

'I know I'm a bit older than you, Ned. Eight and a half years in fact, but I don't think that really matters.'

She unbuttoned her blouse. Took it off, then took off her bra.

'Take your shirt off Ned. I want us to be close.' She watched as he slipped his shirt off, then she pulled his face to her breast, ran her fingers through his hair.

'Ah Ned, I think it's time for us. I've thought about this sometimes and I think now it's time.'

She chatted on. This all came as a surprise to him, but he didn't resist. It had been a long time since he'd been with a woman, but in a few seconds, he felt the old stirrings.

Nora ran her hand down and undid his pants, pulled them down as best she could and wrapped her fingers around his erection. They stayed like that for a minute 'til she said,

'Lean back a bit Ned so that I can take the rest off.'

He stood up while she removed her slacks and knickers and lay back on the sofa.

'Be gentle with me Ned. It's been a long time since I did this.'

She knew she didn't have to say that. Knew he would be gentle, but, being the chatterbox, she was, somehow felt she wanted to say something to keep the intimacy of the moment. Ned undressed and lay on top of Nora as she opened her legs wide, and as he pressed his erection against her, she said,

'Reckon you could find it in the dark?' They both giggled at that and Ned pushed. It had been many years since Nora had been with a man and so she had contracted to such an extent that Ned had to push very hard. Finally, he entered her. He watched her face, her eyes and mouth opened wide and then she relaxed with a look of bliss. They made passionate love there on the sofa for quite a long time, then lay close for quite a while, each wondering at the direction their lives had just taken.

After a few minutes Nora extricated herself and stood up, 'O.K. Ned. Let's have coffee.'

Chapter Forty-Five

Miriam

A couple of weeks later, Rose met Ned in the street. 'I didn't really get the chance to thank you for that talk you gave the children. I want to thank you so much. It was exactly right for them. Been brought up in class and talked about many times. It has made quite a bit of difference to those young ones, 'specially that young Miriam. I must admit I was very apprehensive when you chose her, but that too was just right. She's blossomed in just the short time since. She's into everything now. Can't keep up with her.'

Ned became a bit emotional at that, and turned away. Rose saw that and was quick to say,

'Why, Ned, have I upset you in some way?'

Rose didn't know, couldn't know, what had upset Ned. He'd been thinking of his little girl, little Louise. She'd been only about ten when he last saw her. Now she'd be in her twenties. Maybe married with kids, his grand-children. Thinking of all the things he would have told her. All those things he'd just spoken to the students about. Thinking of how he would have loved the chance to share his thoughts with her.

Ned regained his composure,

'No, young lady. It's just something that happened to me a long time ago. Some things stay with one forever, just don't go away. Think no more about it. I tell you what, I really enjoyed the chance to talk to those young 'uns. It did me a lot of good too.'

They chatted for a few minutes then Ned made a decision.

'Tell me about that little girl Miriam.'

'Well, she lives with her mother. Her father left quite a few years ago and left her mother to bring Miriam up.'

Ned had seen it before, understood what it was like.

'Miss Rose, I want you to do something for me.'

As Ned paused, she said,

'I will if I can Ned. What is it you want me to do?'

'I take it they don't have much.'

'I think you're right about that. The mother does some cleaning and that at some of the shops and some homes. I guess they get by.'

'I want you to arrange for that little girl to have her teeth fixed. She's a cute little kid and I'd like to do something for her. Oh, and get her a different pair of glasses. I want you to get all this done and send me the bills. Oh, and find some way of doing it without mentioning my name. Just say there's a scheme of funding and you think she may qualify or something like that. You'll work it out.'

'Gee, Ned, that'll be great. Thank you so much.'

'I'll leave it to you.'

Rose was to learn some time later what Ned had been through. She heard the story from Nora. The story of Ned's wife and the other girl who'd drowned, and how his wife had taken Louise and left. Then she understood.

Quite a few weeks later Ned ran into little Miriam and her mother in the street. One of those chance meetings which occur from time to time in small country towns. Ned hadn't met the mother but it was evident to him that this was indeed Miriam's mother. Their physical similarities were striking, even from a distance.

They had been shopping and hadn't seen Ned across the street. Ned watched them for a minute and was pleased to see Miriam skipping along in front of her mother with apparently not a care in the world. Ned almost let the moment pass without contact, but then on an impulse called to them as he crossed the street. Miriam turned, saw Ned, then ran straight to him and wrapped her arms around his waist, calling to her mother,

'Hey Ma. This is Mister Ned, the man who made me get up in class that day.'

Her teeth had been straightened and she was wearing a very attractive pair of glasses. He'd had the bills for both of those and was very pleased to see how it had improved Miriam's looks, made her face bright and glowing.

Miriam's mother came up to Ned, held out both hands to him and said,

'I want to thank you so much. You have made my little girl shine. She was always a shy, meek little girl but since that day she has blossomed. Thank you so much.'

'I'm so pleased for you both. So glad I could help. So, tell me, what do you do?'

'I'm a research associate in the field of childhood development.'

'What does that entail?'

'It means I'm a mother.'

'And it seems you're doing it very well.'

Ned thought — what an incredible woman.

Ned thought of his Louise and before he became emotional, he nodded and walked away.

Chapter Forty-Six

Mr Woon's Fence

Bob Creewell had been in the bar talking to a couple of young lads for a while when he said,

'I'll have to go now. Got to see some people about a fence.'

'What sort of fence?' asked Terry.

'Mr. Woon's fence.'

'You mean the old Chinese joker who lives in Carringdon Close, amongst all those upper-class sods.'

'Yair that's him?'

'Doesn't Ned live there too?'

'Sure does.'

'Yair. I bet the snobs'd love those two to leave their little corner. Reckon they lower the tone of the neighbourhood.' Terry's mate was a bit puzzled. He was new to the town and was about to learn a bit about the people of Archerville. He listened as Terry went on,

'How come Ned lives there among all that toffy lot?'

'Yair, how come that?'

Bob was quick to reply,

'Well, see, Ned was there first. His is that little old weatherboard at the end of the road. He's had that forever. It was originally just a weekender on the river and Ned bought it and then they sub-divided housing blocks all-round the place and Ned just stayed where he was. They all hoped he would sell out and leave, but that wasn't Ned's way of thinking at all. He just stayed.'

'What about the fence?'

'If you'll stop bloody well interrupting me, I'll tell ya.'

'Fair enough, go on.'

'Well, Mr. Woon is much the same as Ned. His house was there before all the sub-division happened too, except his is half way up the street, not out on the end like Ned's place.'

'And ...?'

'Well, old Mr. Woon likes to grow his own vegetables. Nothing wrong with that but he grows them in his front garden so that they extend right to the footpath. Nothing wrong with that either but then comes the tricky part. Some of the local dogs've been getting amongst his veggies. Scratching and piddling and that, you know the sort of thing.'

The two listeners nodded.

'Well, Mr Woon didn't like that very much so he collected stuff to make a fence. He used anything he could lay hands on. He had old beds and bed heads, broken pallets, stuff like that. He even had an old car door. He propped all this stuff up with a few iron posts and sticks he'd got from the bush down near Ned's place. Things like that. He's even got a sheet of corrugated iron for a gate. So, you can imagine what they think of that. They didn't mind the garden, in fact some of them used to get veggies from him. For nothing mind you. He'd never take anything for them. He'd say, 'no pay, you sleep, you eat, you like, velly good'. They are too. Better than the shops. So that was all right till the fence went up. Christ it looks funny. All these nice neat houses. You know, all these tidy front yards, manicured lawns, perfectly trimmed hedges and all that sort of affluence and fair in the middle of it is this God-awful conglomeration of crap making up Mr. Woon's fence. I can understand the locals being a bit put out having this abortion of a thing right in the middle of their patch. And the funny thing is Mr. Woon's got no idea his fence is the subject of so much consternation.'

Terry bought more drinks. He wanted to hear the rest of the story.

'What're they gunna do?

'Well, being the type of people, they are they've called a meeting of all the residents of Carringdon Close. Actually, they're all right those people, they just have a few quid and they don't understand how the rest of us live but they're okay really.'

'And you're going?'

'Too right.'

'How come?'

'Well, I live on the corner, and anyway I'm interested. Yair, interested. Any way I'm off now. Got to see some people about a fence.'

Bob left, went home, then strolled round to Carlton Jones's place where the meeting was to take place. Carlton

Jones was probably the snootiest one of them all. He'd set up a table and a few chairs in his neat, tidy, back yard. Bob noted the manicured lawn and trimmed shrubs. Not a thing out of place. Even rakes and shovels hanging on pegs on the side of the shed and the hose neatly rolled up. Bob thought, must've taken him five minutes to roll that up.

There were ten or a dozen people there. Amongst them Ned, Nora, and a couple he didn't know. Must be the new people in number seventeen, he thought. Bob noticed Mr. Woon wasn't among them. They hadn't asked him to come and state his case. They just went ahead trying to decide what to do about this bloody fence. No one objected to the garden. It was just this fence.

Carlton Jones had set himself at the table, and like a pompous school master in front of some errant school children he called for order and declared the meeting open, once again with the pompous arrogance of a man who liked to feel superior and be seen to be superior.

There was some general discussion,

'There must be some council by-law that covers this sort of thing,' said one.

'We could take legal action. We've got a solicitor here. He could handle it,' said another.

'I think we should elect a committee of say three or so,' was another comment.

Various other suggestions were put forward. They were getting pretty wound up till Ned got to his feet. He waited for silence then he started.

'I notice Mr. Woon's not here. Why is that?' Some of them mumbled that seeing he was the cause of the worry they should decide something then go to him afterwards, and all those sorts of pithy comments. Ned listened for a while, then went on,

'Let's get this thing clear. No one's objecting to him growing the vegetables it's just the fence, is that right?' There was a general agreement that that was right. Then he went on,

'It seems to me there might be another way to go about this.' Then Ned showed them a thing or two about what neighbours ought to be about. There was a bit of shuffling and coughing, but Ned just sailed on,

'First, has anyone any idea why he put the fence there in the first place?' No one seemed to have an answer and,

'Has anyone asked him about it? Or even spoken to Mr. Woon about this fence?'

Silence.

'And does it occur to any of you that maybe Mr. Woon doesn't realise his fence might be a problem to them?' Silence again. Nobody had spoken to him. There were a lot of blank looks, and some of them seemed to be a little uncomfortable.

'Well, I've spoken to him.' At this stage Carlton Jones interrupted. Carlton Jones, the local architect who, it seemed to some, thought his buildings were just a little better than the rest, and for that matter, it seemed to quite a few, felt the same about himself.

'Look, I'm not all that concerned about the whys and wherefores of the thing, I just want to see the fence come down and let's have our street tidy like it used to be.'

Ned bristled,

'It may have been a good idea if you had found out why he put the fence up in the first place. I took the trouble to ask him and I'll tell you. He put it up because the neighbourhood dogs were getting amongst his veggies. They used to come in and scratch and piddle and whatever else dogs do. Now Mr. Woon didn't like that so he put up his fence. And I'll tell you something else Jones, that big mongrel of yours was the worst of the lot.'

The silence was deafening. No-one had heard anyone speak to Carlton Jones like that. They were amazed. It didn't bother Ned. He didn't just think it, he said it. The only sound was Nora Jeffery trying to suppress a giggle. She was one of the first people to build a house there. They all knew she didn't like Carlton Jones. After a few seconds silence Ned went on,

'I've heard legal action mentioned, has anyone any idea how much that would cost? Once those jokers start there's no telling where it'd finish. Has anyone asked Mr Woon if he would consider a new fence?' There was another silence, then he went on,

'No... well I did, and he says he would be more than happy but he says he can't afford it. That's why he put up that abortion of a thing you're all whinging about. He just grabbed anything he could find.'

Ned waited while there was a bit of muttering.

'Now, it seems, we've got to the crux of the matter. Has anyone got any idea how much a new fence would cost?'

No-one spoke.

'No... Well I have. A plain ordinary picket one would cost three hundred and sixty to four hundred dollars for the materials. That includes a gate. There's eighteen houses in the street. That's about twenty odd or at most twenty-five dollars per household. Which would you prefer? Spend months writing letters to the council for no action, or pay some lawyer God knows how much to write letters and go to court and all that crap and this time next year we'll be no further advanced, or, all put in twenty-five bucks, buy the materials and then help the poor old bugger put it up.' He walked to the front, threw thirty dollars on the table,

'There's mine.' Then sat down. Nora was the first to recover, she placed her money on the table with a -

'Well said Ned.' The pile of money grew. Carlton-Jones went up in everyone's estimation when he threw a fifty on the table.

'You know Brannigan, I think you're right.'

He knew when to back off.

Ned got up again and said,

'Well it looks as if that's decided, I'll get the materials tomorrow and we'll start on Saturday. Say, about ten.'

Ned then turned to Carlton-Jones and asked would he like to ask the other people in the street to contribute. He could hardly refuse. He was about to pompously 'declare the meeting closed' when he was interrupted by Wally Barnley. Wally Barnley, who'd lost a leg and got a withered arm in a farm accident several years earlier and had had to rely on a crutch, rose to his foot and started speaking. Ned was interested to hear what old Wally had in mind.

Listen most carefully to he who says little. Ned had heard that quotation somewhere and as he considered this might be an opportune time. Wally waited for silence. Then,

'I've listened to what all you people have said and I've got a bit to add. I'm not going to be much help at putting up a fence but I can cook a pretty mean sausage. How about you lot do the fence and I organize a barbeque after? Just all bring chairs and we'll have it in the street.'

Bob called in at the local later and, as often happens in a small town, the same young blokes, Terry and his mate were still there. Terry couldn't wait to hear how the fence saga turned out. Bob told them the story, finishing with the bit about Jones saying I think you're right.

'That sounds a fantastic idea. Did they all agree?' asked Terry.

'All them that were there. Then Ned rubbed it in to Jones.'

'How do you mean?'

'He suggested Jones should go and ask the ones that weren't there for their twenty-five.'

'How did that go?'

'Well, Jones could hardly refuse. I thought it was a neat touch.'

'He's an interesting joker this Ned.'

'Ah, yes, he is that. See, Ned reckons peoples' rights end when they deprive others of theirs, and he set out to look after old Mr. Woon, and at the same time, show that lot a bit of what being a community is all about.'

'Hey that's a bit of good old homespun philosophy.'

'What is?'
'That bit about peoples' rights ending or something...'
'Oh, yair, well that's just how Ned is.'

The fence went up the next Saturday morning. Ned brought the materials on his trailer which was quickly unloaded, the old fence pulled down and loaded.

Most of the residents of the street were there, including Carlton-Jones who surprised everyone by turning up in some old work clothes. The whole operation took only a couple of hours, and the whole time Mr. Woon walked around looking very pleased saying 'velly good, you velly good people'.

The barbeque lasted well into the afternoon.

Chapter Forty-Seven

The Church fence

Ned saw Chapman in the street one day...

'Well, Chapman, what're ya doing for the next few days?'

'Not much. Why?'

'I've got a couple of jobs coming up. I could use a bloke like you.'

'Yair, O.K. Ned. Sounds alright.'

'O.K. Be round at my place about eight tomorrow. Just you. Oh, and bring your lunch. Never sure where we'll end up.'

'O.K. Ned I'll be there. See ya then.'

It didn't occur to Chapman to ask about wages or anything. He'd known Ned long enough to be confident that that would not be a problem. He knew whatever Ned paid would be fair and reasonable.

Next morning, in Ned's ute, they headed out to the end of

town and pulled up beside the church. The old church had a big sign at the front. Chapman could see the old Methodist sign leaning, tired, against the fence, and a large new sign announcing the Uniting Church very prominently displayed at the front. Ned went to the house next door and was met by a short plump woman. An older woman who Chapman thought might be about sixty or so with a very pleasant face. She seemed to always be smiling as she gesticulated, pointing here and there.

Ned motioned to Chapman.

'Right. Now we have to pull down this old fence and load it up.'

Chapman didn't see all that much wrong with the old fence, but, remembering one of the lessons he'd been taught by his first boss, Mr. Watkins, he kept the thought to himself. As they worked, he also remembered someone saying once that a closed mouth gathers no foot, so he kept quiet. They had been working only a couple of hours, when the lady appeared with a jug of cordial and some plastic mugs and poured drinks for them.

'Thanks Mrs. Harbutt. And by the way this is Chapman,' he said waving his hand in Chapman's direction.

'Hello Chapman,' she said and continued without a pause, 'What're you doing for lunch Ned?'

'We brought our own Mrs. H. Never know where we might be, come lunch time.'

'Well now, you just bring what you've got inside later and I'll make you a nice cup of tea to go with it.'

'Well, thanks Mrs.H. That'll be great.'

They worked on through the morning, Chapman finding it very easy to work with Ned as he soon was able to see how Ned worked and was able to see where Ned was headed, and to predict his next move.

They had half of the old fence down and loaded, when Mrs. Harbutt called them in.

'The kettle's boiling and I've made a pot of tea Ned. Come and have it while it's hot.'

They sat at the kitchen table. An old wooden table which had obviously been there for a great many years. It matched the rest of the kitchen furniture. An old glass fronted dresser and a large wooden bench. They engaged in some small talk until Mrs. Harbutt said,

'I'm a bit worried about paying you for this Ned. Would it be O.K. if I pay you a bit at a time?'

'You won't have to worry about that Mrs. Harbutt. We'll work something out.'

'I didn't really want a new fence. Them church people insisted on it. The old one was O.K. really.'

'Well, you know how these people are. Someone gets a bee in his bonnet and wants something new. I agree there wasn't much wrong with the old one, I could see that. That's why I took the job.'

'What do you mean Ned?'

'Well I thought if they got one of the local tradesmen to do it, they might charge you the earth, whereas I'm not going to charge you much at all. Not much at all.'

'Oh, Ned, you still have to get paid.'

'Oh, don't worry about that. I'll see some way of doing it.'

A plan was already forming in Ned's mind.

As Chapman was carrying a heavy fence rail he tripped and fell. Laying there with Ned standing looking down at him, Chapman was expecting some sort of sympathetic remark or at least some help with the piece of timber but no... all Ned said was,

'Don't feel bad. A lot of people have minimal talent,' and went on with what he was doing.

Chapman was to hear a lot of these little gems in the next few days. By the afternoon they had most of the old fence down and loaded when a small boy appeared. He was about seven- or eight-years old Chapman guessed. With curly red hair. A sort of tousled headed kid. A sort of Ginger Meggs look alike. He bustled in on his bike. Came in the gate at speed, jumped off his bike, leaned it against the wall, then stood with his hands on his hips and said,

'By Jees, Grandma's gonna be mad when she sees this.'

After they stopped laughing at that, Ned explained to the little fella,

'It's O.K. She knows we're doing it.' Ned then lowered the tailboard of the ute, sat there and the small boy sat beside him. Ned took the trouble to explain to the small boy,

'See, the old fence was a bit rickety and we're going to put up a new one. Do you think Grandma'll like that?'

'Oh yair, I reckon. Will it be a wooden one?'

'No. It'll be a colourbond one. What do you think about that?'

'What's that?'

'It's like tin.'

'Oh. That'd be alright I reckon. What colour will it be?'

'We haven't decided that yet. What do you reckon'd be a good colour?'

'I reckon a white one'd be good.'

'Might be a bit hard to keep clean.'

'Oh, I'd come and wash it for Grandma.'

'How would you do that?'

'I'd just get the hose and go swish, swish. That'd soon get it clean.'

Ah, the enthusiasm of youth thought Ned.

'I reckon a green one'd be better. Same as the grass.'

'Yair that'd be O.K.'

By this time Mrs. Harbutt had come out and had been watching this exchange.

'Now Danny, don't you go bothering the men.'

'Grandma they're going to put up a new fence.'

Little Danny spoke as though he had some breathtaking news for her. Then with all the enthusiasm of a little eight-year-old,

'And it's gunna be colour bound. Won't that be great?'

'It's colourbond.' Ned corrected the little fella. 'Yair. Colourbond. Won't that be awesome?'

Mrs. Harbutt smiled.

'And it's gunna be white and I'll come and wash it with the hose. Yair, I'll just go swish, swish and it'll be clean.'

Chapman watched all this and was quite amazed at the tenderness Ned showed to this small boy. Big, rough Ned, and yet he had sat with little Danny the whole time and made the effort to chat with him like an adult. Chapman commented to Ned on the way home, 'That was great the way you treated that little boy.'

Ned waited a while before he spoke, 'I learned a long time ago to listen most carefully to the little ones. Oh, and don't dampen their enthusiasm. What may seem of little consequence to us older people may be very significant to them. Yair, we gotta listen most carefully to the little ones.'

Ned thought — God knows, I could have grandkids that age.

Next day, half way through the morning while they were digging holes for the posts, the minister from the church appeared. A sombre looking joker. Ned had met him before but he was quite new to Chapman and straightaway he made Chapman feel uncomfortable.

Fancy, wearing a clerical collar at mid- morning on what could be described as a construction site. Reminded him of a pompous prick he had seen at the church when he was a small boy. Made him think of a couple of observations his father had often made.

'I can't afford the luxury of religion', was one thing he often said, and

'People use religion for their own purposes.'

Funny, he thought, how these things spring to mind in a few seconds. Chapman had these thoughts running through his mind when Ned introduced them.

'This is Reverend Carboon. This here's Chapman.'

'Very pleased to make your acquaintance Chapman,' he said with a pomposity that made Chapman wince. Gawd what a prick, he thought.

Ned sailed on,

'Now Reverend I've got something to ask you. Since it was the church people's idea to put up this fence, and there was'n't much wrong with the old one, would it be within the realms of possibility that the church or their people might consider paying for it?'

The Reverend was quite taken aback. He spluttered for a few seconds.

Seizing the moment Ned went on,

'Like, there's Mrs. Harbutt. She hasn't got much and it would be a very charitable gesture.'

Only a bloke like Ned would have the affrontery to suggest such a thing.

The Reverend spluttered some more, then, 'Well, I've not met her. I hadn't thought of it like that.'

Mrs. Harbutt had been listening to all this from behind the window, and with impeccable timing came out and said, 'Are you coming in for a cuppa Ned. I've got the kettle on.' Then pretending to see Carboon for the first time, 'Oh, and you too Reverend, I've just made some nice biscuits.'

The Reverend could hardly refuse.

As they approached the house Ned leaned toward Chapman and said in his ear, 'Don't slurp your tea. It's not done in the best of circles. I had an English teacher at school who said that. Never forgot that.'

Chapman thought about that as they sat down. Realised he must have been a serious tea slurper or Ned wouldn't have mentioned it. He sipped his tea very carefully.

Ned said, 'I just knew you had something cooking Mrs. H. Been smelling that aroma all morning.'

Mrs. Harbutt had heard most of the conversation between Ned and the minister, remembered the 'we'll work something out' Ned had said but pretended she hadn't heard anything. They sat at the table in Mrs. Harbutt's old fashioned kitchen. An unlikely looking combination, Ned and Chapman in their work clothes and the pious minister in his back to front collar. Mrs. Harbutt produced a selection of unmatched cups and plates and those magnificent biscuits. Chapman tried a biscuit and it was delicious, just as he knew it would be. Still warm and soft. Just like his mother used to make them.

'Sorry the cups don't match Reverend. I expect you're used to something better.' Then, with a cheeky grin and without waiting for a response,

'Now, with milk?'

As they left Carboon said,

'I'll think about what you asked Ned. See what I can do.'

As he disappeared into the church Chapman said,

'That was a cheeky act. You know I think it might just work.'

'Well, you know, if you don't ask you don't get anything. What a parsimonious prick he is.'

'Hell Ned, that's a big word.'

'Stick around, there's plenty more where that came from.

Did you notice he never smiled once the whole time he was here? He must be a bundle of fun when he preaches.'

Then, after a pause,

'You know, it's times like this I thank God I'm an atheist.'

It took a few seconds for that to sink in. Chapman started to speak,

'But an atheist doesn't believe .... Oh.' The words trailed off when he realised Ned was being funny.

Chapter Forty-Eight

Elliot

After work, Chapman and Cree strolled to the fish and chip shop.

Chapman saw him coming. Recognised him immediately. The walk was still the same. He said to Cree, 'You remember me telling you about a teacher I had once. A bloke called Elliot?'

'Yes. The bloke with the funny hair.'

He pointed to a man across the street.

'That's him, there.'

'Where?'

'There.' Cree saw a man across the street. Her memory of how Chapman had described him came back.

'Ah, I see who you mean.'

'I don't think I'll talk to him.'

'I think you should. And anyway, I'd like to meet him.'

'You would?'

'Yair, I reckon it'd be interesting.'

'Ah, I dunno. Not sure I want to be bothered with all that again.'

'Too late now. He's spotted you. Look, he's coming over.'

'Well if it isn't Chapman. Fancy running into you again.'

'Hello Mr. Elliot.'

Chapman didn't have anything more to say. Felt he'd rather be somewhere else. Elliot went on, 'Well. What brings you to this town?'

'Oh well, I left the farm and got a job here. I s'pose I might ask the same of you.'

'Ah. Well. I've been transferred to the school here. Teaching some of the youth of the town. Actually, I'm glad I ran into you again. I seem to remember we parted on a somewhat unusual note.'

Chapman didn't want to introduce Cree but since Elliot seemed interested to continue the conversation, felt he should.

'This is Marion. This is Mr. Elliot. He taught me back home.'

Cree spoke for the first time.

'Yes, I remember you mentioning him.'

Then she asked Elliot,

'How long have you been here in town?'

'Just since the start of term. A mid-year transfer. They don't often do that but one of the teachers here got sick so they got me to take his place. Elliot continued,

'I s'pose it doesn't matter much now but for what it's worth, the reason you may have thought I didn't like you much, or I may have given you that impression was because

I felt you could have done a lot better, and I wanted you to try harder.'

Chapman thought about that for a second, then said,

'Well, why didn't you just come right out and say so?'

Then he added,

'Actually, as you said, I s'pose it doesn't matter now.'

After a pause he said to Cree,

'Come on, I think it's time we went, I've got things to do.'

He moved on, but Cree waited a few seconds and Chapman could see her talking to Elliot.

They exchanged a few words, then Cree joined him.

'What was that about?'

'I just wanted to tell him what you said.'

'What about?'

'How you said you'd begun to appreciate him when he got you to stand up and say what you did.'

'Oh that, yair well maybe I did a bit.'

'What?'

'Get to appreciate him.'

'Yair, well, I just thought I'd let him know 'cos I reckon you're bound to run into him a bit now that he's here in town.'

'Yair, well I dunno if I want to be bothered with him. Like I said to him, he could've just said what he was thinking.'

'But don't you think he had your best interests in mind?'

'Well, yair, maybe he did, but he could've at least said it like that.'

Chapter Forty-Nine

Austin Woller

The next job Ned had taken was out at the farm next to his old farm.

Ned said as they drove out,

'Don't come out here much,' then as they passed a farm with a small weatherboard house, 'That used to be my place.' Chapman noted a tinge of nostalgia in Ned's voice.

'Oh, by the way, you remember me asking that minister chap if the church might pay for the fence?'

'Yair, I remember it well. Think I said you were a bit cheeky or something like that.'

'Well I was and it worked. I went to the church with the bill for their share of the job and that reverend chappie just said, like 'is that just our half?' and I said yes and he goes 'well if I double that will that cover Mrs. Harbutt's share, and I said yes and he sat down and wrote out a cheque for the whole amount.'

'Well I'll be buggered. So, it worked then?'

'Yair. He said he'd asked the local stipendiary committee; I think that's what he called them and they'd agreed. And they are going to pay for all the materials as well. So how about that?'

'Fantastic.'

Chapman thought — I can learn a lot from this bloke — and he began to wonder if maybe he might have learned a lot more from his father if they had related better. Maybe should've listened to him a bit more. He decided then he would try to do just that.

They drove into the next place, a rather attractive place with painted fences down the driveway which led to a very attractive older house with a veranda all round. At least Chapman assumed it would be all round even though he could see only the front of the building. Ned drove straight past the house and directly to a couple of sheds where they were met by an older man, a dignified man, dressed like an English gentleman farmer complete with leggings and all. Chapman was rather taken aback by this man's appearance. He couldn't imagine what sort of a job he had in mind for Ned. Thought he was the sort of joker who would employ two or three men to do the work while he just supervised.

After the usual how are yous and haven't seen you for a while type of exchanges Ned introduced Chapman.

'This is Austin Woller,' and turning to Austin and indicating with his thumb, 'and this here's Chapman.'

They shook hands and Chapman instinctively felt that this Austin chap felt it was a bit beneath him to shake hands with a mere labourer. Chapman had seen his type before when he was working with Mr. Watkins.

'Now, there's some things I want you to do Ned. I want you to put a fence down here to connect with that fence there. Post and rail job like those down the drive, and then I want you to put a couple of doors on the shed. The old ones are a bit past it. I've got the new doors here. They wandered into one of the sheds.

But first I want you to connect the water to this shed. Just connect a pipe from that tap, out there in the yard. It can come over that wall and then down here.'

Not once did he look at or address any comment to Chapman.

'O.K. Austin. Now which do you want us to do first?'

'Oh, the water job would be good. I've got some pipe and the fittings, like, a tap and all that.'

Chapman was fascinated watching how Ned was completely unfazed by this man's standoffish manner.

'Very well then I'll leave you to it.'

Chapman was quite pleased to see him leave, couldn't imagine what it would be like having him breathing down his neck while they worked.

After about an hour Austin reappeared. Ned said,

'We're gunna have to cut this brick to get the pipe through Austin. Have you got a saw?'

'Yes, I'll get it.' He reappeared again after a few minutes and gave Ned his saw and Ned proceeded to start sawing the brick. Chapman was about to protest. Bloody hell he thought. That's a wood saw and Ned was attacking the brick. Austin was obviously thinking the same thing but both men kept their thoughts to themselves, Chapman because he still remembered Mr. Watkins saying sometimes you just shut up, just say nothing, and Austin because he couldn't believe what he was seeing.

Ned hacked his way through the brick and returned the saw with all its teeth pretty well worn flat. Chapman was incredulous and the look on Austin's face was something to behold.

Finally, he sputtered,

'Why couldn't you use your saw?'

Ned's reply was succinct,

'Cos it stuffs 'em.'

The look on Austin's face was even more incredulous. Chapman had to turn away. Look somewhere else to try and hide a grin.

As they drove home Chapman said.

'I can't believe what you did with that saw. It's a wonder he didn't clobber you with it.'

'Now don't you worry about Austin. He might appear as though he's a bit superior but underneath that he's a great bloke. He was always a good neighbour to me and everyone else for that matter. He'll soon forget about his saw.'

Next day as they were working on the fence, they heard the sound of a horse galloping. Coming down the lane was Austin in a horse and gig. Coming at great speed with Austin trying to control his unruly steed. Ned and Chapman jumped clear as the gig swept past and continued towards a small creek at the bottom of the lane and they were just in time to see Austin jump out of the gig, land, roll over and bounce back to his feet like a nimble Olympic gymnast while the panic stricken horse continued on and finished in a tangled heap in the creek.

Ned had had quite a bit to do with horses over the years and felt Austin should have been able to control this runaway.

'Jees Austin,' Ned said as they ran to his side, 'Why did you jump out?'

Now it was Ned's turn to be amazed as Austin, still puffing from the exertion, said,

'Plenty more horse and cart, no more Austin Woller.'

They worked on over the next couple of days and after they had finished and Austin handed Ned his cheque Ned said,

'I'm thinking of going back into farming Austin. Do you reckon you'll ever sell this place?'

Austin drew himself to his full height, stuck out his chest and said,

'This place won't be sold while I'm alive.' Then after a pause, 'They might sell it when I die.'

Ned said with a cheeky grin,

'Oh, yair, right. Let's know will ya.'

Austin was still standing, staring as they drove off.

Chapter Fifty

The finale

The sun came up that cloudy Sunday morning, on schedule, as it usually did, and greeted the local citizens.

By mid-morning the clouds dissipated a little and the sun elbowed its way through the gaps and sent cheerful shafts of light down on Archerville. It was a typical Sunday morning. Thin, bright shafts of light shone down on Archerville, selecting various significant spots around the town. Significant spots and significant people. Kids playing in the park, on skateboards or throwing sticks for some useless dog to fetch. Maybe not really a useless dog, for it kept the young ones amused with its antics.

Just the usual Sunday morning one might expect in any small Australian town. People strolling to the shops, or just talking, passing the time of day, always taking time to stop and chat. Even though they saw each other most days, there always seemed to be something to chat about. People were occupied doing things, important or otherwise. Digging in gardens, mowing lawns, lawns which seemed to require attention of a Sunday morning, or sweeping. Doing the things which keep a town thriving. And thriving Archerville certainly was.

Shafts of sunlight selected various significant spots in Archerville.

The museum, Mr. Woon's fence, Tom Fraser's cottage, Marjorie in her car, or Rose Attwill's school room, or the park bench where Quentin had sometimes sat, either talking to someone or just sat, thinking, or dozing as he had that first day he'd come to Archerville, or Chapman and Marion and maybe Scott, sitting in the car eating chips, or Ned, working at some job, or with Nora, as one might expect him be. Or little Miriam skipping down the street. Life was continuing around Archerville at its usual pace. A slow meandering pace. Nobody in any real hurry.

A typical Sunday morning.

All that changed when Nora decided to buy some chips, a decision she was ever thankful she made.

She strolled into the fish and chip shop. Didn't often do that but she just felt like a nice hot bag of chips. Something to warm the body on a cold day.

'Just a bag of chips please Margot.'

'Right'o Mrs. J. Won't be a minute.'

Margot was a new girl in the shop but she'd learnt a lot of the locals' names.

Nora turned towards the tables, looking for a chair. The

next few minutes were dramatic. Several lives were to be suddenly changed that morning.

Her mouth dropped open. Sitting there with a man and two small kids was Louise Brannigan. Nora let out an audible gasp. Sure, she'd grown up and changed a bit but Nora recognised her immediately, even after eighteen years. Some features don't change. The shape of her nose, the few freckles were still noticeable, but the eyes were unmistakable.

'Good heavens, it's Louise.' She stood, staring.

'Hello, Mrs Jeffery.' Louise said quite calmly. She'd recognised Nora as she came in. Sat watching, wondering if she should speak up. Decided not to. Thought maybe it was for the best but of course she had no choice when Nora came over and pulled up a chair. As soon as she realised who it was, she'd made a decision. She wouldn't be letting her out of her sight.

'Well now, Louise, tell me how you are. I want to hear what you've been doing. This your husband and little ones?'

'Yes, that's right.'

Louise's husband knew immediately who Nora was. Over the years her name had been mentioned often. They had been back to Archerville once before, with the intention of finding Ned, but Louise had chickened out. The children giggled between mouthfuls of chips. Louise introduced them.

Nora chatted a while then asked,

'Now, tell me, Louise have you seen ...'

She stopped when she saw the children were looking and listening quite intently. Two little pairs of eyes, all eager and bright and starry, hanging on each word. The thought occurred to Nora that maybe they didn't know about Ned and what happened here all those years ago. She started again,

'Have you seen, .er, like...er, anyone else around?'

Louise gave her a thankful look.

'No, not really.'

'Will you?'

'I'm not sure.'

'Well, I am. Now there'll be no argument about this. I know I'm right.'

She spoke to Louise's husband,

'There's a park across the road. Why don't you take the kids to play on the swings?'

Her question then to the kids,

'Would you like that?' was greeted with very eager yesses.

'Your mother and I have to go for a little drive.'

She addressed Louise's husband,

'This could take some time.'

He looked at her with the most grateful smile, and said, 'Thank you, thank you so much.'

As they were about to leave Margot called,

'Here's your chips Mrs. J.' Nora put some money on the counter.

'Give them to the kids,' Nora said over her shoulder. She didn't want anything to interrupt the moment.

As they drove, Nora talked,

'I'm just so thankful I decided to buy chips today. I get the feeling you might have just driven away. Would I be right in that?'

'There's a fair chance I might have chickened out. I came here once before. I squibbed it then so there's a good chance I would've done it again.'

'Promise me you won't this time. Er, actually, there's no need to 'cos I won't let you. I'm not letting you out of my sight 'til we find him. He'll probably be home now.'

Half way down Carringdon Close. She could see Louise was getting fidgety. She leaned over and patted her arm,

'No need for you to worry about this. It's exactly the right thing to do. I know. I've had a lot to do with Ned over the years. I know how your mother leaving and taking you away affected him. That broke his heart that did. Absolutely broke his heart. He's never really gotten over it. Today will be the happiest day of his life, and yours and mine. He's never been happy since your mother took you away.'

Louise sat staring apprehensively out the car window. Nora patted her arm again.

'It'll be OK. Don't worry.'

They stopped in front of Ned's place. His ute was there in the drive.

'Ah, ute's there. Means he's home. Now, I'll go in first. You know, make sure he's presentable, then I'll come out and get you.'

She knocked on the window as she walked up the path as she often did, calling,

'You decent Ned?'

'Yair, course I am. Aren't I always?'

'Not always.'

She walked in.

'This time I want to make sure you look Okay.'

She looked him up and down.

'Just go and comb your hair for me.' Ned was wearing an old singlet.

'Oh, and put on a clean shirt.' Nora wanted this to be just right. Rough and tough as Ned was it was always the same between them. He always did as she said. Sometimes quite grudgingly but inevitably he would do as she told him. He put on a shirt as she directed and combed his hair, all the time wondering what she had in mind.

She looked him up and down, 'I s'pose you'll do. Not much to look at really, but I s'pose you'll do.' He was used to this sort of comment. Took it all with good humour. No one else would be game to say those sort of things to him.

'Right, now come out here, there's someone to see you.' He stood, wondering.

'Come on.'

She went out and beckoned Louise. Ned stood at the door, saw her get out of the car, recognised her immediately. He didn't move for a second. Louise walked towards him, slowly at first, then she broke into a run, wrapped her arms round him and said,

'God, I've missed you Daddy.'

And the tears flowed.

www.ingramcontent.com/pod-product-compliance
Lightning Source LLC
Chambersburg PA
CBHW060904190726
48286CB00002B/360